ROCK, PAPER, GRENADE

T0357149

ROCK, PAPER, GRENADE

a novel

ARTEM CHEKH

Translated by
OLENA JENNINGS and
OKSANA ROSENBLUM

SEVEN STORIES PRESS
New York • Oakland • London

Copyright © 2021 by Artem Chekh

English Translation Copyright © 2025 by Olena Jennings and Oksana Rosenblum

All rights reserved. No part of this book may be reproduced, stored in a retrieval system, or transmitted in any form, by any means, including mechanical, electronic, photocopying, recording, or otherwise, without the prior written permission of the publisher.

Seven Stories Press
140 Watts Street
New York, NY 10013
www.sevenstories.com

Library of Congress Cataloging-in-Publication Data

Names: Chekh, Artem, author. | Jennings, Olena, translator. | Rosenblum, Oksana, 1976- translator.
Title: Rock, paper, grenade : a novel / Artem Chekh ; tranlsated by Olena Jennings and Oksana Rosenblum.
Other titles: Khto ty takyï?. English
Description: New York : Seven Stories Press, 2025.
Identifiers: LCCN 2024040147 | ISBN 9781644214275 (trade paperback) | ISBN 9781644214282 (ebook)
Subjects: LCGFT: Bildungsromans. | Novels.
Classification: LCC PG3950.13.H45 K5813 2025 | DDC 891.7/934--dc23/eng/20241029
LC record available at https://lccn.loc.gov/2024040147

College professors and high school and middle school teachers may order free examination copies of Seven Stories Press titles. Visit https://www.sevenstories.com/pg/resources-academics or email academic@sevenstories.com.

Printed in the United States of America

9 8 7 6 5 4 3 2 1

PART ONE

~~~

A Polonaise for Felix

Lida had never been afraid of anything. Maybe because she did not watch TV or read the newspapers. Lida would listen to the radio and knit. She would sit in her small, cramped room on the bed under a monochrome tapestry (a naked woman on a riverbank), knit, and, of course, listen to the radio.

Lida swam in the Dnipro all year. Almost every day, fearless and hardened by nature, she went to the river, resolutely crossed the long sandy beach covered with islands of ice and mounds of snow, walked out on the frozen surface, looked for an ice hole left by fishermen, took off her clothes, but for a faded-pink and at one time red swimsuit, firmly rested her hands on the edges of the hole, and dove in. And all this happened year after year, until one February day she didn't resurface from beneath the ice. For almost a minute, an unexpected force carried her away from the ice hole through the dark waters of the Dnipro, farther from the light and closer to death.

Felix rescued Lida. He often accompanied her when she was swimming. He walked into the distance, smoked, walked carefully along the icy quiet surface of the reservoir, looking toward the fairway, as if expecting desert caravans of *dushman*[1] armed with Stingers to swim out of the frosty haze. But, of course, there were no caravans. And, of course, no dushman either. And when he looked back, there was no Lida. Felix rushed to the ice hole and beneath the murky ice he saw her gray flailing body. He threw off his jacket, plunged to the waist, slid his fingers along her body, looked for something to grab onto, finally grabbed her hair, pulled. Lida hit her head on the bottom of the ice, scratched her face and hands, had almost stopped breathing, and, as was made clear later, had said goodbye to life. In the murky crystal of the cold water, she managed to catch a glimpse of the light edge of the sky, remembered the summer and the sound of reeds in the backwaters between the villages of Chervona Sloboda and Lesky, the tall pines of the Sofiyivka Park, and the spring morning draft that swayed the whitewashed lace curtains hanging in the cottage's summer kitchen. And most of all, she thought about how it was a pity that there was so little and that there could have been a little more: summer, reeds, sunshine, forest skirted with dried mushrooms, limitless lawns of heather, and silver poplars in the wind, pouring over the transparent afternoon splendor. And this was the most frightening of her fleeting thoughts.

After this, Lida didn't swim in winter anymore.

Perhaps the river's ice was the only thing that frightened her.

◇ ◇ ◇

Felix was discharged in '89. After he was wounded, shell-shocked, and held in captivity, the Moscow leadership started to seriously doubt his usefulness. According to the law, while waiting for retirement, he had to work somewhere, so he was taken on as a truck driver for a pasta factory. His influential friends from the Soviet party got him the job. At first, before he got used to it, Felix wandered around the factory open-mouthed. He hardly understood anything and did not trust anyone. The consequences of the shell shock did not let up for a long time. He was allowed not to work, so he wandered between the shops, sat for hours beneath the leaky shed roof, and smoked, watching the measured flow of factory life. Curiously, he repaired the fence around the flowerbed, poisoned a hornet's nest near the public toilet, and drew a realistic penis for the funny bear on the May Day poster.

And finally, he found his way. He joined a group of veterans of the Afghan war (some criminals among them), who drove around the grounds in a truck with black plates, while workers, those who couldn't get away with not working, filled the truck with groceries: Soviet cognac, condensed milk, butter, sacks of flour and pasta, boxes of candies and cakes. After the truck passed the checkpoint without obstacle, it rolled in the direction of the Eastern Borderlands and finally unloaded on the right bank of the Western Bug River. The patrons of the party got part of the money, something was thrown to the director of the factory, and everything else was divided and spent on booze. At the same time, Felix collected payments at the central market. They resold purchases there, provisions bought from the villagers. The payments were small, but the market was big. Sometimes he took goods instead of the money. A silver-haired Azerbaijani with a missing ear got him sweet peppers and tomatoes. Fat-bottomed Ada specialized in meat. One agreeable old man brought eggs and farmer's cheese directly to Felix's apartment.

The building he lived in was right across from the market. It was a new, brick building from '86 with large bright rooms and glassed-in balconies. The neighbors were mostly officers of the 40th Army of the Soviet Ground Forces and their families. Felix got a three-room apartment on the fourth floor. His wife, Tanya, and daughter moved in while Felix was still stationed in Afghanistan. Just like a thousand of his army friends, he outfitted the apartment with Japanese appliances hauled on donkeys and camels by caravanners from Pakistan and covered the living room with a fluffy, patterned rug requisitioned from the Bagram market. The furniture, however, was from Romania, but beech wood, a bespoke order from the factory in Baia Mare. His wife took care of decorating the apartment. In the beginning, Felix did not care about the apartment, the appliances, not even the rug, though he had taken a long time selecting it and was anxious about it, asking the seller detailed questions and bargaining for each afghani, and having reached an acceptable price, he came away with it for free. And when he returned, he still did not care. He was used to an austere life; he couldn't care less about the cozy apartment. Then he came to his senses, looked around, but it was too late to change anything.

"Tell me the truth," he turned to his wife. "What is it, do you have gypsy blood?"

His wife did not answer. After all, what could she say, and who knew what was in his head. After he returned there could have been anything in there.

"Only gypsies furnish their apartments like this. And you're like a gypsy yourself. Gold and leather. You're all in gold. Your arms are in gold, your ears, your teeth—everything is in gold. And in leather. You stink of a goat."

Even before his return, their relationship had been failing, now it was like a squished mulberry in July, and he couldn't put anything back together. Tanya was afraid of Felix and did not understand, although what is there to understand when you are afraid? He never laid a hand on her, but she would wake up in the middle of the night, looking with fear at her husband, and it seemed to her as if some sick dog were lying next to her: he breathed hard, he gasped, he coughed, he moaned. His heavy, helpless moan annoyed her the most. And scared her, of course. But what could she do? Once, she decided to pet his head. Felix grabbed her hand, squeezed it tightly, almost broke it.

Felix did not love Tanya and did not want to love her. He was clearly not in a state to love: he had served for twenty-five years, eight at war. What kind of love was there to speak of? And he wasn't used to her anymore. He wasn't used to civilians. And this woman constantly annoyed him. He didn't know where to hide from her attacks of sudden passion, when she began to kiss his face with her dry, cracked lips. Her thick blue eyeshadow made him nervous, and so did her hoarseness, her habit of quoting films he had never seen. And all this small talk about school, about a new sofa, about money. And even when you start to talk about something else, it ends with money. He wanted to speak out, to cry, to reveal all he had lived through, give it all over to scrutiny, like a service weapon, and forget it like a lesson he hadn't learned well. She wanted a new plush sofa and an entrance to the kitchen decorated with pilasters and ornamental molding like General Chervonopyskyi's.[2] Their only option was to break off into different rooms, which they did.

Even though water was not his element, and he was totally indifferent to it, Felix called his doghouse, the smallest of the three rooms, a ship's cabin. His wife's room was a museum, and his daughter's was a cave. He did not enter the museum, which his wife called a hall in a gypsy manner, just as he did not enter the cave. In essence, Felix and his daughter were strangers. His daughter, not understanding her emotions as she should have, also began to fear him. He didn't really know how to act around her. How should one act around teenagers? How should one act around children in general?

His cabin was densely decorated with maps and newspaper clippings. During his service he did the same in his barracks, it made him feel calmer. The floor was covered with an old rug in a number of uncertain shades, taken from his mother and laundered. A glass jar served as a lampshade.

Felix thought about moving to his mother's, helping her take care of his brother, Yurka, after their father died. Yurka drank even though he didn't know how. How many times did Felix drag him from the police station? And how many times did he look for him in the hospitals? Yurka, having found out, yelled, "It's like they want a rottweiler to guard me." But who would do it? The one with shell shock?

So Felix just wandered around the city. He was either at the market or at the factory. He chatted with someone, got tipsy with someone else, and the day passed that way. In the late evening, when there was nowhere to go, he went home, crawled into his cabin like a bear, sat in an armchair for some time, glancing at the biting darkness outside the window or at the ceiling. Sitting in an armchair, he drank, sobbed quietly, and when his eyes grew dark and an unpleasant current of memories pulsed over his skin like convulsions, he fell on the bed and into a deep sleep, moaning and coughing. And then again, a new day. Just like the one that came before it. Empty and dead, like a village after a purge.

One day in August he was wandering the city center. There was a sticky heat wave; everyone who was able dispersed among summer cottages and the sea. In the morning, Felix called his friends, but no one picked up the phone. He remembered that he had to take care of some documents, went to the Veterans' Affairs building, argued a long time with the secretary, slammed a chair, broke its leg, and left empty-handed. He went to the bar, Chaika, and ordered Soviet cognac and sandwiches. He got a little tipsy from the cognac, so he decided to get some air to clear his head. He walked to Kirov Street, and near the factory. Maybe, at least, he could talk to the guys, even though they were boring and always discussing politics. Or maybe go fishing: small bream, pike, spinners, bait. He walked a little around the grounds of the factory, looking into the noisy workshops. He glanced into the pasta factory, there were only women, of course, all similar, in laundered white coats, plump, permed heads, loud. And yes, they shouted.

But they shouted tensely, hysterically, howling. They surrounded one woman and were yelling urgently. Were they going to fight? It didn't seem so. But they were yelling. And the only one who wasn't yelling, the one who looked like a young, energetic bulldog, broke away from the circle surrounding her, and ran from the crowd along the conveyor belt, toward the light of an open door. Felix became interested, looked closer, and suddenly saw blood, a lot of blood. Liquid and light, like cherry juice, it was dripping from the fist held to her chest, flowing down her forearm, and dripping from her elbow.

"Ambulance! Felix, call an ambulance!" the women clamored from the depths of the shop, "Ambulance! Ambulance!"

It turned out that Lida had been adjusting dough on the conveyor belt close to the blades, and then one of them sliced off half her finger.

"Call it yourself!" Felix shouted to the broads and rushed to Lida. "Apply pressure to your finger!" he ordered.

"I already did."

"No, now. Apply pressure."

"I am." Lida showed him her bloody fist as if saying, here, look! Her finger was in her fist. More accurately, half her finger.

In the meantime, they called the ambulance. The foreman ran over, pale and alarmed. He always kept his hands in the pockets of his uniform, even when he ran.

"And where is it?" he asked Lida.

"What?"

"The finger that was cut off?" the head of the shop said anxiously.

"Somewhere in the pasta," Lida said.

"Maybe we should look? They'll sew it back."

"It went through the holes with the dough," Lida explained. "There's nothing to look for."

It seemed that was all the boss was interested in. At least, the alarm on his dry-shaven face disappeared.

"Take it easy," he said and returned to his business.

The women again surrounded Lida and, sighing, stomped around her. The scene was reminiscent of a ceremonial harvest dance.

"And how is it that it went through the holes with the dough?" Felix asked. "And now people will eat it?"

"They will."

"*Donnerwetter.*"[3] Felix laughed sharply and merrily. Then he came to his senses, covered his mouth with his palm, but Lida had managed to see the absence of his two front teeth. She had problems with hers, too, but the front ones were still there. Even some on the side.

The ambulance arrived. Felix volunteered to ride with Lida.

"Can you mind your own business?" she asked along the way.

"I'm here to help," Felix answered uneasily.

"Be my guest. You're not afraid of blood?"

"I am," he admitted.

And two months later Lida brought Felix to meet her daughter.

◊ ◊ ◊

A handsome man in his forties, shaven almost bald, with a bright, but heavy face, like a prisoner of a Soviet camp who had just found out about his amnesty. That's how Olha, a first-year student of Russian philology, and her son, Tymofiy, who for two weeks had been celebrating his fifth birthday as if it was a remarkable achievement, saw him. Olha had been working as a daycare teacher for seven years, but felt an irresistible need to get a higher education, and at the age of twenty-seven enrolled in a continuing education program.

Felix made a good impression. He was polite, even gentlemanly. Lida made dinner, opened the wine in advance so that it could breathe.

"Felix was a soldier," Lida started the conversation, pouring the Crimean wine into glasses and leaving burgundy stains on the starched white tablecloth. "An officer. He was in combat," she added with gravity, so that her daughter would properly appreciate the guest.

"And where did you fight?" Olha asked indifferently.

"Against the fascists," Tymofiy joyfully exclaimed.

"He was in Afghanistan. How many years, Felix? Six?"

"Eight," Felix answered briefly, chewing.

"Eight years. Rather than the mandated two. And also," Lida continued, as if warning, "He's royalty, an earl."

At those words, Olha came to life. An *earl* was respectable. There was even something of that in world literature, which she greedily fed on, like oxygen, so as not to suffocate in the provincial plebian society. She remembered Prince Myshkin. He and Felix had something in common. There was confusion on his face or something. It seemed the signs of Felix's shell shock were visible.

In those days, he was often still, all of a sudden and for a long time, as if he had seen something unusual beyond this colorless reality; he slowed down, spontaneously opened his mouth, stared into one corner, remained silent and aloof, and then suddenly woke up and returned to the usual pace of existence, began to say something, to top off the wine and even to joke. He was funny. The most banal anecdote caused him an attack of sharp, loud laughter. Then he would quickly cover his mouth with his palm, hiding the food and the missing teeth, quiet down, and return to calm conversation. He put a napkin to his lips with unusual frequency and used a knife, which made him seem like an aristocrat from those books. In classic Russian literature, everyone ate with a fork and knife. Even the kitchen staff and their children. It was that kind of era.

They sat together at one table, talked about everyday life, slowly washing their food down with semisweet wine brought that year from Yevpatoria. However, it was mostly Lida who spoke, excited by the appearance of Felix in her apartment and by his acquaintance with her daughter. She laughed a lot and loudly, putting food on Felix's still-full plate, asking Tymofiy the whole time if he liked what he was eating, carefully catching Olha's eyes. Olha was fiddling with her napkin, occasionally adding awkward comments. Felix, armed with a knife and fork, was tensely cutting up the liver.

Finally, Tymofiy knocked over a glass of fruit compote, and relieved, Olha began to wipe the table and take off her son's wet T-shirt. She had to take him to some preparatory classes, anyway, so she excused them both and hurried out.

Felix and Lida continued their meal.

After the Crimean wine, they opened the Georgian wine. Lida drank from thin cognac glasses. Felix switched to vodka. And the more he drank, the more he hung out in the dimension that was open only to him. He reacted painfully to Lida's voice, grimacing and waving it away. Some moments he was falling asleep, then was suddenly waking up. He grabbed for his fork, threw it in disgust, fell asleep again, whispering curses. And when he began to sour completely, shedding tears and sobbing, Lida panicked. But Felix continued to drink. He drank, cried, and feverishly repeated the same phrase: to hell with this war. At some point, Felix totally lost control, the only possible option to calm him down was physical intervention. Lida dragged him to her room.

Felix woke up late the next morning. Lida was still at the market. Little Tymofiy had gone to his uncle's for a few days. Olha's husband, Lyosha, had just gone to Moscow to buy some goods, so the apartment was empty and quiet, like a village house in the afternoon. Only, in the bedroom, behind the wardrobe covered with QSL cards, in a soft and deep armchair, Olha was hiding with the Andreyev[4] book she had bought the day before.

She was reading with concentration. Her mood matched her surroundings.

Totally disoriented, Felix did not notice her. He was feverishly rushing around the apartment, trying to find if not a living soul, then at least some clues that might help him to remember the previous day, evening, and night. He wanted to find out what kind of apartment this was and how he had ended up there. He couldn't find any clues. There were no explanations. Everything—objects, thoughts, feelings—got tangled like a fishing line in the reeds, and memories spread like raindrops on the windows. Here is an empty three-room apartment, where he, yesterday's counterintelligence officer, soldier, and Soviet Army paratrooper, was locked up. What special services had locked his drugged body in these quiet rooms? If they were enemy forces, he could fight. He was used to it, he killed people with one blow. If these people were on his side, then it was over. Fight or not, they will find you and destroy you. And before that, interrogations; and may God grant your heart the privilege of not having to endure this torture to the end. First you killed, and then you were killed. He had learned it well and, finally, was ready to face the consequences of working for the system.

Felix carefully examined the objects, fixed their details in his brain, looked for entrances and exits in a panic. The door to the top floor was closed. A piano. Why was there a piano there? Who would need a piano in a safe house? Anton Pavlovich[5] looked on phlegmatically from the bookshelf. A catalog of works by Voloshin.[6] A ballerina, frozen in a porcelain fouetté. On the table, a bobbin tape recorder. The picture, a boy and a girl beneath an umbrella, was taken from a prewar German postcard. In the hallway, a pile of women's shoes. In the kitchen, plastic wallpaper that looked like tiles, old colorful linoleum. Absolute quiet.

On the piano, there was a phone, potbellied, black, with letters on the dial. Some kind of suspiciously high-end phone.

Felix picked up the heavy handset. It was working. He remembered Hrysha the Saboteur's number and dialed, but after the first ring he pressed the hang-up button. Were they listening? No matter. He dialed the number again. Hrysha answered immediately.

With the despair of yesterday's special fixer, counterintelligence agent, soldier, and Soviet Army paratrooper, Felix described the situation to Hrysha.

"What do you see outside the window?" Hrysha asked in a businesslike manner.

Felix rushed to the huge window.

"Some shops, pipes. There's a sign that says D-O-K."

"I know where it is. District D. How high up?"

"Fifth floor."

"You'll break your legs. You won't get far."

"Fuck, Hrysha," Felix shouted, "I can't run away on broken legs! Come here!"

Felix tried for a long time to remember everything, hit his palm against the piano, which made it hum alarmingly, cursed loudly, and from time to time put down the phone and froze, just listening to the sounds from the entrance. Hrysha promised to come.

For some more time, Felix rushed back and forth, trying in vain to open the apartment's front door, which could be unlocked with a key on either side, found a knife and a meat tenderizer in the kitchen, ran with them between the furniture, like a restaurant cook between stoves, and cursed.

It was then that Olha lost her patience and emerged from her reading nook. Either under the bizarre influence of Andreyev, or from the general absurdity of the situation, Olha, wringing her hands, indignantly and at the same time hopelessly spoke in a voice that did not sound like hers: "You have a dirty mouth."

"Me?" Felix stared at her in surprise, hiding the knife and tenderizer behind his back.

"You!" Olha almost cried.

Felix looked at her, scrutinizing the seemingly familiar figure in a long plaid dress and wool sweater, for a moment caught a confused glimpse of her dyed-blond hair, moved to red plastic clips, looked closely into her large angry eyes. At the same time, something stirred in his head, fragments of the previous night quickly surfaced, clarity of thought returned. He remembered where he was and what he'd had for dinner last night: mashed potatoes and fried liver. A bit dry for his taste.

Relief and shame came over Felix.

"Mademoiselle," Felix said. But he fell silent when he heard the front door open.

Lida entered the hallway, bringing the street's pure coolness and the smell of fresh bread with her into the house.

At the same moment, someone shouted hoarsely and loudly from outside: "Petrovych! Petrovych!"

"It's Hrysha," Felix explained, looking at Olha and then at her mother, "Hrysha the Saboteur."

◇ ◇ ◇

From then on, Felix began to stay at Lida's often. For Tymofiy it was the happiest year and a half, without worry and with a drunken lightness, as one often remembers the time before a war or an epidemic.

His father, Lyosha, opened an auto parts store, and the family met the beginning of the nineties in prosperity. Olha worked at a daycare, so she was always around, Grandmother Lida worked at the pasta factory, so there was always flour and plenty of pasta in the house. The boy went to kindergarten and various preparatory classes. He read a lot, watched TV, and had blissful confidence that the chewing gum brought from Moscow or Lublin would never disappear from his father's pockets. At the same time, Lyosha's parents bought a summer home. They loaded meat, wine, and peaches into the green Lada and drove to a small village, to their cozy piece of land. When Lyosha asked how much money she needed, Olha, following the example of the heroine of *Goodfellas*, squinted slyly and showed the thickness of a stack with her index finger and thumb. The money was dwindling, but it was enough.

When you are five, you can hide the whole world in a matchbox. Everyone around you loves you, and you carry this love like a beetle caught on the burdocks. It is all yours, your power over it is absolute, and it is up to you to decide whether to let it go or to tear off its legs and wings slowly and with a lot of focus.

Those were the times of innocence. Tymofiy's consciousness was captured by bright images and alluring scents. Around him, families were falling apart, the country was crumbling, many years of foundations were rotting, and crushed was the certainty of their daily bread. Living on hope became the norm. There were people who couldn't even do this. Tymofiy was protected from meanness and pain, from hunger and fear. The large rooms of the apartment, the limitless city, where here and there familiar landmarks sprouted, clearly outlining the known territory, unspeakably comforting books with daring illustrations from the perestroika times, a clear daily routine with those rare deviations, when he was allowed to finish watching a movie with his whole family, hearty breakfasts in the kitchen filled with steam and cigarette smoke, Sunday trips to the playground, where he spent most of his time near the giant wooden figures from Pushkin's tales. And these dark-brown figures, polished by nature and children's palms, seemed to be faithful guardians of his peace.

But, above all, Tymofiy's matchbox protected him, and he believed in its strength to the end.

◊　◊　◊

This strange man was neither a relative nor a friend. He woke up late and washed up for a long time in the bathroom, sniffed and snorted like a wild animal in a watering hole, scratched his goose neck, almost dry, with a razor, cutting off the upper layers of epidermis together with the fuzz, dried himself with a thick waffle towel, came out of the bathroom with a face red as a ham, looked at Tymofiy with a seemingly loving look, as adults usually look at someone else's kid whose affections they want to gain. The boy felt it, and so, instead of offering a greeting, he turned around and disappeared into one of the rooms.

At the same time, Felix brought unpleasant changes to Tymofiy's life. Before Felix's appearance, almost every morning, Tymofiy, excited in anticipation of a small daily miracle, would run into his grandmother's room, the smallest in the apartment, with an indelible smell of dried herbs and rose oil, crawl under her covers, and look for a gift under her pillow. If she worked second or third shift at the factory, then on the way back she always met Uncle Boba. The kid believed in him, as people sometimes believe in God, without a hint of hesitation and reluctance, blindly accepting the existence of the mysterious Uncle Boba as an integral part of his world. Usually these gifts were Fakel candies. Sometimes they were Kara-Kum, or even a mango, a fruit that was totally foreign to him. But when Felix arrived, Olha forbade Tymofiy from entering his grandmother's room. Especially in the mornings. The realization that Uncle Boba's gifts were just lying under the pillow where he couldn't get at them depressed Tymofiy, as if it were his fault that this strange man with a goose neck was there. Finally, he ran into his grandmother's room anyway. Waiting until Felix went to the bathroom to snort and scratch his cheeks, Tymofiy would quickly dive under the covers and put his hands under the pillow. But under the pillow, which now smelled not of his grandmother but of something else, only disappointment waited for him.

"There was no Uncle Boba," Lida said guiltily. "I didn't meet him."

And later she forbade him from climbing under her blanket. The kid understood everything, now, these were not only her covers but *their* covers. For both of them. And the room was now for both of them. And her love was divided in half. Half for him and half for this strange man.

And sometimes Felix drank. Then something hung in the air, like smoke from burnt toast, some bitterness and dirty, silenced truth. Something cracked in the family, and this sound of fabric tearing penetrated every corner of the apartment. After this sound, an alarming silence fell, which they were afraid to break, so as not to tear the fabric even more. It was uncomfortable and frightening, and Tymofiy could not find an explanation for these feelings for a very long time.

"Don't go there," Olha said. "Just don't go. Don't go out into the hallway," she sternly ordered.

From the hallway, you could get to Grandmother's room, the kitchen, and the bathroom with a tub. The most interesting places in the apartment. But he was told not to go, to stay here, finish reading his book, finish drawing, finish watching his cartoon, to follow instructions. What was the point of Uncle Boba or the mangoes? Everything was falling apart.

Tymofiy saw how the relationship between his mother and grandmother was deteriorating. How coldly they spoke to each other, how quickly it began to get dark outside the window. When you're a first grader, it seems that the world in general has ceased to be comfortable and understandable. The world no longer exists in you. You exist in the world. It does not fit in a matchbox. And you have lost your matchbox. You hardly remember where or when.

◇　◇　◇

In '92, when Tymofiy went to the first grade, Lyosha's business folded. The goods coming from Russia were stopped either by customs or some crooks associated with customs. They confiscated everything, or more precisely, cleaned them out, without any explanation. Olha insisted that they not give up the profitable business. Lyosha had no debts, he had a lot of useful connections, he had a place to live, enough to eat, and could make up for lost money in six months or a year. But the incident at customs shattered Lyosha's faith in himself and in some of his friends, and later it became clear who framed him and why. For some time, Lyosha walked around in low spirits, silent, with the corners of his lips turned down as if in grave doubt. But what doubts can there be when everything is taken away from you? Only despair and emptiness remain. So he firmly decided to choose an easier road for himself. He would get a job. Yet even there he failed. Factories were closing and hundreds of people like him, still young but already afraid of the unknown and devastated by their own insignificance, roamed the city streets.

Tymofiy remembered his father constantly sleeping. In his thirties, his father slept so much it was as if he planned to stay awake for the next thirty years. Later, Tymofiy understood. Perhaps, if Tymofiy had been thirty then he would also have been sleeping a lot: to block out all that social turmoil around him, to shove his own responsibility deep into sleep, a heavy and alarming daytime sleep. Well, at least he had no debts. Not yet, anyway.

In the end, Lyosha jumped ship just in time. Those who continued did not continue for long. And even if they plunged into shady commerce, they did things that Tymofiy's father did not want to do and wasn't capable of doing. Much later he told his son things that you begin to understand only late in life. In '89, in order to open a store, he and his friends had held an old man in an apartment for a long time and put hot brass nickels on his body. Tymofiy never found out who that old man was. Money was smuggled across the border in their asses. Later, they started checking asses. Some man stitched money into his belly; he was killed by Poles somewhere near Chelm. The pathologist got richer by three thousand dollars.

Lyosha mindlessly stared at the TV or made plastic model airplanes with manic concentration, causing the apartment to smell of silicone glue. Sometimes he disappeared with his friends, sat for a long time in their smoky kitchens, talking about cars or perfumes. At least he didn't drink. He didn't go down dirty, but he didn't fly high either. During one of his naps, a man called him and suggested going to Slovakia, though not entirely legally. But, what is legal nowadays?

Thus began the long epic of money making, the winding, overgrown path to material well-being. Not everyone was able to overcome it. One day Lyosha woke up and went in search of treasures and victories. He found neither the former nor, especially, the latter. Instead, he had experiences that he would have been better off not having, which once again reminded him that the best thing in the world was a nap—heavy, disturbing, but sweet.

◇ ◇ ◇

Gradually, Felix began to play a significant role in Tymofiy's life. For the longest time, Tymofiy could not understand who this man really was and if it was worth focusing on his behavior, habits, manners. Each was immediately labeled as negative. Drinking was especially bad. Tymofiy realized this without any help, although for a while he kind of liked it when Felix drank. There was something funny about it, something Tymofiy had never seen before, but that now he was witnessing.

In October '92, Felix was sitting with Lyosha in the kitchen. Felix drank, telling stories from his recent past: it had only been three years since he returned from Afghanistan. He talked about the war, about friends, and about legs, especially legs.

Lyosha could get along with almost anyone, so he humbly sat, listening as if to an old friend, playing along, and even enjoying the terrifying attraction to someone else's experience.

A single bulb in a dusty lamp shone a heavy, suffocating light, laundered curtains fluttered beneath the open window, and a school uniform was drying over the gas stove. There were a lot of onions and some lard on the table. Felix chain-smoked and ate mushrooms in oil with boiled white beans. At first, he and Lyosha had a respectful conversation, and in it there was obviously some kind of reconciliation. In Tymofiy's opinion, something right, something understandable and honest was happening. After all, if we live under one roof, he thought inadvertently, then we should all eat at one table.

However, at some point Felix's lively story was interrupted by tears. His face suddenly changed, darkened, dried up, resembling a giant prune. These tears did not surprise Tymofiy, but rather interested him. His father and his grandfathers never cried, at least not that he had seen before. And here was a grown man, with a courageous though wrinkled face, crying. The reconciliation came to an end, the right and understandable was replaced by the elusive and incomprehensible, a disgusting kitchen frankness from which one wanted to hide. Anywhere. Even in a matchbox.

Felix kept repeating the same phrase. "To hell with this war."

Sometimes he jumped up and shouted, spitting in Lyosha's startled face: "How do you stand in front of an officer, you bastard."

"Okay, okay," Lyosha said quietly, smiling confusedly with beautiful lips, "I'm not even standing."

"Who the fuck are you?" Felix was riled up.

"All right, all right. You're scaring the kid."

Tymofiy sat in fear on a stool hidden by the refrigerator.

Felix glanced cautiously at Tymofiy, calmed down, briefly tamed his inner lions, sat down, lit a cigarette from the burner, scorching his eyebrows. He shook the ashes into his palm. Lyosha handed him an ashtray, Felix waved it away.

"Okay, okay," Lyosha repeated. He looked indifferently through Felix, through the yellow space, at the profile that slowly swayed over the fire, at the blue flame of gas, turned his gaze to the window and the edge of the black sky. Obviously, he was tired. But something kept him from getting up and leaving.

"Donnerwetter," Felix sobbed, "I killed." He looked at his hands thoughtfully. "With these hands. I killed."

"Don't cry," Lyosha said childishly.

"Don't cry?" Felix jumped up again. "What do you know about tears? I had generals crying in my cellars!"

Tymofiy would hear the line about generals in cellars hundreds of times, and he imagined that Felix had sheltered generals in his cellar during the war, and they were crying. Either from pain or from fear.

"Who the fuck are you?!"

At these critical moments, and they would inevitably come, he would start punching the wall, growling, baring his teeth, completely losing himself. His wrinkles deepened and his eyes darkened, sinking into his sockets as if he wanted to hide inside himself. Crying, laughing, screaming, and taking aggressive stances, changing every minute, as if he were surrounded by dozens of opponents. Sometimes he froze, put his head, weighed down with pain, against his hand, and looked at the floor for a long time. Then his cigarette or hand-rolled smoke would burn down to his fingers. Felix did not notice it. His fingers were constantly burned.

Sometimes it seemed to Tymofiy that he, together with Felix, could see the bearded faces of the dushman around him and hear distinctly the desert sounds of the sitar, the long *adhan* that seemed to come from nowhere, and the whirring of the helicopters in the hot air above the house. Together with Felix, he wanted to wave away the cruel and intrusive genies, so that they would not squeeze his throat with their paws dried under the Kandahar sun, so that they would not bite his face with black stumps of teeth. If only they did not exist.

Tymofiy liked it when Felix drank. Up to a point. The short period somewhere between the second and fourth glass. His voice would become cheerful, his movements smooth, almost graceful, he would talk about his life outside the army and the war: about his childhood, adventures in love, about the fact that he had a daughter, he spoke with admiration and tenderness about the Dynamo soccer team and arrogantly about politics. But, suddenly, something exploded in him like a landmine in the middle of a column of airborne combat vehicles: his lips moistened, his eyes darkened, and all of a sudden the good-natured retiree transformed into Lieutenant Colonel Ignatiev of the Airborne Troops, who fought and was still ready to fight, if only alcohol had not knocked him down.

It was that October evening of '92 that Tymofiy remembered as the first real time he witnessed Felix's nakedness, candid and dirty, when all the insides were out, when scent and taste were especially acute. To some extent, even then he understood that it was all because of the war. He imagined the war yellow and flat. And on this yellow plain, soldiers were moving on armored personnel carriers, they tightly clung to their armor, and Felix was sitting on a hot barbette and pointing, like Ilyich.[7] That way! That way! And then at some point, everything explodes, the soldiers are blown off the platform, splash wetly in the sand like overripe tomatoes, everyone is dead, and only Felix remains, sitting near a large, pointed stone, looking at the bloody mess in green uniforms, and crying. And now he is here, also crying, remembering that minced meat in green rags, and that hot armored personnel carrier, and that dead space: yellow sand, yellow stones, yellow sky.

At the same time, something flashed in the small space of the apartment, as if a clot of dark aggression had scattered in sticky pieces all around. Felix smashed a porcelain teapot, bent forks, jerkily grabbed knives, fell in the hallway, grabbing the yellow lacquered moldings with dry fingers, screamed, sang Hnatiuk's "Two

Colors"[8] in a false basso, cried again, then remembered something painful and froze, kicked the wall, searched for his briefcase for a long time, and finding it, broke the lid with his elbow.

Lida shoved him into bed with difficulty, then hastily apologized to her grandson: it happens, don't mind it. Lyosha, frightened, and therefore lethargic and apathetic, was silent. Olha cried in her bedroom. Tymofiy felt some strange joy. There was something unusual in all this. Something fun and unusual. Now he was a part of it.

◇　◇　◇

Lyosha was in a Slovak prison. His first trip to work abroad turned out to be a failure just like most of the ones that came after.

Slovakia had just become Slovakia, a separate country, not very wealthy, still dependent on the economy of the former Soviet Union, but Western nevertheless. Suspicious documents did not prevent Lyosha from welding kiosks and other small, temporary architectural masterpieces in the capital's downtown. But only for a while. The raid took place on an April night on the outskirts of Bratislava, where workers from Ukraine lived in the basement of an old building. They took Lyosha too.

Raids were often instigated. The unemployment rate in Slovakia was already off the charts, and then these newcomers from Eastern Europe took away jobs from the locals. The locals, however, also fled in search of fortune farther west. Dzurinda's[9] time still hadn't come.

The local authorities had problems not only with honesty and the rule of law but also with solving particularly serious crimes, so somewhere there, in the wide hallways covered with synthetic carpets, it was decided upon to pin all the cold cases on the Eastern European illegals.

They hung a murder on Lyosha—a difficult, substantial, hopeless case. He was arrested and summoned once a week for interrogation. However, Slovakia, despite everything, was a European country, so thanks to Lyosha's stomach ulcer, he was prescribed a special diet: steamed chicken cutlets, boiled vegetables, and unleavened bread. Lyosha had contradictory feelings. On the one hand, he had gratitude for such attentiveness. On the other hand, he was not ready to put up with the twelve years of imprisonment that the investigator predicted for him. In truth, the investigator predicted much more. He banged on the table with a plastic mouthpiece, farted shamelessly and repeated: "*Sto rokov samoväzbou. Sto rokov samoväsbou, Oleksiy.*"

"*Vyser si oko,*"[10] answered Lyosha.

Finally, after a month he was provided with a public defender, a student who was doing an internship. Law students mostly gained their first practical experience on such cases: illegal immigrants charged with murder and robbery.

The student's name was Pavol. Thin-mustached, with a wavy black mullet, like a young Clooney, he desperately defended Lyosha. He said that Lyosha looked very similar to his older brother, who moved to Prague in '83 and stayed there to live with some widow. He squinted his small eyes, hidden behind large dark glasses in silver frames, and asked a lot of questions. He also called Ukraine, uncovered all possible documents, found useful witnesses among the Slovaks. And finally, on a hot July morning, he began his speech in court.

"Are you aware that Alexej Vjačeslavovič is a father? And that his son is waiting for him at home?"

◇   ◇   ◇

Lida worked the last year before her retirement, but she was no longer paid. Olha worked too. The daycare teachers were paid little and irregularly. Olha used to go to work too early in the morning, when it was still dark outside, frozen in an old fake fur coat from her youth, and walk past the boarding house for scoliosis patients to her daycare, where she was surrounded mostly by has-been women in their forties who did not like children. She didn't like them much herself: they were poor and sick, had crazy parents who worked in factories that produced almost nothing but heavy industrial groans. Parents came in the evening, tired, hungry, shouting at their children, shouting at Olha because there was no one else to shout at. They took out their anger on her, blaming her for their poverty, their fatigue, their hunger. And the children screamed. Because they were afraid, because of their parents, because of Olha. Olha did not shout at anyone, she just shook her head with a sense of doom, aloofly agreeing with all the accusations, as if it were all just a stupid dream that would pass, as soon as thin crimson stripes flashed on the horizon, and there would be no more of the harsh provincial cries, no more snotty screaming, no more poverty, no more of that surrounding reality that flaunts poverty aggressively, like the beggars in crosswalks flaunt their festering stumps.

And when the screams subsided, when the smells of chlorine and stewed cabbage dissipated, when the city was overcome by gloom and darkness, Olha would go home. Fake fur coat, icy asphalt near the orphanage, and in the evening, the grocery store. At home were notes and preparation for class: Lomonosov, Cantemir, Fonvizin.

Occasionally Tymofiy ate at the daycare. He came after school or after clubs and finished whatever the children had not eaten. Mashed potatoes with fish or mashed potatoes with chicken meat. Though there were only occasional white streaks of meat, it was enough to feel that rare taste of satisfaction. Sometimes there was porridge or lazy dumplings, and jelly instead of compote. But, still, this was better than lean homemade dishes of oatmeal and millet with the thick taste of rancid sunflower oil. Tymofiy filled up on bread. That was what his diet mainly consisted of: bread with jam.

Because of his poor and unvaried nutrition, his hair began to fall out. A rather noticeable bald spot appeared right on the top of his head, which he tried to hide with moderately long hair, but in vain; people noticed it, laughed at it. Someone in his class called him professor. The doctor sent him to get electrophoresis and intravenous drips. Olha was advised to improve her son's nutrition at any cost. She had to sell some of her gold. Olha jokingly called herself a blockade runner. In December '93, Tymofiy was fed the kind of food that he had not seen for a long time before and would not see for even longer afterward.

The three of them lived together. Tymofiy, Olha, and Lida. Sometimes the four of them. The fourth being Felix. He did not live with them permanently, but he often came over. Sometimes he stayed for a week or two, sometimes he just spent the night. He burst in drunk and disheveled, as if it were Christmas, sat in the kitchen for a long time, occupied the bathroom, screamed terribly in Lida's room, smashing his fists against the wall until they were bloody. He and Lida had a strange relationship. He was seven years younger than her, which she did not like to remember. He loved her. She put up with him.

Drunk, hugging Tymofiy's neck as if he were an old battle comrade, Felix would often repeat: "I love your grandmother. I love this woman."

And he would always add: "To hell with this war!"

When he was not drinking, it seemed that they really loved each other. There was even something touching about it. Suffering, sometimes painful, but touching. He often called her a poor *Slobozhanochka*.[11]

And she really had had a poor childhood in a village near Bohodukhiv. Her father, the son of a sorcerer and a wealthy man, who until the 1930s wore an embroidered shirt and zupan and went in them to Temnikovsky Labor Camp, died in 1942 on the

Don steppes. Back home, a drunk German was driving a Panzer on a nearby field. Rockets dragging their tails rustled merrily over the village, and in the surrounding forests savage partisans ate frozen pinecones and small rodents.

In the postwar years, her mother often left her daughters alone in the starving and half-dead village. She herself walked around the farms and villages, drank, stayed with some one-legged man, got hired with rogues and tramps from Donbas for temporary work, returned again to the one-legged man, giving him the money she earned. She rarely visited the girls, who went around begging from the neighbors, stealing, or getting food from relatives in neighboring villages in exchange for housework. At the age of thirteen, Lida, having finished the seventh grade, moved to Kharkiv and became hired help. She cared for children, cleaned, cooked. After two years, her mother gathered her daughters and took them to Abkhazia. There Lida mastered the skills of a confectioner: baked cakes, pulled caramel, boiled syrup. Tired of the hospitality in the Caucasus, in the sixties the sisters fled back to the serene landscapes of Ukraine. Her sister Tonya settled in the capital, while Lida was more suited to provincial life. She did not like the hustle and bustle. She married an engineer, gave birth to a daughter, then a son. In the seventies she divorced her husband, who, despite his great love for the children, was neither distinguished by puritanism nor sobriety.

Sometimes Lida visited her mother in the village, waiting half a day for the bus in Bohodukhiv, and when she got to the old yard, abundantly sown with the black peas of goat droppings, she rushed to return home. It was hard with her mother because, although they had similar beliefs, they were strangers, unwavering in their dislike for each other to the point of open contempt and violence. Eventually, when her mother was overcome with diabetes, Lida took her in, settled her in the smallest room, and simply waited for her death. She did not die for a long time, blamed her daughter for her illness, complained to the neighbors, and generally behaved as if she were not going anywhere any time soon. She smelled bad, ate and took a lot—took kilograms of unnecessary medicines until her liver failed and killed her.

Lida had never been afraid of anything. She lived all her life in mystical socialism—the black, quiet, biting mysticism of the dead collectivist system. Lida worked at the pasta factory for more than thirty years. People were always disappearing there. They disappeared routinely and easily, without warning. They disappeared right in the middle of the echoing factories; they dissolved in the flour fog. Sometimes, managers died at production meetings. Serpents and toads crawled from their nostrils. And at forty days, those who took their place would surely die too.[12]

Lida was repeatedly visited by a household ghost and her deceased acquaintants, but she was not afraid of all that, she was immune to such things. She was used to seeing half-decomposed corpses on the coast or in the forest or dark human silhouettes outside the fifth-floor window. She spent almost all her free time in the forest, where she collected berries and medicinal herbs. In those dark coniferous forests Lida met ghosts, forest spirits, onanists. And, of course, the dead: murdered women with their breasts cut off, hanged men, babies abandoned by their mothers. And this did not scare Lida either, she carefully walked around them, from time to time putting copper coins on their eyelids. If a mushroom grew on one of them, say, a Suillus or a white mushroom (she was not picky), she would carefully cut it off without hurting the mycelium, so that later she could return and harvest more.

Lida's grandfather, a trader and a rich farmer, was a sorcerer and had also never been afraid of anything. He predicted his own death. As he predicted, so he died. Having expropriated his entire farm along with livestock and equipment, the Soviet authorities sent Lida's grandfather, at a very old age, to Mordovia, where he, a teetotaler, exchanged all his clothes, except for a *chumachka* and underwear, for two bottles of vodka, got drunk, went out into the yard at night, and froze to death in a snowbank. It was probably from him that Lida inherited that wealth of fatalism, which was like a sinister trail following her life. And when Felix appeared, she shared all this mysticism, all this otherworldly frenzy with him. Obviously, he found some explanations for these events that Lida spoke of, and at the same time, like Lida, he was not afraid of anything. Except for blood.

Olha often emphasized that her mother was an adventurer. In a positive sense, of course, she clarified for Tymofiy, explaining his grandmother's eccentricities, which, of course, he never noticed. After all, what could he notice? What did he have to compare it with? Grandmother was grandmother. The forest, the Dnipro river, household spirits, a thick and indelible mushroom scent in the apartment, dozens of types of herbs laid out on the floor, on the cabinets, on the tables. They were dried to make tea in winter. After all, in winter you must drink herbal tea. In summer you should walk barefoot. Berries were not to be washed, grapes were to be eaten with seeds, burns and cuts were to be moistened with urine, money was to be spent on oneself, and in winter, one was to bathe in an ice hole.

When Felix wasn't drinking, everything could be endured. Even poverty. Tymofiy loved to be with him. Together they went to the beach or to the forest. Lida would take the lead, and the two of them would slow down, as if for their own, exclusively male, frank conversations that only the two of them would understand. Despite Tymofiy's age, Felix spoke for a long time. About his family, about his daughter—whose heart was on the right side of her chest and who was about to graduate from school—about Hrysha the Saboteur, about some aide-de-camp, about chess, soccer, even about women. That was probably the first time an adult told Tymofiy about sex, about death, about rage and honor. Such things are usually talked about either by people who have known each other for a very long time or by accidental interlocutors.

Those were nice days. They were few, but they were imprinted in Tymofiy's memory as something happy and good.

Once, on the way to the river, Felix took Tymofiy aside and opened the briefcase he almost never parted with. In it, among torn cigarette packs and shabby hardcover notebooks, there was a disassembled Kalashnikov.

"Does it shoot?" Tymofiy asked, timidly stretching out toward the greased iron.

"It kills," Felix answered.

"Can I do it?"

"You can, but not now."

Tymofiy grimaced.

"You're still just a private," Felix explained, but then, sitting on a deserted winter beach under a sprawling willow tree with thick roots washed by the waves of the Dnipro, he juggled his long fingers like a street hustler and showed Tymofiy how to assemble the gun. Tymofiy did not remember how exactly, but the sounds of assembly remained with him forever. Metal, clear, barrel shroud, spring, bolt.

"But don't tell anyone, or they will put you in jail."

"Of course, I won't tell anyone."

Tymofiy told everyone he could the next day about the machine gun. Fortunately, no one believed him.

And, of course, there was chess. Game after game, Tymofiy lost to Felix and stubbornly rearranged the pieces. Felix quickly and easily smashed all his naive defenses (Tymofiy almost never dared to build attacks) not even thinking of surrendering, as if he were not playing chess, but playing the board game Chapayev.[13] After ten minutes, on Tymofiy's half of the board there was a defenseless king surrounded by a few powerless pieces. Tymofiy was nervous, angry, and came to tears, but the desire to win was stronger than the bitterness of defeat, so he again arranged both his and Felix's pieces, so that he could play one more game, doomed to a quick checkmate.

"That's how Old Petro taught me!" Felix said. "He never gave in, the old bastard."

Felix called his father Old Petro, although he had died when he wasn't that old, at sixty-eight.

◇ ◇ ◇

Old Petro was born in '22 near Cherkasy. He did not know his father, because his father died in the forests of Kholodny Yar.[14] Already surrounded and defeated, the defenders of Kholodny Yar fired their last bullets blindly. One of these blind bullets pierced the young Red Army soldier's skull. The body was not taken away, it remained in the forest under the January snow until the enclave was completely cleared. The human remains that were thrown into a common pit were not identified. It was not known who they belonged to, Cossacks or Bolsheviks. At first, a wooden plaque was affixed nearby, but it disappeared. And then, on the sandy expanses around the Tiasmyn river, green plants began to grow well.

Petro's mother was a simple peasant from the village of Lesky, who in '23 moved to the neglected Cherkasy. Old Petro grew up in those first years of the young Soviet republic. He met the war when he got out of school, was mobilized, but not to the front, served in the rear headquarters, engaged mostly in paperwork. In '43 he caught Russian Liberation Army soldiers near Kharkiv, in '44 he separated out the ideologically opposed in the villages around Lyuboml'. In '45 he returned to his hometown, where he married a schoolteacher. And after the war he quickly climbed the career ladder, receiving the rank of officer in the Ministry of State Security. Blood or office dust, who knows what that career ladder was covered with, but when his son was born in '47, he had the authority to sign documents in the building on Karl Marx Street. It was then that the family moved to a new house built by Hungarian prisoners of war.

The schoolteacher, Lyudmyla Pototska, was a native of Podillia, and her father bore the Silver Pilawa coat of arms.[15] Her father was shot in the early '30s in Sosonky near Vinnytsia. Lyudmyla and her mother moved to Uman. In the final months of the war, she was sent to teach in Donbas, but the train was stopped at the Shevchenko station near Cherkasy. She and seven other young teachers were transported to the city, settled in dilapidated barracks near the Dnipro river, and assigned to different schools. Lyudmyla got the first one. That's when she met Old Petro, a young long-legged security officer who paraded around starving and wounded Cherkasy in shiny boots and had access to special rations, which he used to feed the young girl from Podillia.

Felix had a fulfilling and, by and large, carefree childhood. The family of a state security officer had everything necessary for a comfortable life, free from poverty and everyday fuss. They had one of the first TV sets in the city, a maid, a tutor, a company car. In general, his childhood was joyful. Detached from reality and detached in general. But joyful. Except for his brother Yurka, who had an untimely birth in '53 and took all the attention. He was loved, pampered, allowed more than Felix. At the age of six he was sent to the choir. Choir? Why the choir? Later, Felix saw this as the basis of Yurka's alcoholism. "It's all because of the choir," he explained to no one in particular, "and because of the sailor suit. Yurka is a faggot and wimp, so he hides his fear and his failures in red wine."

Felix almost never drank wine. He got drunk for the first time at nine, on diluted spirits.

About twenty children lived in their building. All of them were sons and daughters of influential people in the city: elite workers, first and second secretaries of district and regional committees, judges, and, of course, KGB officers. At the age of ten, Felix had already formed a gang of clean, well-groomed kids of the same age. Later, he'd call them his "cruel neighbors." Each had his own nickname. These were the names of the SS, or as Felix not quite appropriately called them, "the elite." Jodl, Himmler, Heydrich, Eichmann, and even Goebbels. Felix was Kaltenbrunner because of his height and his KGB father. Himmler was called Fima at home, and his father was a famous architect. However, no one could ever remember what he designed, except for that hideous building on Kirov Street. Heidrich, also known as Volodka Lutsenko, was Felix's best friend, and the two of them headed the gang. Goebbels wore glasses. Jodl's grandfather was a hero of the Soviet Union, and his father was a retired tank colonel. Eichmann was always bothering Himmler and trying to take off his pants so that everyone could see his circumcised dick. And although Himmler insisted that there was nothing circumcised there, Eichmann did not stop.

For a while, they all ran around the city center like a pack of hunting dogs in a stable, playing Gestapo and Buchenwald, sneaking into the neighboring school, tracking down girls, throwing themselves at them, frightening them, and touching their private parts "by accident." They ran to the Dnipro and stole fish and crayfish from fishermen, destroyed pigeon nests, and looked for the remnants of German weapons near the destroyed bridge. Their most beloved pastime was catching rats. Jodl had an old hunting dog, which his father, a colonel of tank troops, brought from Pomerania in 1947. Rats settled in dilapidated houses, or rather, under their debris. The dog eagerly sniffed for burrows, and the boys pushed a bent rebar into a burrow and turned out a mound of sand, and from there, rats. The rats were caught and put in a cage, which had once, apparently, belonged to a parrot. Up to three dozen of them were stuffed into the cage;

they screamed, fought, eating each other's noses and eyes. Then the rats were sold to a crazy old man who lived in the Kazbet district. The old man paid twenty pre-reform coins per rat. He would put the rats through a meat grinder and stuff them into the minced-meat pies he sold at the Kazbet market.

Felix was supposed to be educated by his tutor Ilarion, a young philology student, but he turned out to be a drunk. For a while he conscientiously taught Felix English, watched his manners and social circle, but soon Felix discovered Ilarion's weaknesses and bought him a liter of wine with his pocket money. Felix ran off to join his gang.

Their house was almost opposite the newly built School No. 17. After Yurka's birth, Lyudmyla taught there. The entire SS elite was eventually transferred there from various city schools. Immediately behind their Hungarian-built house was a chaotic neighborhood of small single-family homes, inhabited mostly by old people. Half of the houses were never rebuilt after the war. Among the squat, sometimes straw-covered huts along the long and deserted streets of Cherkasy, stretched the workers' barracks. Cold, stove-heated, with leaking thatched roofs and clay walls on which moss and dandelions grew. Various bums from the cargo and river ports settled in the barracks, as did children of the builders of the Cherkasy dam and the first chemical giants. Clashes constantly broke out between the SS and this proletariat. There were attacks from both sides, honest fistfights quickly turned into the waving of rebars and chains. It was dangerous and fun to divide the territory. The SS called it an intervention. The port people didn't call it anything at all; they just beat everyone around them, their own and others. Once, in the basement of one of the destroyed houses, the SS found a Maxim with a loaded ribbon and a somewhat rusty turret. At night, they dragged that machine gun to the port, put it in front of a construction trailer, where their fiercest enemies usually gathered, and fired at the dark-green tin can. One was killed, three were hospitalized. State security took over the case. Felix was also interrogated. A young lieutenant with a burnt ear was assigned to him. The lieutenant obviously knew that he was talking to the son of a major, his superior. He followed the protocol. He asked questions in general terms.

"Whose idea was it to shoot from a machine gun?"

"What machine gun?"

"The Maxim," the lieutenant clarified, moving his thin bloodless lips.

"And what happened to your ear?"

"It happened in a fire." The lieutenant was confused.

"Did it hurt?"

"I don't remember, I was a child. It was before the war." Then he remembered that he had to interrogate. Questioning, but not pressuring, he said, "So, whose idea was it? To shoot at the working class?"

"The White Guard[16] shot at the working class."

"Yes, the White Guard," the burnt man agreed happily. "And you guys, with the Maxim."

"We didn't shoot at anybody."

"Is that true?"

"It's true," Felix confirmed, waving his hand, and the interrogation ended.

He and Volodko Lutsenko were whitewashed, while some of the others were searched. The security officers found Polish zlotys from the time of Piłsudski[17] in the sideboard among the books that belonged to Goebbels's parents. After a month of paper-pushing, the frightened Goebbelses exhaled with relief. A Nagant revolver was found in Eichmann's nursery. Eichmann was the least lucky of all of them. He went was sent to the colony. For the sake of justice, one of the wounded was also imprisoned.

The proletariat promised to take revenge, and there were rumors that the entire cargo port was collecting weapons to strike at the downtown guys. People from the camps, coastal sailors, and veterans joined in. They talked about a box of grenades and a dozen Soviet submachine guns. Eventually, the barracks began to be replaced with high-rise apartments. Entire blocks of brick and panel four- to five-story buildings were built in different parts of the city. The hostility subsided, and the case was hushed up.

Remembering Old Petro, Felix especially liked to talk about one episode, emphasizing his father's honesty and integrity. Although, he would add, what kind of honesty can a KGB bastard really have? After graduation, Felix wanted to get into the Airborne Troops at all costs. He had been dreaming about it since he was thirteen years old, when he met a resident of the neighboring building, an old one-armed man, who he generously treated to drink, receiving fantastic stories about paratroopers and reconnaissance during the war in return. The old man's name was Adolf. He was completely gray, with big white eyebrows. He walked around the city in a worn tarpaulin robe, the left sleeve tied in a knot. He smoked Kazbeks, spoke quietly and surreptitiously, gladly accepted gifts of alcohol from neighborhood kids, and then took his time inventing strange stories from the frontlines that, of course, did not actually happen to him, but could have happened. It was around this time that Lukinsky's *Jump at Dawn*[18] was released on Soviet screens. The film was nothing special—just patriotic junk about the honor and courage of the Soviet Army. However, the cute and somewhat phony paratroopers still managed to make all those impressionable Soviet youths fall in love with them.

Having already finished school and begun preparing for the army, Felix was firmly convinced that Old Petro would easily satisfy his heroic aspirations. He would call where necessary, arrange with whomever necessary, and, if necessary, have a drink with whomever necessary. But Old Petro was fundamentally stubborn and seemed to dream only of ruining his son's life.

"Serve your term, and then we will decide," Petro said dryly.

"Dad, can't you?"

"I can. But I won't. Do your time, then join anything you want, even the construction battalion."

And Felix did.

It took two weeks to prepare for the oath. They marched, sang, hung out for hours beneath the white-hot sky. The mocking July sun hung over the pine trees, the thick, cool scent of needles spread over the grounds, Soviet marches sounded out from a loudspeaker mounted to a wooden pole grayed by the rain. Along the central building, lined with glazed tiles, soldiers and parents ran carrying bags and suitcases filled with homemade food. Someone was stuffing his son with cutlets right near the grounds. A young lieutenant from the headquarters, with a round and acne-strewn face that looked like a burnt raisin roll, was leading the civilians. There were not many of them, mostly locals. Conscripts from other Soviet republics, whose relatives had not come, looked enviously at the bags of sausages and jars of dumplings.

Old Petro, Felix's mother, and Yurka came to visit Felix. Yurka did not want to go, so he continuously expressed his dissatisfaction: heat, mosquitoes, no place to sit down. And, in general, what was so important about this oath that he had to travel three hundred kilometers? Petro's silk lieutenant colonel's epaulets and cornflower-blue gorget patches obviously caused anxiety among the officers, but he behaved with restraint, shyly even. Felix's mother, on the contrary, was fussy and nervous, listed several times all the food she had brought to her son, asked him to drink more water, calmed Yurka, and was clearly embarrassed by her husband.

Felix continued to put pressure on his father. He could arrange everything but did not. He ordered Felix to wait for the buyers[19] to serve where he had to, and then, if he wanted to continue along the military path, he would get everything he wanted.

"Then go to your construction battalion!"

He repeated this phrase five times.

Felix was angry, he did not talk to his father, but instead hugged his mother, who also insisted to her husband that he arrange everything. Finally, he suffered through the oath, dryly said goodbye to his father, kissed his mother, gave Yurka a used shell casing, and headed to the barracks with two canvas bags of food.

The buyers were more supportive of Felix's dreams. They took him to Zhytomyr to jump from towers and run ten kilometers instead of having an aperitif before breakfast. Anthropometry and physical data allowed this. Until the end of his military service, Felix was sure that his father had made all the necessary calls, arranged things with whomever he needed, and when necessary, had had a drink with them too. Later, Old Petro denied it, saying that he was not of that rank and, moreover, that he was not in the service so that he could drink with people. A phone call would have been enough. But no, he hadn't called.

Having received a sergeant's shoulder mark, Felix gained confidence. Without asking anyone for anything, he entered the Ryazan Guards Higher Airborne Command School. This entry was preceded by a short assignment in neighboring Czechoslovakia. Dubček wanted more freedom there and, sadly, did not want to share his access to power with the Soviet authorities, so he had to hold back that access, and at the same time restrict freedom. Huska[20] was assigned there to restrict freedom, and Felix, together with half a million people, successfully helped Huska.

He swore that while there, he had not hurt a single soul. They captured some airfield, blocked it, finally. They were following orders, that's all. So what if they rode a tank over some old pavement. It wasn't like they were cutting throats in hand-to-hand combat somewhere near Bagram. After the successful operation in Czechoslovakia, Ryazan welcomed a young and promising paratrooper into the red banner Komsomol ranks, blessed by Lenin.

While he was studying at the school, the GRU, the military intelligence agency of the Russian Armed Forces, became interested in him. Calls to Moscow became commonplace. "Business trips" to Angola, Sudan, Nicaragua. These were the happiest years.

Somewhere in the mid-seventies he met Tanya, his future wife. The most important thing was that she was approved by the headquarters. He got married, a daughter was born, and although her heart was on the wrong side, it did not seem to affect her health, so they didn't worry too much. Training, marching exercises, business trips, paperwork, Yurka was drinking again. Old Petro retired with the rank of colonel, their mother continued to teach. They were not poor, were in good health, spent winters in the city. In the summers, they visited their maternal grandmother's village near Uman. Felix had spent a lot of time there as a child. A quiet village on the river, without forest, unfortunately, but with endless meadows and pastures. They had friendly and sometimes close relationships with the locals, who affectionately called their place the Yagoda House. A large farmstead, officially ten acres, but in fact a hectare of arable land. Then there was an apple orchard, which turned into a state-owned field, which was never plowed because of its distance from the main collective farm fields.

In ten years, Felix visited his grandmother only twice. Her death caught him in training somewhere in the forests near Orel. He missed a lot of things then, dedicating his whole life to the service. He forgot about birthdays, missed the weddings of friends from the past, and the funerals of their parents whom he had known since childhood, spent little time with his family, or frankly, did not spend any time at all. And why family then? Why all this? For whom is this service? For the state? For the Central Committee of the Communist Party? For himself? Yes, for himself. He had already gone too far, there was no turning back. Only ahead. And this way ahead—through shitty barracks and dusty fields, through damp forests and endless sky, through hundreds of kilometers of marching and constant secrecy, without which you can't even go to the toilet—gave him the strength to keep going. You have to keep going. Even if you miss the birthdays and funerals of your loved ones.

He was close only with his mother. Old Petro always stood aside, as if watching a game, and did not interfere. His mom was always at his side. Even thousands of kilometers away. When he read letters from her, and she wrote a lot, he could smell chalk and soap. His mom always smelled of chalk and soap, even when she retired and stopped teaching; it seemed to him that this smell from her body and clothes would never disappear.

She maintained her Polish identity to the end, unbearably irritating Old Petro, for whom any manifestation of nationalism was unacceptable.

"My father did not strangle yours enough," he sometimes repeated not so much with anger as to annoy her. Old Petro's father did not take part in the Polish war. All his military victories were limited to local clashes with the town's insurgent leader.

Felix inherited this Polishness from his mother, hearing Polish folk songs and poetry since childhood. The folk hero Kościuszko stood next to Margelov in his imaginary altar. Mickiewicz was no less important than Shevchenko. Ogiński's[21] music, in particular his polonaises, was the trigger that revealed all the hidden sensitivity and anguish of his nature.

◇   ◇   ◇

Their living room was a peeling but expressive fresco. While it had torn in some places, the wallpaper, brought by Lida's ex-husband from Ulaanbaatar, was still quite interesting. Tymofiy had never seen anything like it. Lemon, carmine, emerald. These stunning colors and patterns had been glued in August '68, just as Felix was trampling the Bohemian pavement in his boots.

Tymofiy especially liked the armchairs. They were part of a Czech set that Lida bought with all the money she had saved, about a thousand karbovantsi, and gave to Olha as a wedding present. A foolish purchase, in her daughter's opinion. Everything was huge, bulky, not suitable for a cozy three-room apartment. Wardrobes and cupboards, veneered to look like ebony, stretched to the ceiling, the sofa brazenly occupied half of a bedroom, chairs and armchairs stood awkwardly, as if on display in a furniture store. The tables were assembled only on holidays when friends and relatives crowded into the apartment. Only the kid enjoyed all of the furniture to the fullest. He built shacks, stacked all that tasteless malachite-black furniture in a pile, covered it with cotton blankets, raising an invisible cloud of dust in the cramped space, which made his eyes water and his voice squeak like a beggar child's. But nothing could compare with the chairs. No one else had such chairs. Soft, deep, it was easy to drown in them, as if in mud, warm and treacherous. It was good to read books in them, wrapped in a blanket or his mother's bloodred terrycloth bathrobe, but the best thing was to sleep in them. It seemed to him that he would live in those chairs for the rest of his life, filled with bitter lack of freedom, endowed with the hypnotic immobility of a manatee.

And there was a piano. It was a rust color, covered with lacquered cedar veneer, from the Austrian company Bösendorfer, produced in the early twentieth century. It was bought for Olha in '70, her father having spent four of his foreman's paychecks on it. Throughout her early childhood, Olha dreamed of playing the piano, of how she would conquer cities, countries, friends, husbands, and the husbands of her friends with her music. When she did not yet have one, she went to ballet, because there it was. After dance lessons, Olha would linger for at least ten minutes, mindlessly running her fingers over the factory-made Ukraine-brand piano and pretending to be an concert pianist. But she was not very good. She failed the two last years of music school and vowed never to take up the instrument again. However, as soon as Tymofiy turned five, she sat him down to play piano.

Every Thursday, he went to the home of his teacher Iryna Pavlivna. There would be no visits to music school! They could go ragged and hungry, but his training was to be private, as it was done in decent families. The teacher was one of those outwardly exhausted people who aged early and for whom the commercialization of daily life was of paramount importance. She devoted herself to earning money and invested all of it into the repair of her apartment. She kicked out her husband, a good-natured and lazy mustachioed man, for his good-naturedness and laziness, and brought up her son alone. He was Tymofiy's peer, a cruel bully who always flaunted fashionable clothes. Feeling independent and strong, Iryna Pavlivna smoked a lot and drank endless cups of coffee, ate little, and took up to seven students a day, after which she fell onto the soiled sofa, covered herself with an old refugee blanket, and wailed from exhaustion, frightening her son.

Music lessons were a serf's duty for Tymofiy. Every day he had to spend one and a half to two hours at the instrument no matter what. Only a fever above thirty-eight or a broken arm could release him from this musical torture. Tymofiy was cunning and tried to avoid classes in every possible way: he threw tantrums, screamed, cried, sobbed, bit, gave ultimatums, threatening to jump from the fifth floor, go to an orphanage, or live on the streets. Olha, each time promising herself to be restrained, cold, and firm, like an Anglo-Saxon warden, quickly gave up and exploded with typical Slavic emotionality.

Felix dreamed that Tymofiy would learn to play Ogiński's polonaise. Tymofiy did not know what a polonaise sounded like, but he said he would learn it someday. Instead, he learned everything from Strauss to Scott Joplin, but not Ogiński. Often, when he was practicing the piano, Felix would listen, sitting on a chair in the corridor behind the wall so as not to annoy Olha.

Tymofiy could hardly say that he learned to love Felix, but he had fun with him. Was he his friend or a grandfather figure? Sometimes Felix asked him to call him Grandfather, but Tymofiy could not get himself to do it. There was something artificial and plastic in it, an outright fiction, an attempt to mask cracks and troubles. And Felix himself did not feel like a grandfather. Perhaps subconsciously he hoped to legitimize himself in this family through this title. Grandfather. It is unlikely that Thatcher was delighted by this.

Felix usually called Olha "Thatcher." Sometimes "Maman," but less often. The first thing he asked Tymofiy when he came to the apartment was whether Thatcher was home. He was afraid of her, afraid of her bitter silence and indifferent gaze. Perhaps, if Olha, with her characteristic emotionality, resorted to hysterics, it would have been easier for him. At least her reaction would have been clear. But here there was absolute disregard. As if Felix did not exist. There were even attempts to reconcile on his part, but he usually came to the truce drunk, drawing the red line of a decisive offensive instead of raising the white flag of surrender and negotiation, so nothing good came of it. Holding his hands behind his back and bending his body with guilt, he slowly entered the room.

"Mademoiselle," he said insinuatingly, "let's talk."

Olha looked up at him with eyes full of exhaustion and empty contempt. They were dead eyes. This is the way one would look at the bad weather outside the window or at the endless fields from the window of a train compartment. Felix, depending on his mood, either gently retreated, muttering something in Polish, or insisted on reconciliation and dialogue.

Lida had to constantly control him, as one controls small children so that they don't get into trouble. Felix was forbidden from entering that part of the apartment. A curtain appeared between

Olha's and Tymofiy's two rooms and the hallway. A heavy burgundy velvet curtain hung like a solemn background in a photo studio. It let in neither light nor sound. Behind it began another world, bizarre and alluring.

At that time, Thatcher hardly spoke to Lida. She could not understand. Why was he here? Perhaps if he quit drinking, some time would pass and she would accept him. Why not? Okay, he was not an intellectual, but he read a lot, knew Polish and English well, ate, again, with a fork and knife. He had many interesting stories, not only just about the war, he knew history, recited Polish poetry. But he did not stop drinking.

Next to him, Lida seemed to change, blindly defended him, ignoring his madness as if she herself was becoming mad, remained unconditionally loyal to his person, cherished this loyalty despite her family. Justifying him to her children and to herself, she considered Felix almost a saint, and to reproach him would be a manifestation of sacrilege. She accepted him as he was, closing her eyes to all the darkness and all the dirt that followed him in a wet, slippery trail.

It is obvious that Lida fell in love with Felix not for his alcoholism. She loved him in protest. *If* she fell in love, of course, because she never confirmed it. Even before Felix appeared, there was someone who used to court her: short-legged, on heels, always in a pressed beige suit and a buttoned-up shirt. A wide silver striped tie added prestige and years to him. On his lapel he wore two badges alternately: Rukh[22] and VLKSM.[23] He waited for Lida near the factory, hiding behind a tree. And when she appeared, cheerfully coming out of the exit, he slithered like a snake out from behind the trunk holding flowers. He stood silently, smiled, wiping his always sweaty forehead with a handkerchief. And each time he gave her flowers. Lida said that she hated the sweet floral blancmange, that flowers made her sick, that it would be better to bring wine or cake for the children, but he kept bringing these bouquets and wondered how a woman could not like them. He didn't drink alcohol, so he took Lida for ice cream, babbled on about membership fees and trade union affairs, went on and on, sweating, about dishonest leaders, and that if he was given the opportunity to govern, he would govern, but you see, the country was falling apart, it couldn't be governed anymore, but he would, of course, just watch him!

"How is it possible to stand him?" she asked Olha. "His shirt is buttoned up to the top! He smells of a Soviet office!"

Then there was the accident on the conveyor. Felix appeared, tall, thin, with the heavy imprint of shell shock on his face. It turned out that he had never buttoned his shirt because he didn't have any shirts with buttons. But he had a dozen striped shirts. He also never brought flowers, and if he took her somewhere, it was anywhere but for ice cream in a children's cafe, because he might accidentally kill someone there due to his extreme dislike of blancmange. The one in pressed clothes called several times, offended, and babbled with a lisp, even tried to meet with Felix, to talk, to air out the situation, so to speak, but at the entrance to the factory, when he saw him with his friends, he deflated like an air mattress in autumn, and never appeared in Lida's life again.

◇ ◇ ◇

In January of '94 Felix was brought home by his neighbor. Frightened but determined, she held him tightly by the shoulder. His eyes were wide open, his lips trying to sound out either a greeting or a curse. But all he could do was open his mouth silently, like a crucian carp caught in a muddy pond.

"Take him," the neighbor said as she let Felix go.

His legs weakened, he folded like a marionette, letting out a long fart.

Felix was frail and helpless, with a face blackened like a fig. Lida dragged him into the apartment, grabbed his Dubok²⁴ jacket with its black synthetic-beaver collar, dragged him down the hallway, shoved him into the bathroom. The apartment filled with an acrid stench. It was the smell of pain, despair, loss. Lida quickly washed him and put him to bed. After a while, Tymofiy came into the bathroom. Somewhere at the bottom of his throat he felt the prickly taste of bile. The bathroom was completely saturated with a pungent sweet smell, which turned his insides and made him feel ashamed and full of pain at the same time. Olha came into the bathroom.

"It's everywhere," she mouthed, looking sad.

"On the floor and on the towel." Tymofiy completed the picture.

The two of them looked at the brown spots on the hand towel and at the floor that was smeared with pieces. They stood there for a while and were silent, staring at the humiliating palette of a mad landscape painter, examining it all like an atavistic exhibit in a natural history museum.

"Ask grandma to clean it up," Olha finally said, holding her stomach.

Tymofiy looked at the puzzled Olga with bitterness and sadness in his wet eyes.

"I don't want to ask her to do that," he said.

"Son . . ."

"How should I ask," the kid nearly cried, "Grandma, clean up the shit?"

"Well, yes," Olha said, looking helplessly at the stains. "Say so. I can't, but you can."

He stood outside his grandmother's room for twenty minutes. He did not dare to go in. At the same time, he was filled with a sense of adulthood and responsibility for Olha. He understood that his mother, most likely, had not imagined her thirtieth birthday this way—standing in the middle of a poisoned bathroom, confusedly wondering about her fate, next to her equally confused son, who was going bald from malnutrition.

If not me, then who? Tymofiy thought, hesitantly stopping at the door to the room. If not now, then when?

He knocked on the door.

Lida answered.

Tymofiy opened the door. In the room, instead of a nightlight, an old TV flashed silently. Lida had taken it to her room from the living room after Olha bought a new Orizon in the summer of '92 with the last of the easy money before a long trip to the Crimean Tarkhankut Cliffs. In an instant, everything came back to Tymofiy: fuzzy peaches, Turkish sweets, chocolate-flavored chewing gum, scuba diving, a white lighthouse melting in the shivering steppe air, a miserable Soviet Independence Day celebration, an endless game of "drunkard" with his friend Natasha—with whom he constantly fought and who taught him to dance the energetic dance to "Soon I Will Be Gray and Old"[25] during the armistice hours—a drowning eighteen-year-old boy whose oxygen tank ran out at twenty-five meters and whose dead body Lyosha pulled from the seabed like a ragged doll's. Young and handsome, with short curly hair and transparent eyes, he was lying on the sharp limestone, and Lyosha stood next to him and trembled, either from fear or from bitterness that this young man had so recklessly ended his life. In a week, Tymofiy was to start the first grade, he was full of dizzying excitement, and everything was bright and wonderful around him. And even the death of the young man did not overshadow the bliss and timid fantasies of returning home from the sea, where school, new things with a special August smell and, of course, a new TV set with a remote control was waiting for him.

"Grandma," he turned to Lida, "Please clean up the shit in the bathroom." That's what he said, word for word. Lida sighed heavily. In the coolness of the TV's light, her face looked old and worn. Then he noticed for the first time that she had wrinkles, dark eyelids, and the sagging, faded skin of her cheeks. She was tired and old. She was already fifty-three. This realization lasted a few moments, stretched into an infinity that lasted a minute. He looked down, blushed, backed away.

"I'll clean it up," Lida said firmly, "I'm sorry. It happens sometimes."

It doesn't happen like that, Tymofiy thought, it never has and it never should.

He turned to his mother. She was sitting in a chair with a book, but not reading it. She was looking into the cold darkness outside the window, nervously ruffling her dyed hair.

"Did you ask?" she asked.

"I did," Tymofiy answered.

"And?"

"She said that it happens sometimes. Can I watch TV?"

"Have you finished your Ukrainian?"

"I'll do it later."

"Then you can't," Olha said. "Finish your Ukrainian."

"Mom."

"Finish your homework and watch whatever you want."

Tymofiy sat at a wide desk, heavily scraped and scratched with pencil, and wrote out the adjectives from the given text. A single table lamp illuminated his notebook, firecrackers were exploding outside the window, probably leftovers from New Year's, and the radio was grumbling behind the wall next door. Lida rustled in the bathroom.

After that, Tymofiy also stopped talking to his grandmother. And he did not talk to Felix either. Now he was on his mother's side. It seemed to him that they were sailing in the same broken boat, rapidly filling with water, which they were trying with all their might to scoop out, but the more they scooped out, the more poured in. Felix ceased to exist for him. He didn't feel sorry for him. On the contrary, he wanted him to suffer, to let his pain finally drive him crazy, to bring him to a frantic state in which his head might hit the concrete. Let him get drunk, Tymofiy thought, get drunk and freeze somewhere in a foyer. Or smash his head against a concrete wall, torture himself for what he had done and not done, or let him shoot himself with his rusty gun. But Felix just got drunk. He came, bringing his dark past to their quiet peace, his fears and defeats, which he shared with them like the last piece of bread, tearing it apart and generously giving away the larger piece.

Their refrigerator was divided into two sections, like in a dormitory. Their time in the kitchen was strictly regulated. In the morning before school and in the evening between six and seven o'clock was Olha and Tymofiy's time, and neither Lida, nor Felix, appeared there. Of course, their paths crossed. For example, you couldn't go to the toilet according to the schedule, but even then, they behaved like sworn enemies at someone's wedding, sitting at the same table, giving each other cold electrified glances.

Tymofiy was on Olha's side in this war, although, of course, he knew that his grandmother loved him, loved him more than anyone else. Olha knew it too and constantly emphasized it. Still, she was even less clear about why Felix was still there. Really, why? Tymofiy also did not have any sound explanation that would satisfy him with logic and consistent evidence.

However, the boy had no doubts that they would certainly get out. They would get out. And his father would come, he would definitely come, and hair would grow over his bald spot, it would definitely grow, Felix would go somewhere, and they would start being friends again. They would definitely start being friends.

And then, the universe seemed to have mercy on them, hearing their mean, desperate prayers. Felix disappeared.

He was gone for a week, a month, half a year. Everyone seemed to have forgotten about Felix. He disappeared the way an inconveniently placed old wardrobe or a clumsy cupboard usually disappears from a house. At first, you are happy to get rid of this heavy and bulky junk, and after a while you don't even remember that it was there, except for a random old photo that sparks something in your memory for a moment, and then goes out like a damp match. Together with Felix, the musty smell of vodka and the tobacco scattered across the kitchen table disappeared. There were no night terrors and morning scratching in the bathroom, worn-out shoes by the door, soaked handkerchiefs in the basin. His black leather coat, which he wore all year and called the ceremonial coat of the Obersturmbannführer, no longer hung in the hallway.

Family relationships were on the mend. Olha spoke to Lida without that metallic tone in her voice. Of course, it was not a true reconciliation, but a truce, though the atmosphere changed, nonetheless. Lida herself changed: she smiled more often, hid less in her room, cut her hair to look like a boy's. And even the sun seemed to look in the windows of their home more often, gently illuminating the furniture, wallpaper, and books on the shelves, giving them the warmth and color of those photographs printed in new photo studios.

Tymofiy became closer to his grandmother again, as if he had returned to those times of Fakel candy and mango under her pillow. However, growing up was inevitable and irreconcilable. Movements, gait: everything became different. Thinking: deeper. Silence: longer. Only his gaze had not changed. It was still clear and bright, like a strawberry field during a blustery storm.

◊   ◊   ◊

Summer came and Tymofiy spent almost three months with Olha in the village, except for two humiliating weeks at camp built on collective obedience and seasoned with childish cruelty. Milk from their neighbor Fedir, wild berries, and vegetable gardens somehow made their existence possible. It was not so bad, because the village is never as bad as the city, at least in the summer, when there was a lot of space, a lot of sun, and even more elusive daily joy.

They had a small, shingled house with three rooms and a summer kitchen made of plywood upholstered with resinous tar, which boiled like oil on hot days. In the summer kitchen there was an old cupboard, a cot, and a large, perhaps oak table, where they usually had dinner or tea. There was also a stove that had not been used for many years. Lyosha's father, Grandfather Slava, had painted it with Petrykivka village designs, but over time they faded away, like everything around them. The house was not in the best condition. The tin roof leaked, which quickly rotted the rafters. The porch was damp. There was no money for paint, so Lyosha dissolved some resin he found in the barn in gasoline and rolled it over the rotten tin surface and on the rotting gable. And so, their house, with its black roof, kept standing. Superstitious people crossed themselves as they walked by.

In the house there was an old painted chest, an open plywood wardrobe, a Rigonda[26] with a small collection of Soviet pop music on vinyl. There was a black-and-white TV and pliers to change channels. However, there were only two channels, national and local.

The two inhabited rooms were cozy and bright, but the third was a winter kitchen that Tymofiy was afraid to even enter. No one had ever spent the winter in it or ever lived there. It was cold and empty, as if someone were dying there all the time. Herbs dried on the floor; the stove was a sparsely stocked country library, consisting mainly of Soviet novels of patriotic orientation and binders labeled *Youth* and *Change*. The yard was green and shady. A white mesh hammock hung between a pear tree and an apricot tree. In the middle of the yard grew a tall and ancient maple tree, which Tymofiy equipped with an observation post (a stool nailed to the trunk and an umbrella tied to it). From the post on the tree, you could see the whole village and even the neighboring Shelepukhy; you could see the PAZ 672 bus, yellow and rounded, rushing between the fields, like a single loaf of bread on a black conveyor belt. The yard from that height seemed fake. Several outbuildings were huddled together, creating an architectural ensemble reminiscent of the Russian hinterlands: grayed wood, small windows with sooty panes, black asbestos chimneys.

In early August, Lyosha arrived quite unexpectedly. Straight from captivity, that is, from prison. Pavol, the young lawyer, had been able to prove that at the time of the murder, Alexej Vjačeslavovič had been in Ukraine. Lyosha received compensation of three hundred korunas.

He brought some sweets, supposedly from abroad, but obviously bought at a train station kiosk somewhere.

Lyosha looked tired, sickly. The day before, he'd had a hellish time on the Ikarus bus crammed with people. He had clearly gained weight in prison: they fed him well, some of the rations were donated by a generous local religious community, Pavol brought good cigarettes.

He sat in the summer kitchen and rubbed his temples with his thumbs and kept silent, obviously wanting to sleep. And he probably would have slept, if not for the family he had not seen in over six months.

Tymofiy ran around and climbed on him like a puppy, unable to hide his joy, proudly showed his father a bag from the Billa supermarket, in which Lyosha had sent a package in the spring: pâté, a bar of chocolate, and two packages of Polish margarine. He showed his treasures: a dried, perfectly preserved frog found on the road, nunchaku he made by himself from a sawed-off rake handle, and an army flask given to him by Felix. He talked about Felix, who was gone, about his baldness and that he looked like his father's friend Uncle Koka, about rubella, which he had in

March, and about the camp, where you had to fight every day, whether you wanted to or not, because others wanted it.

Olha, on the contrary, first asked her husband to tell a story. In the viscous fog of half-sleep, Lyosha began to recall something, some emotional episode from prison life, a carefree smile appeared on his face from the fact that the experience was already behind him. He sleepily stretched his thoughts, trying to catch the lost thread of his story, but Olha, sensing his stumble, immediately interrupted him and told him herself. Excited by his appearance, upset by his unsuccessful trip, she, as if going through a string of troubles, talked about illnesses, debts, and the head of the day-care, Prokofieva, who turned half of the building into a warehouse for building materials. She talked about Prokofieva the most. She also talked about Felix. She talked about him a little, saying how good it was that he was gone and how tired she was of him, of his dushman and the pissed-on walls in the bathroom.

"I saw him," Lyosha said. "Yesterday."

"Where did you see him?" Olha did not understand.

"In the kitchen."

"In which kitchen?" Olha shuddered. "Don't tell me in ours."

"In ours," Lyosha replied calmly, trying to hide that strange smile that sometimes appears when you give someone unpleasant news.

"Oh my God!" Olha cried out in horror. "Drunk? What's so funny, Lyosha?"

"It's nothing funny. No, he was normal, I mean, not drunk. He was afraid of me. Then he hugged me. He was eating cabbage soup. So, I ate too. It was delicious. Your mother made it. She said that you were here, that you would be here all summer," Lyosha yawned, twisting his head.

"And what?"

"Well, I came over," he answered.

"Not you. What was Felix doing?" Olha got nervous, ran her

fingers through her hair, and bit her upper lip. And then froze with her lower teeth bared and a hand in her hair.

"He finished his cabbage soup and went to the beach."

They returned to the city in late August. Felix, swollen with silent shame, sat for a long time in Lida's room, which he called a bunker. He read or watched TV, afraid to go out, lest he accidentally run into Thatcher. He was glad to see Tymofiy. Felix shook him by the shoulders at length and excitedly, as if trying to shake love and forgiveness out of him, gave him a set of army pots, put his hand in his trouser pocket, searched for something for a long time, obviously some kind of surprise, but, having found nothing, he shook Tymofiy's shoulders again.

Tymofiy, to his surprise, to some extent rejoiced at Felix's return. As long as he didn't drink. Or drank in moderation.

In early September, Lida took a step that was difficult for her. It seemed to her that everything could be fixed, saved, or at least not destroyed completely. Her retirement would help with Tymofiy, and with the atmosphere in the house. Felix returned on the condition that he would not drink. And all this seemed to amount to a reconciliation.

"He has a job, in security," she explained. "He will bring money to the house. Maybe it will be easier."

Olha did not react to that statement, just shrugged her shoulders, as if to say that it would not be easier for her. She was not going to put up with him. His very presence, sober or drunk, was unbearable. Although, of course, more bearable when sober. For Tymofiy's sake, the most important thing was for Felix not to lose control. For him to eat his cabbage soup, scratch his neck with a dry blade, even if he yelled while watching soccer, yelled as if during artillery training, unable to hear himself: "Kick! How do you kick, you bastard!" Let him bring or not bring money, let him wear the ceremonial coat of the Obersturmbannführer, in the pockets of which there were always dried fruits covered with tobacco, seed husks, and breadcrumbs. Let his striped sailor's shirt with yellow armpit stains hang over the stove next to the school jeans, let the towels smell of laundry soap, and cigarette butts float in the toilet. As long as he doesn't snap.

Only Lyosha did not care. He slept for the second month, occasionally crawling out of the apartment to visit his parents or old friends. Apparently, he was planning to go somewhere like Tyumen.

◇　◇　◇

It was the middle of autumn. Tymofiy was in third grade, walking home from school slowly, kneading the fallen leaves with his soft blue leather shoes, wandering into the sun-drenched parks full of large trees or around the faceless white building of the theater where he studied acting. There with Timur, a boy also in third grade, chasing an old rubber ball in the park near the Hill of Glory, Tymofiy was in no hurry to go home, knowing that he would certainly sit down at the piano, which he hated with all his being.

Lyosha finally left. Olha was coping, but not very well, with the kid who got Cs and bronchitis, with Felix, with hopeless provincial boredom, and with the cat that should certainly be taken to the vet. But where can you find one in a weathered and dead city where you can't even find a regular pediatrician?

The cat had gotten fleas and worms during the summer in the village. She was walking, grooming her soul out, defecating liquid, smearing it all over the carpet like oil paint on canvas. They had to treat her at home. Lida decided to put her in a plastic bag, leaving only her head exposed, and spray dichlorvos insecticide into the bag. No one had any doubt that this was the way to treat pets with fleas. And so, that is what they did. Lida held the bag with the cat, Olha conscientiously sprayed dichlorvos. The cat was panting, trying to break out, letting loose long meows, making terrible human sounds, and tearing the bag with its hind legs. Finally, they released her, caught her again to wash her, but just then the water was turned off, so they released her again, and by the time the water was turned on again, the cat had already managed to lick off all that wild mustard gas. The fleas died, and the next day the cat began to die too.

"Maybe we shouldn't have done that," Tymofiy commented timidly.

"Perhaps," Olha agreed sadly, conscious of her guilt and helplessness in the situation. It had not made the cat feel better. She walked around the apartment and vomited yellow-brown mucus, a bit like plum jam. In a few days, her fur, along with pieces of skin, came off in clumps, revealing a raw flesh covered with ulcers. The cat collapsed. The gray-pink carcass, like those skinned rabbits hanging in the market with fluffy remnants of fur on their legs, lay under the radiator, shaking continuously and refusing to eat. Even in peacetime, she refused to eat ordinary human food: porridge, soup, potatoes, but now she would not even sniff it. She could not even move: her whole body was in constant pain, piercing and all-consuming, like death itself. This was death. Long and agonizing. This was probably how the saints died, flayed alive. This is how heretics died, drunk with liquid lead. That's what you are, death, thought Tymofiy, looking at the half-corpse of the cat and into its blind, wet eyes. That's how you will die, cat.

One day Lida and Felix came back from a walk on the autumn beach with a full bag of river mussels. They often walked there, catching the cold Dnipro wind as it filled their hoods and jackets. Lida swam. Felix walked along the shore, sinking his boots in the damp sand, and keeping an eye on Lida.

"There are thousands of them, just lying on the sand near the water," Lida said happily.

They determined that they were called toothless river mussels. Once pulled from the salt water, they opened their dense shells, showing their vulgar insides. Felix liked these grayish mollusks, swollen like chestnut buds. They also gave them to the cat to try, and she ate them, weakly, barely chewing and swallowing with difficulty, but she ate them.

For a few months, Lida went to the Dnipro every week and collected toothless river mussels, which she fed to the cat and to Felix. Tymofiy did not dare to eat them, smelling rotten fish and death. They were almost all dead, because after the water receded, they were left lying on the sand under the harsh sun and dry wind. But their death helped the cat not to die and they enriched Felix too. He consumed them by the bucket—with cabbage and pickles, seasoned with onions, and doused with vinegar, with rice and mushrooms, with potatoes and pasta. One day, coming home from school, Tymofiy saw Felix making dumplings, carefully putting a cooked mussel in each one. The apartment was filled with a fishy smell, which remained there until spring, when the water in the Dnipro rose, burying dead shellfish under its thickness.

"It is a gift from above," Felix joked, "God himself had mercy and gave us a part of himself. Flesh of my flesh, so to speak."

Felix took responsibility for the cat, he fed it mussels, cooked and pushed through a meat grinder, wiped its skin with a cooling balm mixed with honey and aloe juice, and for some reason dripped sulfacetamide in its eyes. It helped. Tymofiy was grateful and Felix was comforted. The kid spent more and more time with him again, when, of course, he had the time. He attended many clubs and private lessons, had to practice the piano every day by himself and every Thursday with Iryna Pavlivna, not to mention his schoolwork and his English tutor. Dark evenings, blackouts, brief sleep. He had to go to school on the other side of the city, to the same school where Felix's mother used to teach. He returned in the dark, sometimes very late, when only black shadows moved through the streets. It was especially scary to wait for the bus at a semi-abandoned stop downtown. Will it reach you today, or will you have to schlep dozens of blocks in the damp darkness? And this darkness, peering into you, into your soul with its black gaze, will you withstand it? Will you be able to reach your home? Do you have a home at all? This darkness was so thick that you could touch it, feel its cold and stickiness, like a dead body.

Calm, confidence, and some kind of security appeared only in the dimly lit kitchen, from the sight of Felix reading an old newspaper or sports magazine. If he is home, then Grandmother is home. The bustle around dinner, familiar sounds and smells: mushrooms, mussels, tobacco, something else, fresh laundry, bitter cologne. Mom in her territory, as always, behind a book or sewing. Concentrated, firm.

Tymofiy struggled to throw off his backpack, take his coat off, do his homework, or sit down at the piano.

◇ ◇ ◇

"I was eleven then, like you."

"I'm ten."

"Well, I was eleven. And she was a little older. Maybe twelve. Her name was Katyusha. We were sitting under the fence in the wormwood, and I was sticking my finger inside her."

"Where? Right there?"

"Yes, right there. Although she was older, she was still small. She was pleased, because something was moving there. So, I put my dick in her. Not directly into her, but on top of her. What a redneck. First she squealed, and then told her grandmother everything."

"And what?"

"Nothing. She told her and that was it. Then her grandmother gave me a lecture. She said that if I kept doing this, my parents would have to take Katyusha to their apartment in the city."

"And did they take her?"

"*Psiakrew!*[27] Are you crazy? Nobody took anyone away. I did it with her a few more times. I've never had anything leak out. Do you have any idea what I'm talking about?"

"Yeah, I do."

Tymofiy and Felix walked along the endless green fences, deeper and deeper from the center toward the suburbs built around the factories thirty years ago. From time to time, they plunged into the blue shadows of the sprawling fruit trees, picked ripe apricots from the ground, ate their generous pulp, leaving the dirty rough skin. They stopped near a water fountain. Felix pressed the lever with one hand, leaned on the ground with the other, greedily drinking cold water. Tymofiy stood, weakly peering into the green distance and thinking about Katyusha. This thought confused him with something secret and even magical, that incomparable rural mysticism, into which only selected townspeople are initiated, those to whom Katyusha entrusts her puppylike body, tender and untouched. There was something teasing and exciting about it. How did it even happen? Why did she allow it? He tried to imagine one of his classmates in her place and got even more excited. At that time, he was not in love with anyone in particular; his childhood affections were reserved only for Alicia Silverstone. Tymofiy tried to imagine Alicia in Katyusha's place, but her image under the fence in the wormwood blurred, resisted forming one clear picture, slipped away, and melted in the hot air.

They passed the last of the private houses and approached the stretch of squat ochre-colored four-story buildings.

"Listen," Tymofiy asked, "what's with her now?"

"With whom?" Felix did not understand.

"Katyusha, who else?"

"Oh, with her," Felix thought, smoothly moved his shoulder. "Well, she became an alcoholic."

"What do you mean?"

"Well, like me, only a woman. She became an alcoholic, lost her beauty, and lived by the holy spirit of a full glass. She kept walking around, people poured her drinks, and then, apparently, she bought the farm somewhere."

Tymofiy stopped for a moment, imagining Katyusha with a large farm behind her, walking from house to house, from afternoon to late evening, pouring into herself all that holy spirit (vodka or moonshine), which the owners keep for some special events. And then somewhere, under a streetlight, she chokes on her own bile, swallows it, coughs it up, spitting the remains of her insides on the gray asphalt, and finally, without realizing what's happening, dies.

"Do you feel sorry for her?"

"What the hell, do I have to feel sorry for everyone?"

"I don't know," the boy sighed.

"I don't know either."

They came to the entrance with a burnt door. The house itself had tiles peeling off like a vocational schoolgirl's nails. Nearby, there was a cart without wheels. In the front garden, there were flowers overgrown with weeds. It seemed that it had been many years since anyone lived in the house.

They went up to the third floor. All the doors to the apartments had the same entrance: wooden, painted with brown paint.

"That's it," Felix said, stopping in front of number twenty-four. "Here we are."

It was important for Felix to introduce Tymofiy to his friend, in fact, his only friend, Hrysha the Saboteur. Tymofiy was alarmed by this.

"Do you want to go with me?" Felix asked in the morning. Somehow easily and naturally. He had never taken Tymofiy anywhere, except for the usual trips to the beach or forays into the forest, but now he wanted to. Hrysha was *that* awesome. A rock.

Tymofiy grimaced in disbelief.

"A mountain!" Felix added, after a pause. "So, will you?"

"I'll go," Tymofiy agreed.

"Hrysha is decent. Unlike me. He killed people without being noticed."

Obviously, Felix wasn't going to drink. And when you're not going to drink, the chances of doing something stupid go down to zero. Why not take the kid?

Like Felix, Hrysha joined the defense as a junior officer. He was an excellent student of intelligence work.

Felix was loud, active, and he had a huge presence, like an uninvited relative at a wedding. Hrysha was as modest and unremarkable as a Soviet coat. Felix showed off his rank and valiant past as a Soviet officer. Hrysha cowered and did not like to remember the past.

A unique time in their lives was a special operation in Nicaragua, organized by the Second Main Directorate.[28] Felix said almost nothing about it, and that almost nothing only in a semiconscious state. "Fat faggot Somoza," Felix kept repeating.

Only once did he manage to say something coherent about this top-secret raid. The punishment for disclosure was the death penalty. More precisely, about two raids. The first one took place in '78. The civil war was in full swing. The forces of the Sandinista National Liberation Front seized parliament, and armed confrontations between government troops and Sandinistas were happening throughout the country. Destruction of companies, national strikes, and protests, US and USSR intelligence, hostages, and torture chambers, in short, a typical situation for a Central American country at that time. The task of Felix and his partner Hrysha was not fully understood. Felix managed with his, but Hrysha failed.

At the end of the operation, they were immediately summoned to Moscow, and were driven from Chkalovsky base through the city along wide avenues. There was a lot of sun, it was shining so inappropriately, so contrary to their mood, and the driver, a psoriasis-riddled silent man, did not respond to their questions. As if he knew, idiots, where he was taking them. It was so anxiety provoking, and it would be so sweet when finally this anxiety would end. Only no one knew how or when this would happen. How do half-failed operations usually end? Would they get demoted? Ended? They were taken to the general's office. The office, however, looked more like a banquet hall: long massive tables, chairs under the window, a fluffy red carpet that stretched to the oak altar with a marble inkstand and a malachite lamp, a general's throne upholstered in green plush, lacquered oak, a three-meter coat of arms, a pale Brezhnev. And the general himself, short-legged, gloomy, and alive. Though it may have been better for Felix and Hrysha if he wasn't. He took a few steps towards Felix, hiding something behind his back. Fuck me, Felix thought then. He will end me, and that's all. It's a pity about the carpet. It's a beautiful carpet, fluffy.

"Come here," the general commanded, pointing his little finger at Felix, his other hand still held behind his back.

Felix approached.

A sly smile emerged on the gloomy and gray face of the general. That's how you look at a victim who has been caught but not yet killed, Felix thought.

He'll end me for sure.

"Captain Ignatiev!" the general shouted. "You are no longer a captain!"

"Thank God," Felix thought. "Private. Not killed. Just a private."

"You are no longer a captain," the general repeated, "you are a lieutenant colonel!"

And he handed Felix new shoulder marks.

Hrysha was standing at the door. And he dreamed that he would just be ended, that he would be killed quickly and, preferably, suddenly, without cellars, without interrogations, without pencils between his fingers and oxygen under the skin, to just be led down a long corridor past the concrete offices of people like him, and then pop! He was ready for it, he had failed, he was in intelligence, and he had no right to fail, he had been taught not to fail. At least they would return his body to his mother. But they probably would not give it back, they would probably just bury or burn it somewhere. He had heard about crematoria for those who made mistakes. They were burned. First, of course, oxygen under the skin, and then, into the oven.

The general slowly approached his desk, stopped, turned around just as slowly, pointing at Hrysha with his little finger.

"And you, motherfucker," the general said quietly, "will be a lieutenant until the end of your service."

The next time Felix flew to Nicaragua was the following year. Before that, they had hinted at the difficulty of the operation, hinted at possible non-return, so you can say goodbye to your loved ones, but not explicitly—visit your father, mother, spend a day with your daughter. Felix visited his parents, took his daughter to the park, his wife to buy new shoes. In the morning he left for Minsk, and from the military airfield there, he and several other specialists were taken to Havana. They spent the night and, in the morning, flew to Nicaragua. Felix had three sealed bags of documents at that point. In Nicaragua, he was to be told which one to open. The rest he was instructed to burn. So, he stayed at some base near Managua for a week, but the order didn't come through. He slept on boxes filled with shells, ate bananas, baked cassava, and some kind of barley syrup, and was given a carton of Marlboros. As he smoked and looked at the tropical night sky, listening to the insistent singing of the Amazonian motmot bird, the Sandinistas overthrew the fat faggot Somoza, the revolution won. They flew to Cuba. From there, to Moscow. He did not know what to do with the packages if none were opened. There were no instructions for such a scenario. He brought the packages to Moscow. When he was asked whether he had burned the packages he had been instructed to, for some reason he said that he had, although in fact all the documents were in his hotel room. By the time he got to the hotel, his hair had turned gray almost completely. If they had searched the room and found them, they would have killed him. No other possible outcome. And then they would have burned him. Everything was simple here: if you do not burn them, they burn you. The bags were in place, there were no searches. It was dangerous to burn the documents in the room or flush them down the toilet, and even more so to attempt to take them out of the hotel. He had no choice but to eat them. And so he ate them—after thoroughly soaking the papers in water. And, of course, without reading them.

The door was opened by a thin man of medium height wearing soft slippers. He was wearing a wrinkled white T-shirt with yellow and pink stains on the chest (probably from ketchup and scrambled eggs) and blue trainers tucked into high gray socks. He didn't look like an intelligence officer. Rather, he looked like a retired warrant officer, who had spent his entire service in the booth, making tea and giving mattresses to the rookies. His face was inexpressive, faded, as if he was merely disguised as an average guy. It was difficult to focus your attention on his appearance. His lips, nose, and forehead were all there, but somehow it was impossible to distinguish it all.

"Come in, but don't make noise," Hrysha greeted coldly. They came in.

"This is my grandson," Felix introduced Tymofiy, letting him go forward.

"Hryhoriy Ivanovich," Hrysha extended his dry hand. Tymofiy shook it.

Hrysha had a small two-room apartment, almost empty. In one room, the bigger one, there was an old red sofa with the armrests shredded, obviously, by a cat. Opposite that there was a similar red armchair and a dark lacquered chest of drawers with golden handles. On the wall immediately above the chest there were two shelves with books. Pikul,[29] Viktor Suvorov,[30] fairy tales from various parts of the world. In another room there was also an armchair. There was a Swedish wall with a horizontal bar, two weights (16 and 32 kilograms), a locker, a TV set on a stool. What else did the old lieutenant need? He didn't have a wife, his daughter had been married to an animator at Disney for several years, lived in Orlando, Florida, on the shore of Lake Hope, surrounded by giant trees with eerie garlands of Spanish moss. Sometimes she called, not so much to talk as to make sure her father was still alive. But Hrysha was in excellent health, he did gymnastics. Though he smoked, he drank only in moderation. It seemed that Hrysha did everything in moderation. Even lived. In this way he differed from Felix. It probably brought them closer together.

He walked quietly and spoke quietly. He was obviously being shy because of Tymofiy's presence. Hrysha offered to turn on the TV. The kid declined.

They sat down in the kitchen, as ascetic as the rest of the apartment. A Dnipro-2 refrigerator, a table, stools, an aquarium with Madagascar cockroaches on the windowsill, a gilded crucifix with a surprisingly sad Jesus above the stove.

"I don't suggest eating," Hrysha said. "It's what pigs do. Let's drink?" He looked first at Tymofiy, then at Felix.

"I'll have tea," Tymofiy said, looking disgustedly at the cockroaches.

"Tea for you. Petrovych?"

Felix pouted, looked at Tymofiy then at Hrysha.

"Get me some water."

"Then I won't drink either," Hrysha said. Still, he did not put the kettle on.

They sat at the bare table.

"Well, out with it," Hrysha said. Felix spun on the stool.

"Hryhoriy Ivanovich, I'm not going to break your balls for nothing."

"Well? What do you want?" Hrysha tapped the table with his index and middle fingers.

"Hryhoriy Ivanovich, we have a *muy importante* task here."

"Just say it!" Hrysha almost lost it, but he stiffened and even let himself slouch a bit.

"Hrysha, give me the pistol," Felix said dryly.

Hrysha turned his gaze to Tymofiy. He looked, not taking his eyes off him. His look was calm, balanced, and therefore unpleasant, so Tymofiy turned his to Jesus. Felix noticed Hrysha's confusion, waved his hand at the boy, saying that it was okay to discuss such matters around him.

"So, you give it to me? I'm not just asking for nothing. If I need it, I need it."

"Well, it's your pistol," Hrysha calmly said. "If you need it, you need it."

Hrysha stood up heavily and disappeared into the hallway.

"Makarov. Bullshit." Felix turned to the kid.

"What for?" Tymofiy asked timidly.

"Be quiet, rookie."

Hrysha rustled around in the hallway for a long time, turned the light on and off, climbed around in the attic, took out boxes with Christmas decorations from somewhere, and then kept pushing them back in place. An old brass faucet fell to the floor, something burst, as if glass had shattered, Hrysha cursed, somehow pushed everything back, finally pulled out a brown sports cap with a pistol wrapped in it, and somewhat angrily went into the kitchen.

"So here," he held out the hat, from which plaster dust was spilling. "You sure you won't have a drink? I have some."

"I have some too," Felix said, looking into the cap and clicking his tongue with satisfaction. Then he put the cap in his briefcase.

They stayed for another twenty minutes, mostly silent. Felix thanked Hrysha for his hospitality, famous throughout the city, stood up, looked at Jesus, crossed himself with a sweeping motion, raising his hand high, and went to the hallway.

"Should I call?" he asked, grabbing the white plastic handset. "Password twenty-five," he said hoarsely, pressing the disconnect button.

"Total secrecy," said Hrysha ironically. He was standing next to him, folding his arms across his chest.

"Hryhoriy Ivanovich, at ease!" Felix commanded. "Follow me, rookie!"

Tymofiy lagged behind Felix.

They were going back the way they came, along the green fences and apple trees, along the empty and hot summer street. They walked in silence. Tymofiy was embarrassed by the pistol in the briefcase, Katyusha was still on his mind. He had come too close to forbidden things, felt distressingly like a bad guy from a gangster movie. However, he looked at Felix, at his sweatpants, blue shirt, worn brown shoes, like a Saracen's, and at this briefcase. If the shoes and shirt could still be attributed to poverty, the briefcase undoubtedly gave him the appearance of a madman, even without the gun inside.

Having reached Ilyin, a street lined with one-story buildings that cut the city lengthwise, rapidly tearing it into rectangles, they turned left, in the opposite direction from home.

"Where are we going?" Tymofiy asked.

"Well, we're together, right?"

"Yes, together."

"Then be silent, rookie. It's not far," he quickened his pace.

They passed a daycare with splintered acacia trees, a city market where they sold Turkish goods, rugs, jeans, and jewelry, and came to a lonely nine-story building that stood in the middle of the commercial district like a minaret. They entered the courtyard, clean and green, and sat down on a bench in the shade.

"Are we waiting for someone?" Tymofiy asked again.

"We're waiting," Felix answered irritably.

"For whom?"

"People."

They sat for about twenty minutes. The sun was hanging high in the sky, the house opposite cast a short shadow, which, despite all its efforts, did not quite reach the playground. In the neighboring yard, someone was trying in vain to start a moped. It seemed that this day would never end.

Tymofiy was bored. He threw his head back, exposing his face to the warm wind, looked at the shining whitened sky, which made his eyes fill with warm tears, drew swastikas and stars on the ground with a piece of broken glass, picked celandine, and drew more swastikas with the thick yellow juice from the stems, but this time on his hand. He thought about Katyusha. It was impossible not to think about her, or at least, about her probable death.

"They're coming," Felix suddenly said. "Alrighty, get out of here."

"Where?" Tymofiy did not understand.

"Get lost! Over there!" Felix waved his hand in a random direction, pointing at a children's swing about ten meters away.

"All right," Tymofiy conceded, offended. But then he changed his mind. "And if I don't go?"

"Get the fuck out of here!" Felix shouted.

Tymofiy shuddered, muttered "retard" through his teeth, but obeyed.

Two guys entered the yard. One, with hair slicked back, was dressed in long shorts covered in a palm tree pattern. The other looked more serious: half-shaved head, jeans, white Sprandi sneakers, a black T-shirt. They stopped at the first entrance, stood, talked to each other. A scene somewhat reminiscent of two penguins struggling to decide whether to jump into the winter water or stay on the ice. Finally, the one in shorts jumped, that is, began to walk toward Felix. The one in jeans remained standing, constantly looking around, fidgeting, and glancing nervously at an apparently dead pager. Tymofiy was angry with Felix. He sat on the swing and swung his legs, unsuccessfully trying to shake it.

"Who is that?" the slick one asked nervously.

"My grandson," Felix calmly answered.

"Your grandson? Okay. Did you bring it?"

Felix opened the briefcase with respectful indifference, took out the cap. The slick one took it, looked inside. He stood and looked, clenching his jaw.

"No bullets?" he asked Felix.

"Well, check," Felix said mockingly. He felt confident and even relaxed.

"Okay."

The slick one was telling Felix something hurriedly, but too quietly, as if he was praying. No matter how hard Tymofiy strained his ears, he could not hear anything.

"Okay," the slick one said again, looked back to his accomplice, pulled money from the deep pocket of his shorts, and put it on the bench next to Felix.

"I don't fucking understand, why did you bring the kid?" the slick one asked, with a half grin.

"None of your fucking business," Felix answered.

"The old man and the sea," the slick one said. He put his cap under his armpit and moved toward the man in jeans. When they disappeared behind the house, Felix waved his hand for Tymofiy to come over.

"Did you sell them the gun?" Tymofiy asked disappointedly.

"Yes," Felix answered. "Why? You need one?"

"I thought we were going to shoot."

"We will, but not now," Felix said dryly. "Let's go." They emerged onto dusty Ilyin Street. The sun was slowly slipping behind a skyscraper, the wind was picking up, the trees rustled, evoking anxiety. Tymofiy could hardly drag his feet, tired of the heat, the long walks, and still angry with Felix. Felix, though, felt elated and began to tell one of his stories. This time it was about a general who pronounced his *r*'s like *w*'s, and how when the general flew out to a particular military unit to carry out an inspection, no one could understand what he wanted. And he just wanted to be given a refreshment.

"Where to now?" Tymofiy interrupted him.

"Where do you want to go?" Felix asked.

"I want to go home."

"Home—stand down! We're going to the market."

"You go to the market." Tymofiy got angry. "I'm going home."

"Hey, you! Don't start sobbing! The market is the end point of this operation."

Tymofiy grimaced helplessly, wanted to say something offensive, but kept silent and followed Felix.

Felix started talking again, and without finishing the story about the general, began to retell, probably for the tenth time, some story about Hrysha the Saboteur. Again, he complained about his brother Yurka and his drunken binges. He also complained about his daughter, saying that he gives her all his Afghan pension, almost five hundred hryvnias, and she still does not appreciate him, she despises him, but does not refuse the money.

"It's half a thousand," he said desperately. "People don't get such salaries, and she is just like her mother, all gold and leather. Like a gypsy."

Felix was silent for a few seconds, as if thinking over what he had said.

"There are only gypsies around," he continued, spitting into the road dust. "What can I say about them, they have a national dish: hedgehog."

"Hedgehog?" Tymofiy was surprised. "You can't be serious!"

"I have nothing against the Jews," Felix continued, "but the gypsies . . . There was once a Mr. Höss . . . do you know who Höss is?"

"I have no idea," Tymofiy answered.

"An interesting gentleman. The commandant of Auschwitz. He dealt with gypsies every day . . . passed through their barracks . . ."

"You know, I think you just admire them, all these . . . fascists. I've seen *Schindler's List.*"

"Give me your hand!" Felix said forcefully.

"What for?"

"Give me your hand!"

Felix grabbed Tymofiy's left hand and held it up to his eyes.

"What is this?"

"A hand."

"No, what's on your hand?"

"Skin."

"Donnerwetter, don't be ridiculous."

"Well, a swastika." Tymofiy gave up. "But I just . . ."

"And I'm the one who admires them?"

They turned into a low, open gate with peeling blue paint. It was evening, the man making shish kebabs was extinguishing the coals on the grill, pouring yellowish water on them from a plastic bottle, the vendors were all winding down their trades, hiding the goods in oversized checkered bags, drinking wine while sitting on their sacks and duffle bags and waiting for the loaders, who would take the goods to the metal trailers on wide pallets with wheels bolted to them. Lazy wasps were circling over a garbage can filled to the top with cardboard and rotten fruit. Some of the vendors stood to the last minute, waiting for random buyers. Although what buyers were there at this time? Everyone had made their purchases before lunch. Without visitors, the stall looked orphaned, like a classroom without students: only the teacher standing at the blackboard, indifferently rubbing away algebraic equations with a wet cloth.

Felix crouched down from time to time, as if tying his shoe, turning half his body around to make sure there was no one sur-veilling him.

"Never turn around," he said. "Even if you know there's a tail, don't turn around. The tail must not know that you know about it."

"Is that why you brought me along? For secrecy?"

"You're not as stupid as you look," Felix smiled.

Finally, they came to a stand with all kinds of glasses. The vendor, a mustachioed short man, who probably did not expect any customers, perked up and moved his small body toward Felix. Felix reached for the glasses. He took a pair, tried them on, looked in the mirror for a long time.

"Well?" he asked. "Are they too wide?"

"They look fine," Tymofiy answered.

"And these?" He tried on another pair, half-tinted.

"Yury Antonov, 'Moon Road.'"[31]

He stopped at a third pair, like an American cop's.

"I'll take these," he said.

He paid for them. They moved on. They stopped at a stall with fake brand-name watches. The seller was already packing up the goods, hiding watches, chains, and souvenir knives in boxes.

"Which one?" Felix asked.

"Like I know. Take whatever you want."

"You choose for yourself."

"Come on," Tymofiy did not believe him.

"What? It is a joint operation after all."

"Really?"

"Yeah, dude, either choose or let's go."

Tymofiy first looked at the watches, then hesitantly moved his fingers over them, as if reading braille, could not choose for a long time, but eventually settled on the Adidas. They were knockoffs, but in '95—after his Electronika-5 watch—they looked like they were from another world.

"This one." He took the watch and immediately put it on his wrist.

"How much?" Felix asked the vendor.

The vendor, a fat man with big, hairy hands, suggested a cosmic amount for the watch. He obviously overpriced it, having taken the characteristic pause before naming the sum. He felt that the old man was obviously not going to back down.

Felix hesitated, but what the hell, he promised. He counted the money.

"Is it okay?" He looked at Tymofiy.

"Okay," he agreed.

"Tell Grandma and Thatcher that you found it."

"Yes," he agreed, "I found it." After a pause, he asked again: "Where did I find it?"

"On the beach. We were on the beach. All right," Felix held out his rough hand, "we're done, go home."

"And you?"

"I'll be there later."

Tymofiy went out to the evening boulevard, waited for the bus. He rode, passing through the city that was in ruins as if it were on the frontline, kept looking at the watch that cost half his mother's salary, recalled the long and strange day, thought about Katyusha. And also thought about Hrysha. How could such a weakling kill people? And about the gun. And about the slick one. Who would he end with that gun? He obviously didn't buy it to shoot at bottles. He looked at the watch again. It was beautiful.

Felix didn't come home that night. Or the next. He disappeared. Didn't call, didn't show up, neither sober nor drunk. Maybe they ended him, Tymofiy thought nervously, or the cops had caught him somewhere, and now they were charging him with possession and sale of firearms. Although it was unlikely that they would do that. Felix wouldn't give up. He would put away whoever he wanted. He would end whoever he wanted.

But Tymofiy still worried.

He asked Lida cautiously where Felix was. Lida waved him away with obvious irritation, angrily said that she didn't know where he was and that it was none of her business.

"Why do you need him?" she asked dryly.

Why do I need him? Tymofiy thought about it. Felix had promised to come but disappeared with the money. Maybe he got drunk somewhere, got hit by a train, or fell off a balcony, breaking his long legs in three places.

Okay, he would turn up. Sometimes he disappeared for a month. Maybe he had some other special operations? Who the hell knows with that Felix. He was so secretive. Finally, Tymofiy went to the summer cottage. There was still half the summer ahead, sweet and warm, like lemonade on the Crimean beach.

◇ ◇ ◇

In the village, Tymofiy had a friend named Ivan who was two years younger than him. Short, ruddy, plump, with delicate baby skin, but quite skillful and inventive. He loved various mechanisms and building blocks. In the city, he shared a courtyard with Tymofiy and, fleeing the hunger and urban suffocation, also went to a summer cottage. Tymofiy was already reading some anti-Soviet stories in the issues of *Yunost* published during perestroika, which were lying in damp piles in that dark morgue-like room. Ivan did not like to read, but he had many plastic robots and a TV, which, unlike Tymofiy's, had four channels.

Ivan's grandfather was a beekeeper. The flowering plants in their village and surrounding villages allowed them to have an apiary with more than eighty hives. His truck roamed from village to village, stopping in inconspicuous glades and forest edges near collective farm fields, pastures, and meadows. His grandfather loved bees, and he lived with them for several weeks among the blossoming honeysuckles. In the cabin of the truck, he arranged four sleeping places, like in a train compartment. He had been born somewhere in Siberia, he was thin and anemic, somewhat like a donkey, doomed to an empty life. He became fond of beekeeping in his youth, and decided to move to the south, where the climate was more favorable to his hobbies. This passion of his grandfather's had been passed on to Ivan. He knew a lot about beekeeping, if not everything. He could talk about bees for hours, distinguish their species, what flower their honey was made of by taste, what the bees were fed, and whether they were fed at all.

Despite their age difference, they had fun together. Tymofiy told Ivan about Stalin, Ivan told Tymofiy about honey. Together they caught crucian carp in a pond, dissected hornets and beetles on the rocks, made toy planes and boats, made traps and homemade explosives, gathered hazelnuts in Shelepukhy. Or just watched TV. Tymofiy had been the older friend for a long time, and Ivan trailed him like a tin can behind a wedding car.

Tymofiy did not get along with the locals. Despite all his conspicuous poverty, in the eyes of the locals, he looked like some city slicker in jean shorts who should be thrown into the nettles or banally punched in the face. It was easier with Ivan. He was a homely boy with openly pacifist tendencies.

Once in the afternoon they went to the pond to fish. They were walking along the village road, sinking into the melted tar, lazily talking about some of their plans for the coming weeks. Lonely clouds floated in the sky. Flies stuck to their bodies. It smelled like shit and tar everywhere. They turned from the asphalt road to the sandy one, walked past the indistinct gray houses that stretched along the way. They stopped near one of the typical farmsteads. A mulberry tree was hanging over a rotten, warped fence. Large black berries resembled desert beetles. The boys hid under the branches, greedily picking berries, smearing themselves with purple juice, wiping their hands on their T-shirts and shorts.

"Are they yours?" They heard a girl's voice from behind the fence.

They did not answer. What could they have said? Of course

the berries were not theirs, but who in the village couldn't spare a mulberry?

"I'm asking you, are they yours?" The girl would not calm down.

They did not see her, but her voice sounded nasty, like an old gate creaking.

"None of your business," Ivan answered her sharply.

"Jerks!" she squeaked, vanishing for a moment into a blue shadow in a gap of the fence.

After gorging themselves on mulberries, they moved on. Having reached a small muddy pond, surrounded by rough reeds and willows, they chose a clearing and unwound their rods.

The fish turned out to be lazy and reluctant to bite, so Tymofiy and Ivan unenthusiastically cast for blind luck. Unfortunately, there was none.

In the afternoon, the locals began to gather at the pond. Some had fishing rods, some had nets for duckweed. There were a lot of them talking loudly, their voices echoing from one side of the pond to the other. They behaved like they were at an oriental bazaar. There were a lot of dirty children who were strangling frogs with aspen sticks, and when muffled or beaten-to-death frogs floated to the surface, the children, under the approving glances of adults, were very happy.

An eleven-year-old girl approached the boys. Maybe twelve.

"Hi," she said.

"Hi," they replied.

"Well, are the fish biting?" she asked in a familiar voice.

"There's nothing here."

"You have to fish in the morning."

She was wearing a blue dress, her feet were bare, and her hair was cut into a short, tattered bob.

"Have you ever been told that you can't take someone else's things?" she asked, crossing her arms over her chest and putting her left leg forward.

"Okay," Tymofiy grumbled. "Are you counting your mulberries?"

"You could have shouted over and asked."

"But everyone eats from that mulberry bush, no one asks."

"Keep it in mind for next time."

"Yes," Ivan said quietly, "we'll keep it in mind. I'll come tomorrow and burn your mulberries."

"What?" the girl asked again.

"Nothing, clean your ears."

He had no desire to talk to her. Tymofiy and Ivan condescendingly called the locals natives and laughed at their speech, their clothes, even at their children, who knew nothing in this life except goat shit. And respectively, for the urban fascism he unleashed upon them, the local boys despised and physically abused Tymofiy. Ivan, however, was safe. They respected his grandfather.

"Okay, what else?" Tymofiy asked sternly. "We've dealt with the mulberries."

"Nothing else. Can I sit here?" she asked amicably.

"Sure, sit down."

She sat next to Tymofiy while he was fishing in vain and she kept talking. She talked and talked as if she were an old woman dying, wanting to bequeath all her acquired wisdom to her ungrateful grandchildren. She recounted everything about her parents, her brother, her grandmother and grandfather, who sold his motorcycle and went to Russia. And that she herself went to Russia, although it was just for one day, but they went to a wedding at some restaurant, and there was so much Coca-Cola that they even took a few bottles home with them. She spoke about a classmate who ate a lot of beetles in May and had to have his stomach pumped. And about the goats that eat only clovers, and about Muzychykha, whose husband ran away from her to Kaniv, fooled around with whores somewhere, and then when he was buried, the coffin was closed, because there was only minced meat in cellophane bags.

And at some point Tymofiy realized that she was showing off for him. She even sometimes jumped into Russian, as if this Russian would not give away her rural accent. Tymofiy did not encourage her in her efforts to impress him. Ivan got bored and started to get ready to go home, while Tymofiy sat and listened to what she was learning at school. They had also been studying English since the first grade. She was choking as she spoke, laughing to herself, and touching him as if by accident. Sometimes his shoulder, sometimes his thigh. As if by accident, as if by chance, you know. When something's so funny that you just need to hold onto someone. Although he immediately figured her out, Tymofiy began to like her flirtations. Actually, he liked the fact that he figured her out even more than the flirting itself.

"What's your name?" he asked.

"Maryana," she answered.

He looked more closely. For a few seconds, he could not take his eyes off her. Noticing this, she fell silent, her face became serious. But only for a second, only for a few moments. Well, he noted to himself, her face is pretty. A small, slightly flattened nose, blue, almost transparent eyes, mulberry-blue lips, knees, elbows, shoulders, springy legs, though dirty and bitten by mosquitoes, but covered with a strong, rough tan, so that those bites were nearly invisible. Even her nails were clean, cut short, with remnants of pearly polish. She must have borrowed it from her mother, he thought, or from her grandma.

"Do you want to go to our place?" Maryana suggested.

Tymofiy looked at Ivan, who had long ago put down his fishing rod and was waiting either for his friend or until he froze.

The water stank of dampness. The sun hid behind the pines where the dense forest started just behind the pond—tall and resinous pines, smelling of sap and sea water. Ivan sat and looked at

Maryana with distrust. Maryana did not look at Ivan at all, as if he did not exist, as if there was nothing except Tymofiy, except this dark rippling water and blue evening air.

"And where do you live?" Tymofiy asked just in case.

"Where you were stealing mulberries," she said coyly. Tymofiy looked at Ivan again.

"Shall we go?"

Ivan shook his head, took the fishing rods, and left without a word.

Tymofiy tried to stop him, but Ivan just waved his chubby hand in disappointment.

"Do you swim?" Maryana asked.

"I won't go into this swamp," Tymofiy said.

"But I will," she said. And in one fell swoop, threw off her dress, revealing a pair of blue swimming trunks and a bare chest, although her breasts had clearly begun to grow sharper and bulge. Why no top? Tymofiy thought. Maybe she didn't have one? Because of poverty or because they simply have no place to swim here? Except for this pond, of course, where, really, no one swims.

He tried not to look at her breasts. Although, of course, he was looking at them. How could he not? She jumped into the quiet and still water, which could not have been very pleasant because it was not even particularly warm outside. Ivan had frozen and gone home.

After diving several times, Maryana jumped out of the black water, covered with goosebumps. Her skin was stretched like a tablecloth on a wedding table, her legs were stained to the knees with slit, and a piece of dry reed was sticking out from her hair. Tymofiy handed her the dress. She put it on her wet body. It clung heavily to her stomach and hips. Tymofiy thought he should try to warm her somehow but held back. How could he warm her? With a hug?

"Should we go?" he asked.

Maryana, shivering from the cold, nodded.

And they left.

He did not like to be in Maryana's house. The bare floor, a bucket filled with something shredded and sour, the smell of steamed milk and wet wool, huge pillows embroidered in fluorescent colors, icons of the same fluorescent colors in every room. The yard was covered with concrete, a wrecked mini-tractor surrounded by a puddle of black oil, a miserable, hungry sheepdog on a chain, which could not even bark from heat exhaustion and hunger, a broken swing that should have been scrapped long ago, and all of Maryana's family, screaming incessantly. At the dog, at the chickens, at Maryana, at one another.

He would come to her after breakfast and immediately hurry to escape. Then they went somewhere away from the screeching sounds and sour smells, wandered around the outskirts of the village, beating the grass by the side of the road with maple twigs, sat in the quiet schoolyard or the main street near the shops, dove into corn in other people's gardens, destroyed it, and threw it away, raw and fresh.

After a few days, Tymofiy realized with regret that they had nothing to talk about. Everything she told him seemed flat and uninteresting. How long can you listen to these stories about neighbors drowning in each other's wells, running over each other with combines, and hanging themselves in attics?

He wasn't inclined to tell her anything at all. She wouldn't understand anyway, and if she did, it would be in her own way. But they were together. Maryana no longer showed off in front of him, he noticed this with relief, having felt a kind of muffled shame for that false and inept pretentiousness. She never switched to Russian again, but she repainted her nails with the same polish. And she didn't walk barefoot, but in some ugly black patent-leather flats. They must have been bought for school, he thought. After all, he had nothing but those sneakers either.

Meanwhile, he was haunted by Katyusha's ghost. It hovered over him like a storm cloud, whispering sweetly and flatteringly, provoking him to action, and refusing to let him sleep peacefully. Tymofiy fought. He tried to brush it off, but he was afraid. He was afraid to take the first step, afraid to act, although, as it seemed to him, Maryana had been waiting for him to dare to try something for a long time.

And after a week of walks with Maryana, he made up his mind. They were on the playground near the school, hidden in the shade of hornbeams and lindens, hanging on monkey bars and lazily talking about something. Maryana climbed up on a high horizontal bar and tried to balance on it, holding on to a hanging hornbeam branch with one hand. But her plastic shoes slipped on the polished metal, the branch broke, and Maryana fell to the ground, hitting her head on a dug-in tire. She lay there, confused, disheveled, and motionless in her blue dress and black patent-leather shoes, trying to recover her breath. Her eyes filled with tears. Tymofiy ran to her, sat down next to her. He watched her lying there, not knowing how to help her or what to say. And then it dawned on him: it was either now or never, he thought, and he fell on her like he would on an air mattress, trying to put his lips on hers. Maryana did not immediately understand what was happening, but after a few seconds, she slammed her palm into his face, pushing him away.

"You jerk!" she screamed, crying. "What a jerk!"

Tymofiy pulled away from her, picking up his feet, staring at the tears running down her hot cheeks in two identical streams.

"You idiot!"

"I thought you wanted to," he said, frightened.

They sat opposite each other and were silent. He, from embarrassment and fear. She, from anger and the pain in her back and her head.

"Cocksucker!" Maryana finally said, stood up, and slowly walked along the alley, past the silver-painted barrier, past the fallen willow, and finally to the football field. She was walking, crying, and turning around for some reason. Tymofiy stayed, stunned, stood near the monkey bars, kicked the slide, hoping that Maryana would change her mind and return.

When the blue silhouette turned beyond the football field and disappeared into the dark-green thicket, Tymofiy wandered home. He sat in the summer kitchen and remained silent, trying to understand what had happened, why he had behaved that way, what had pushed him to take this step, and most importantly, why she had left. Although it was clear why. He was not as stupid as he looked.

Then in the evening he paced the yard, driving himself to despair with disturbing thoughts. Conscious of his shame, he was afraid that Maryana would go to her grandmother and tell her everything. Everything. How he lured her to the schoolyard, how he threw her off that horizontal bar, how he tried to rape her. Who knows what was in these locals' heads? Each creak of a bicycle behind the gate, each indistinct voice piled on him more and more fear, conjured ominous notions that her grandma would come in now, shifting her legs like a goose, tell Olha everything, and he would stand in front of them, ashamed, pitiful, except for the fact that he hadn't pissed himself, and would listen to her talk about age, about sexual maturation, about encroachment on someone else's body.

But that evening her grandma did not come. And the next day she did not come. She did not come at all.

On the third day, however, Maryana appeared. She was shifting from foot to foot at the gate, afraid to come in. She called Tymofiy in a quiet, choked voice. He came out. He stood motionless in front of her, like a failing student in front of the head teacher. He stood and looked at her. And she stood and looked at him. It was late morning, remnants of dew sparkled in the grass, dragonflies fluttered between the currant and barberry bushes, and the neighbors were hunched over in their gardens.

"Forgive me, please," he said finally, because, finally, he had something to say. And then for some reason he blurted out, "I thought you wanted to."

"I do," said Maryana. "It just hurt me then. Should we go for a walk?"

They walked along the quiet pines in the direction of the forest, passing the water tower, the hospital with its poor squat buildings lined with glossy blue tiles, passing a narrow glade filled with household garbage, the raspberry patch, and a small sand pit dug by locals with garden shovels. And when the real forest began, gray green, with fallen oaks and glades overgrown with hawthorn and elderberry, they stopped. Maryana approached Tymofiy, hugged him, and began to look for his lips. They stood in the middle of the forest and kissed. And when they were tired of standing, they lay down and continued to kiss lying down, touching each other, awkwardly bumping into the sharp corners of their bodies, greedily swallowing the tart forest air with their dry mouths, falling with their palms and knees into the soft wet moss, filled with each other's hot breath and silent, afraid to say anything that might dissolve all this passion and stupidity.

They stayed in the forest until evening. Almost without talking, only kissing and looking into each other's eyes. And when the cold twilight hung over the forest, and mosquitoes dug into their sweaty bodies, they left. Exhausted, they walked along the dry sandy path to the village, licking their swollen lips and holding hands. They walked and were silent. And when they approached the school, Maryana stopped.

"I'll go the rest of the way myself."

"Okay," Tymofiy agreed. He didn't have the strength to walk her home. "Tomorrow?" he asked.

"Sure," she answered. "And also, I'm sorry I called you a cocksucker."

"It's okay," Tymofiy replied. "I'm used to it," he added for some reason.

And he left, thinking that, perhaps, everyone is like that, and there is nothing special in that Katyusha, or in this Maryana. There is simply a time for everything.

He saw Maryana every day, running away to remote places, away from eyes, licking each other like cats, and returning at night, naively confident that their relationship remained a secret. One evening, Tymofiy had just come home, and Olha, pouring her usual tea, asked, "What's going on with you and this girl? You in love?"

"No way! Have you lost your mind?" he answered, frightened, and therefore aggressively.

"Ivan came looking for you several times already. You're not friends with him anymore?"

"Yes, I am."

"But this girl is better?" Olha laughed.

Tymofiy freaked out, overturned his cup of tea, and ran out of the kitchen.

What do you know at all, he thought. You don't know anything, he reassured himself.

However, he felt that he did not know much himself, either. He was floating downstream, avoiding shoals and quicksand, faster and faster, in fact, it was as if it were not he who was floating but the hero of some movie—watch, cheer for him, worry about his fate.

A few days later, Olha's old friend came to visit with her daughter Toma, Tymofiy's former classmate. She had been expelled from school after the third grade for bad grades. He, by some miracle, had managed to remain in school, avoiding outright failures. He was sort of friends with Toma, but only out of desperation, when they were left alone together while their mothers drank coffee and discussed their affairs. Usually, they just sat in the same room, inventing games that were not interesting to either of them and rejoicing when these friendly get-togethers came to an end.

Toma's mother sewed, professionally, and a lot. It was her bread and butter. It was hardly wealth, but there was enough money. Good clothes, delicious food, pocket money.

And now there she was. Toma. Fashionable, emotional, with a brand-new Sony Walkman, wearing ripped jeans and a T-shirt with the Looney Tunes characters on it. She was short, with a small face and a thin ponytail of sparse hair, like dry autumn grass. At first, they walked around and sniffed like dogs in the town square, but eventually they started talking. Tymofiy showed her his air gun.

"Only there are no bullets. But you can shoot with nails," he explained.

"Let's shoot with nails," she said suddenly in a cheerful voice, and Tymofiy was happy to realize that this time he would not have to pretend to have fun.

She appreciated his new watch, let him listen to a cassette player, had a dozen tapes: Bon Jovi, Sting, Mariah Carey. They took turns listening to music, telling their own stories, and discussing mutual acquaintances, staying up almost all night, finding things to laugh about.

And in the morning, after breakfast, Tymofiy suddenly remembered that he had to stop by Maryana's. They had agreed to go to the water tower. Maryana had assured him that they could climb it, and that it would be a great adventure. But he did not feel like climbing the tower that day. And he did not want to meet Maryana. For some reason the thought of her caused some lazy sense of anxiety and boredom. Perhaps, he assured himself, we just spend too much time together. I mean, really, I can't only hang out with her. Maybe we should take a break? For a day.

Or for two, he thought the next day, and then took Toma on his bike to a nearby village to pick some hazelnuts.

Or three. He avoided obsessive thoughts about responsibility and duty, hoping that it would all simply dissolve by itself, like smoke in windy weather. Or maybe it wouldn't. Then I'll see her, he reasoned. Even though I really don't want to.

And then Maryana herself appeared in his yard. She stood confused in her clumsy shoes and looked at Tymofiy and Toma with transparent eyes. It turned out that she had come the day before but hadn't found anyone. Finally, she came up and said hello. Tymofiy felt like a character in a comedy, when you owe everyone something, but you can't do anything, so you behave like a jerk. And he was acting like a jerk. He fussed, said something inappropriate, introduced Maryana as a friend. He introduced Toma as a friend too. Maryana was embarrassed and felt uncomfortable. Toma was obviously uncomfortable as well, but she behaved defiantly. Their conversations did not work, their games fell apart. They sat on the bench outside the house like random passengers at a bus stop. That's when he suggested that everyone go to the pond to fish. The girls did not react enthusiastically to the proposal, but what the hell, he'd take them to the pond.

Tymofiy walked along the shore, carefully choosing the best spot for fishing, eagerly unwound the rods, spent a long time baiting the worm, concentrated, tried to stay on top of the situation. He even told some jokes that weren't funny. Then he sat down on the wet grass and cast the rod. Maryana sat down next to him. At first, just next to him, then closer and closer, until she was wrapped around Tymofiy's waist.

"Wow," Toma reacted.

Tymofiy sat and looked at Maryana's shoes. Why did she put them on, he thought, it would be better to be barefoot. It was a pity and a shame at the same time. He sat, afraid to move, clutched the fishing rod with his pale hands, the float had long since gone under the water, pulled, apparently, by a large or very stubborn crucian carp, but Tymofiy did not pay attention to it. "Fancy shoes," he repeated to himself, "fancy shoes."

"Okay," said Toma and, pulling on headphones, she walked along the pond. Tymofiy and Maryana sat tense and silent. He held the rod, Maryana held him. Maryana was not held by anyone.

Tymofiy felt sorry for her, but he just wanted her to leave. To go back to her sad icons and embroidered pillows, to her screaming relatives and her tortured dog. But she did not leave, instead sat clinging to him as if to the last hope, as if to the hornbeam branch near the monkey bars on the playground.

Although the bite was good, Tymofiy insisted that it was not, and suggested going home. Maryana, leaving with a sad "bye," wandered off in the direction of her home.

"Come on, let's go," Tymofiy called to Toma, nervously winding his fishing rod.

"Where is your girlfriend?" she asked.

"She went home."

"I see," said Toma. "Let's go."

During dinner Toma kept looking at Tymofiy, a mocking and at the same time sly smile on her face. Tymofiy tried to avoid eye contact, but still caught the glint in her eyes. It made him feel strangely tight in the throat, and he suddenly could not swallow the food he had just chewed.

In the evening, when their mothers went to bed, Tymofiy and Toma stayed in the other room, watching TV. They were watching some old German series about a spy. German and uninteresting. From time to time, a moth tried to dive into the screen.

They sat on twin beds and combed their bodies for mosquito bites.

"You need to press an X into it with your fingernail," said Toma. And when Tymofiy focused on the red bubble and his nails, Toma suddenly grabbed his hand.

"Quiet," she whispered.

"Quiet what?" He did not understand and recoiled from her.

"Be quiet!" Toma ordered.

She got out of bed, holding Tymofiy's hand in her damp palm, and pulled him along with her. He gave in. She walked out of the room and into the hallway, dragging him behind her like a blanket. They dashed across the porch and jumped out into the night courtyard, lit by the white August sky.

"Look at me," she said, and then she wrapped her arms around his thin neck and kissed him.

She kissed him for a long time, and he, numb, feeling the sweat rolling down his back despite the cold, kissed her back. They stood in just underwear and T-shirts under the dark canopy of grapes and kissed. Toma smelled different, and she tasted different. She did it more confidently, as if it were not her first time. Of course, it wasn't her first time. And he stood there, confused, thinking that he wanted to get back to the city as soon as possible. To return to his clubs, music, school, that he wanted to have winter and snow, and wet feet in muddy boots, and quiet evenings with some Garin-Mikhailovsky[32] books under the dull yellowish light. And he would certainly tell Felix everything. Felix would burst out with his trademark laughter, and then, having calmed down, would tell a story that would make everything fall into place. He knew how to tell stories. After his stories you wanted to live.

Tymofiy thought about the slick one and about Hrysha the Saboteur. And he thought about Ivan, it had turned out badly with him. He also thought about Katyusha, and how far he was from her, and that all of Felix's story was a pale and faded parody of his reality full of colors, light, and shadows. Maybe he didn't think about it as much as he felt it, in fuzzy, blurred strokes.

Toma touched his body boldly and confidently, she did it in an adult way, and there was something threatening and frightening about it, something Tymofiy was not ready for. She touched his whole body, without inhibition, ran her hand through his thick black hair, kissed his neck and shoulders. And he stood, like a plaster pioneer statue in a children's camp abandoned after the collapse of the Soviet Union, afraid to move.

"Let's go, I'm freezing." Toma twitched, wiping her lips with her pale hand. "And you can lick the bites," she said, and then ran into the house. She was thin, awkward, and angular like a gazelle. With the cold smell of Polish soap.

At night, when they went to sleep on the same twin bed, she kept her hand under his blanket, touching his body. He lay motionless and stared at the ceiling, unable to sleep for a long time out of fear and excitement. He could cope with the fear, but what to do with the excitement, he had no idea. He lay and watched, lay and watched. And he fell asleep. Scared and excited.

They spent the next days distracted and lazy, pretending that nothing was happening between them, and in the evening, they would go out again into the dark yard, full of night rustles and tart, almost autumnal, smells, and kiss, freezing and shivering with cold and excitement.

He never saw Maryana again that summer. He did not visit her. She did not visit him. And a week later, with a backpack full of apples and an armful of country asters for his first day of school bouquet, he went to the city, dry and cold as it should be in September. As if he were an old friend with whom he could swap stories. But Felix did not appear. All that remained were his white cracked sandals in the hallway and a sun-bleached T-shirt that had been hanging in the kitchen above the sink since July. No one moved it, no one threw it away.

◇ ◇ ◇

Felix was gone for a year. For some time Tymofiy thought about him, worried even. In his grandmother's notebook with the hard blue binding, where she wrote down recipes and phone numbers, he found Felix's home phone number, copied it, and finally called. A hoarse, as if with a cold, female voice angrily said that he no longer lived there.

"And who is this?"

"An acquaintance," Tymofiy answered.

"Who?" The woman did not understand.

"An acquaintance," he said more firmly, hearing his voice as if from the outside, squeaky and gentle.

"What acquaintance? Who are you?"

Tymofiy hung up the phone. Probably Felix's wife, he thought. And one day in October he remembered Hrysha the Saboteur. He must have known exactly where Felix was. This one knows, this one knows everything. But would he tell? After school Tymofiy took not his usual bus, but the one that took him to Shkilna Street, right to Hrysha's house. Dead neighborhood, dead yard, the same dead and abandoned house with two dead pigeons right at the entrance to the foyer. Tymofiy got up, rang the doorbell for a long time, waited. Maybe Hrysha had gone out somewhere? At work, Tymofiy thought. Of course. Where else would he be? He was definitely not surviving on a lieutenant's pension.

Finally, he left the yard, walked around the poor neighborhood, wandered into Khimiky Park, wandered there, kicking wet piles of fallen leaves with his worn-out boots. When it got dark, the park was no longer comfortable. Scary. Dead district, dead park. He returned to Hrysha's house. He went up again, called, even tried guessing the passcode. To no avail. Finally, feeling hungry and tired, he wandered to the bus stop. Maybe I'll come back later, he thought.

That autumn he learned Ogiński's polonaise. An endless, endless, endless polonaise. He could play it for hours and hours. Perhaps there was nothing he played as well as this polonaise. But the most important listener never appeared.

For Tymofiy, the year was long and eventful, almost as endless as "Farewell to the Motherland." He got the starring role in the play and hardly ever left the theater, falling asleep from fatigue on the faux leather-upholstered chairs. Entering his dressing room, narrow and long, like a hallway in a communal apartment, with vanities along the wall, he could smell that purely theatrical, lively, and genuine smell—a mixture of petroleum jelly and suede. For him, the theater had always been more than just a theater. He felt this so profoundly because he was too young to simply experience it or not feel it at all. At some point, the theater became his second home, although it was disconnected from heat and without power, so he had to sit in the cold darkness and sniff mothballs.

The theater fit harmoniously into Tymofiy's life. All those backstage quarrels, intrigues, irresponsible actors, the hoarse voices of the ballet dancers, Kolya the prop man, who constantly blinked his eyes because of a tic, all these conversations between adult actors, all this dirt, this lightness, this anguish fused in him the understanding that he wanted to be a real artist. He also wanted to grow old at thirty-five and die at forty from poverty and despair. The theater existed for him exclusively behind the scenes and allowed him to become one of those who tasted this theatrical cuisine with its whole mediocre menu.

On his days free from music, theater, and tutoring, Tymofiy met Toma. They walked in her neighborhood among the sands and gloomy silent high-rises, went out to the Dnipro, held hands, sometimes dove into concrete arches and damp entrances, frozen from drafts, warmed each other, both of them chewing a single piece of gum, passing it back and forth, rejoicing in their adulthood and independence. They carefully hid their relationship from their parents, fearing the discovery of their newfound adulthood and independence. The best dates happened when their mothers visited each other. Then Tymofiy and Toma would lock themselves in a room and no one questioned them. What questions could there be? Children, so grown up, so independent, but even more unprotected and vulnerable. They grow up without fathers, grow up, naive in their cruelty, say hurtful things, leave home, come back, cold and hungry, but no, they do not apologize, they lock themselves in their rooms and hastily live out their childhoods, as if something better awaits them.

All of them grew up without fathers.

Toma's father left the family when his wife became pregnant with their second child. He did not want a second child. Inga, Toma's sister, was nine years older, left home at a young age with a criminal, a native of Bessarabia. She lived separately, maintaining a close relationship with her father. The latter was not sure that the second child was his, so he did not pay attention to Toma, did not show love, although he paid alimony regularly. Toma undeniably looked like him.

Tymofiy's father was constantly traveling somewhere. He would return after a few months: sometimes confused and unhappy, sometimes happy and with money. He resembled a gambler, crazy in his excitement, stubbornly insisting on betting everything on zero, even though it usually fell on black or red. Of course, it also fell on zero, but rarely. And he, happy with an accidental win, returned to his native shores, foolishly spending everything on expensive colognes and brand-name clothes. From time to time, he would throw something to his family, if only just to secure the right to sleep all day, until the money finally ran out. Then he would gather his strength again and go to work. Russia, Poland, Germany, Russia again. Red, black, red, black.

The days passed quickly, but time dragged on endlessly. Evening rehearsals or performances, piano lessons, tender and exciting meetings with Toma. Every Tuesday he had his English tutor.

At home, in their kitchen, Olha's strange and uncultured friends crowded for hours, drank liters of coffee and ate chocolate that they kept secret from Tymofiy. He constantly found the butts of long More cigarettes in the ashtray. He knew that Olha smoked and was surprised that his mother had this childish desire to hide such an obvious fact from him.

And then the father returned again. But for how long? He said that it had become safe in Croatia. But he hadn't been there yet.

◇ ◇ ◇

Felix showed up in the late spring of '96. He stood in front of the door in his Obersturmbannführer coat, in shiny blue Adidas sweatpants, swaying drunkenly, looking at Tymofiy with muddy wet eyes.

"Sergeant!" he said, "I'm promoting you!"

Tymofiy stood leaning on the moldings and looked at him sleepily, not immediately realizing who it was. And then having understood, he dryly noted to himself that Felix was alive. Drunk, but alive.

"Where is Lidulientsia, Sergeant?" he asked.

"She's gone."

"Dead?"

"You're dead!"

Felix smacked his oily lips.

At that moment, Olha came out of the room to see who had come. Seeing Felix, she said, "Oh my God," and hurried to disappear into the depths of the apartment.

"Mademoiselle, I'm already gone! Mademoiselle, my respect!" Felix shouted. He turned around and went down the stairs with slow, shaky steps.

Since Tymofiy traditionally spent the summer in the village, they planned for Toma to come for a whole month. She arrived with a backpack full of canned fish and cassettes with new recordings. She wore short, narrow skirts, showing thin white legs, read one book for an infinitely long time without even getting to the middle of it, ran to the deserted sun-drenched schoolyard to smoke, covering up the smell with currants and mint, and most importantly, hinted in every possible way that she had outgrown Tymofiy and was not interested in him as a boyfriend or as a person. Several times she mentioned some Ihor and his kayak; she would say something out of the blue like "Ihor . . ." And then, not knowing what to say next, she would add, "You wouldn't understand." Because of this, Tymofiy was depressed, but tried not to show his feelings. In the spring they saw each other less often, and by May, he could not reach her at all—always exams, friends, or the wrong mood. So, he went to the summer cottage devastated and broken. He visited Ivan several times, but Ivan was always chattering about bees, hives, drone cells, and the district fairs where he and his grandfather sold honey. He talked about all this with an unhealthy gleam in his cloudy eyes, full of arrogance and manic detachment, which made it both boring and disturbing at the same time. So Tymofiy decided that it was better to suffer alone, and spent his time in his room, watching Toma, studying her lonely gazelle behavior.

After a week, she became bored.

Tymofiy was sitting under an apricot tree in a deck chair with a book. From the heat and the blur of an afternoon nap, the letters seemed to stick together in one black thorny spot, he read the same paragraph several times and each time was surprised to notice familiar phrases. Toma came up to him and stopped abruptly, putting her bare foot on a metal handrail and placing her elbow on her knee.

"Get up!" she ordered.

"What for?"

"Get up!" she repeated. "Are you okay?"

Tymofiy did not answer. Sleepy and nailed to his spot, he slowly raised his eyes to her.

"Do you love me at all?"

"And what would that change?" he asked.

"What would you like it to change?"

Tymofiy shrugged his shoulders in confusion.

"Well, well," she said.

Finally, he put the book down and stood up. She hugged him, squeezing him tightly. She stood there, her skinny knees touching his. She smelled of wet towels and hand cream, breathing hotly in his ear and whispering something. Explicit, but tender.

Those were sweet and hot days, full of perfect childish passion and permissiveness. Shaky pine trees, dry thorny grass, fingers dirty with berries, heady air, languor, thirst, and endless Chris Isaak on Toma's Walkman.

"You have eyes like a leopard," Toma said with alarming seriousness.

"Is that a bad thing?" he asked.

"Like a leopard," she repeated mysteriously, and something sly appeared in her half-smile.

At the time, his only wish was that it would last forever, not get lost in the dirt and rust of the city, not melt in the noisy crowds and stuffy school classrooms, not drain into the dark city sewers. But as soon as you have time to think about it—about the bliss, about eternity, about the sweet hot air—as heavy blocks of routine and responsibility fall on you, you struggle under them, try your best to swallow as much air as possible, but your lungs shrink, like scrap metal in a press, and you can do nothing but fall to the ground and cry. Sometimes there is nothing left but to cry. Especially when you are eleven.

The family returned to the city.

Felix returned to the family. He drank heavily, occupied the kitchen and toilet for a long time. At that time, he extinguished his pain in a particularly loud and brazen way, he felt some weakness within the family, some cracks and rot, so even Thatcher did not scare him. All she could do was close the curtain to the room and stop talking to Lida again.

Tymofiy held on.

◇ ◇ ◇

Lyosha, having borrowed a huge amount of money from Olha's friends, again put everything on zero. He lost. He returned from another trip devastated and broken. There was nothing to win back; his other prospects, crooked and blurred, did not bode well. With demonstrative sacrifice, Lyosha got various jobs, but did not stay at any of them for long, mostly just scraping together money for cigarettes and food. He repaired rotten wrecks at the service station near the sugar factory, did construction for a friend, finally gave up, went into hibernation, hid half-heartedly from creditors, and then went to work again. Not so much to earn money as to escape from problems, which were then left for Olha to contend with by herself.

Tymofiy slipped into monotonous Cs at school, gave up the piano, and, as a compromise, switched to the guitar. But he did not want to learn. The guitar teacher was named Shlosser—a short man with an open spirit and bronze stubble on his chin. Seeing Tymofiy's difficulties, he refused to take money from him and taught him to play not only the guitar but also the flute, drums, double bass, and various folk instruments, from the washboard to the duda to the spoons. Not only did he teach him how to play but he showed him something else entirely: another side of music, simple and kind, where there were no annoying solfeggio and mnemonic excerpts but there was a lot of sunlight, colorful maracas, accented rhythms, and black people in stuffy Harlem basements. Sometimes Shlosser would feed Tymofiy. He brought sandwiches and tea in a thermos, bought nuts especially for him, which, he assured, had all the nutrients necessary for the child's development. Shlosser was thirty years old, and two of those years he devoted to Tymofiy, a stranger to him. Tymofiy was his worst student; during those two years he did not even learn barre chords, only a couple of primary ones. It did not upset Tymofiy at all. But it upset Shlosser.

"What should I do with you?" he said in his soft Kaniv voice.

"I'm sorry," Tymofiy said, and he immediately wanted to cry out of pity for himself and for Shlosser.

Sometimes he did cry. Then they would sit in the unheated plywood classroom, drinking cheap, bay leaf–scented tea from a thermos, blowing steam through their mouths, keeping silent until the sad, cold silence was broken by the sudden breath of an accordion or the raspy wail of a saxophone behind the wall.

"You are a good boy," Shlosser said. "I will teach you, whether you want it or not."

Tymofiy did not want to learn, he wanted to eat instead.

Felix usually ate mussels. Tymofiy lived on bread and soybeans. Lida brought two bags of soybeans from somewhere. She cooked pies, cutlets, pancakes, and made soy porridge and soy soups. Soybeans became Tymofiy's main nourishment. Tasteless, but high in calories. Tymofiy started to gain weight. There came the understanding that life was shitty and unfair. It was felt most acutely when, exhausted from school and extracurriculars, he returned home, where drunk Felix, Lida, and Olha, stupefied by poverty and debts, were waiting for him with smiles of terrible doom, inviting him to pass through the open doors of the adult world. He wanted to run away from it all. It scared him.

And he did run away. If not to the theater or to Shlosser's, then to meetings with Toma, which were quite frequent in autumn and excited him especially. They wandered after school through the cooled, yellow parks, wandered through the city gardens between the black decaying trees, talking incessantly. Tymofiy's excessive sentimentality and visionary nature annoyed Toma, and she, wanting to ground him, would again mention Ihor and his kayak or Ihor and his funny St. Bernard. But he carefully ignored the kayak, Ihor, and, especially, the St. Bernard, and all the time he dreamed, preaching like a presbyter and promising a happy future.

Toma was grimacing unhappily.

They talked, of course, about sex. They loved to talk about sex, trying out roles they hadn't yet grown into. He promised summer and a summer cottage. She was skeptical about their future together, but she skillfully played along and it was enough for him.

In winter, when the city was mired in dirty, smoky snow, they saw each other less and less. Tymofiy disappeared at the theater, while she blamed the mythical busyness and the stern rigidity of her mother. Maybe another time? Let's do it on Monday. But on Monday something else would come up, and Tymofiy imagined a half-naked, muscular, and tanned Ihor skillfully steering a kayak, breaking the crystal thickness of the Dnipro's icy surface with its steel nose, and Toma impatiently peering out from the shore, holding a drooling white and yellow dog by the collar.

In December they went to the nature center. Though it was deteriorating from lack of attention and funding, it was still warm inside and they could hang out looking at sleeping parrots and half-dead salamanders.

He waited for Toma outside her house. The icy wind crawled beneath his clothes, Tymofiy wrapped himself tightly in his unseasonably light jacket and blew on his hands now and then. The dark door creaked, and Toma came out. She was wearing a neat blue coat, new jeans, and sneakers with fur on them. It was possibly the first time she had ever worn mascara. He looked like a younger brother next to her.

They walked along the blocks, bypassing snowdrifts, jumping over possible flower beds, walking crookedly on the sports field between the monkey bars and soccer goals. And when they were about to reach the road that stretched over the Dnipro, two men approached them. Much older, in dark wide jackets and black hats. Tymofiy had noticed them from afar, felt a cold stinging somewhere in his groin and a sneaky trembling in his knees and elbows, which definitely warned of danger. He wanted to go around them, dive into some back alley, and jump on the other side of the yard, onto a crowded street near shops and kiosks, but there was nowhere to dive except for the soccer goal.

The men stopped. Silently and businesslike, they searched Tymofiy's and Toma's pockets, examined their wrists and necks for watches and chains. Tymofiy became even more nervous, snapped, hit one of them on the arm, and immediately got a palm to the face. Tears flowed. Of course, he had no money, but he had a watch, the fake Adidas that Felix had bought a year and a half ago. They took it off, delicately undoing the strap.

Finally, they said something, obviously offensive, but which Tymofiy did not hear. They did not beat him again. They did not touch Toma, although she might have had money.

Offended, he sat down on the snow. His cheek was burning. He wanted to look at Toma, but he was too scared.

"Get up already," she said. "Ugh!"

He stood up, but slipped on the packed snow, fell back into the snowdrift, and made a strange guttural sound.

"I'm leaving," she said. And she really left.

Tymofiy got up and, without shaking off the snow, waddled to a stop. Then he rode the frozen bus and cried. The conductor did not even come up to him. She just stood in a dog fur coat in the center accordion fold of the bus for the whole trip.

When he came home, broken, with a red burning cheek, with snow on his hat and boots, he started to cry again. He sat on the coat rack under the fur coats, looking at his reflection floating in the mirror, grimacing, whimpering, unable to stop. There was no one at home except Felix. He had been drinking all night and all morning, so he was asleep, his heavy snoring resounding throughout the apartment. Hearing the crying, he crawled like a mole out of the dark room. With a swollen face, dark eyes, puzzled. He saw the kid in the corridor, tensed up.

"Sergeant!" he said. "Wipe up your snot!"

"Fuck you," Tymofiy grumbled.

"Come on! Come on! What's wrong?"

"Nothing."

"Sergeant! How do you stand in front of an officer? Stand up straight!

"Piss off."

"Sergeant!"

"Back off, I said!"

Felix approached Tymofiy, grabbed the back of his head with his palm, turned his face toward him, and looked into his wet, pink eyes.

"Tell me what happened."

Tymofiy told him.

"Don't take your coat off," Felix commanded. "Let's go."

"Go where?"

"To Mytnytsia.[33] We'll find those bastards."

"Where will you find them?" Tymofiy mumbled tiredly, rubbing his face with a wet and cold sleeve.

Felix quickly pulled on his trousers, put on his shoes, dove into the ceremonial coat of the Obersturmbannführer, wrapped a woolen checkered scarf around his neck, and gripped the briefcase tightly.

"Sergeant!"

Tymofiy followed him lazily.

They ran through the dark neighborhood, dashed between houses and lonely poplar trees. Felix, his black coat open and the briefcase as black as his coat clutched in his frozen red hand, ran ahead. Barely able to keep up with his wide steps, Tymofiy trailed behind him in a green jacket and his father's hat. They ran around the house where Toma lived, squeezed between the garages to the grocery store, from there out to the wasteland, slipped along the bushes, emerged near the Dnipro, walked along the beach, turned toward the high-rises, and went straight through the enfilade of dark courtyards to the school, empty and dark. It seemed that the neighborhood, like the whole city, had died before dusk. They stopped. Felix coughed but did not lose his zeal.

"Continue on?" he offered.

"But there's no one here. Come on, let's go," Tymofiy panted.

"Well, where are they?"

"They could be anywhere. Let's go home!"

Felix looked at the neighborhood, at the gray silhouettes of houses, at the lights in the windows, turned to the school with black windows, spat. Really, they could be anywhere. Even on the other side of the city.

"How long have you known this Tamara?" Felix asked.

"Toma. She's called Toma. As long as I've known you."

"A long time. Maybe she's with them? Probably not. What could they have taken from you?"

"The watch," Tymofiy reminded him.

"The watch," Felix said again. "Motherfuckers."

"Let's go home."

"Motherfuckers," Felix repeated, spitting again, rubbing the yellow glob deeper into the snow with his shoe.

They walked downtown and stood at a bus stop under a billboard. Near the Fraternity of People's cultural center, the streetlights were shining brightly. Snow was falling. A pre-festive and anxious atmosphere hung over the city.

Buses ran irregularly at that time. One could wait forever and catch pneumonia. But here they were. Felix, disappointed and angry that they had not found those bastards, was moving his jaw briskly, smoking. Tymofiy was devastated, but glad to have avoided a possible clash.

The drive home was long. The almost empty, shoddy trolleybus stood endlessly with its doors open at every stop. Snow was blowing into the bus, forcing the conductor to scrunch up her body, like a huge potato. Tymofiy was silent at first, then spoke about Toma, embellishing and understating at the same time. Felix listened attentively, almost intensely. Then he advised Tymofiy to talk to her, to clarify everything, maybe apologize.

At home, Tymofiy walked around the phone for a long time,

firmly grabbed the receiver, grimaced, put the receiver back, retreated to a safe distance, and approached again. Finally, he dialed her number.

"What do you want?" Toma answered, unfriendly.

"Why did you leave?" he asked.

"It was disgusting," she said. "Why didn't you follow me?"

Tymofiy was silent. He kept twisting the wire in his hands, feeling his tongue go numb and his ear moistening against the receiver.

"Hello?" She shouted, confused by the silence. "Are you there?"

"I'm here," he said quietly.

"No offense, but don't come to my place anymore." He was silent. "Because you're like a bum."

And she hung up the phone.

That evening, Tymofiy tried to hang himself in the bathroom with his mother's tights, which he fished out of a basket of dirty laundry. He tied them to the pipe, wrapped them around his neck, hung on them, barely touching the cold tiles with his knees. He only became red. He unwound the tights, brushed his teeth, and went to bed.

And then everything finally fell apart. He was finally expelled from school. They had put it off until the last moment, so that he could improve his grades, so that he could hold on, and finally they expelled him. It was a good school, his classmates were the children of local businessmen and politicians, grandchildren of the former elite crowd, and simply good students. Tymofiy was a bad student. He had to transfer to one of those regular schools in his neighborhood that taught not so much academics as it did survival skills.

He did not get used to the new school, could not withstand the pressure from his new classmates, who kept pressuring him as if they wanted to squeeze the last semblance of humanity out of him. At first, not understanding the playground rules of such a place, he simply endured, hardly understanding the reason for the harassment and beatings. Soon he grasped their idiotic nature, cruelty for the sake of cruelty, and began to fight back, waving his fists frantically, poking his fingers in eyes, and even biting the skin on the back of one long-legged boy. But it turned out that resistance did not work there either, the gang was winning, the strength to fight back was dwindling, so he convinced himself that it was all temporary. He could manage not to be provoked by a group of mentally retarded kids until graduation. And poverty played an important role in his misery. Tymofiy's was plainly visible. He went to school in his great-grandfather's altered pants, in his father's suede jumper, which was okay in the shoulders, but almost reached his knees, in his father's shoes, again, too big, scuffed, worn out, no matter how you tried to mask the scuffs with polish.

He went to school, sat in the front row, and wrote poems instead of doing dictations. The Ukrainian language teacher noticed, made a remark, saying that all this is great in extracurricular time, and should even be encouraged, but that at these moments the participle phrase is somewhat more important than trochaic pentameter. Tymofiy moved to the back row. He sat there under the portraits of famous writers and historical figures until the end of the year, not giving a damn about his studies. He started a diary, diligently recorded his dreams, and prayed before going to bed. Where did this piety come from? He began to grow out his hair and rapidly gained weight.

Once, in the theater, a seven-year-old girl came up to him. Thin, sickly, malnourished, with cotton balls in her nostrils. She came up, raised her head, and said angrily: "Princes are not fat!" And there was so much disgust and disappointment in her voice that, for a moment, he even felt sorry for her. He wanted to make a joke, to historicize, to explain that princes could be fat. In fact, if not them, then who could be fat? Just think of Buddha or one of the Carolingians. They were all short and round. But the girl stood with such a crooked face that he knew it was no joke. And what could she possibly know about the Carolingians, anyway? The stupid hen.

At first, writing poems did not cause him shame, only excitement. He read them to his friends, and they said they were extraordinary and sensual. One of them even brought out a synthesizer to set the poem to music immediately—striking while it was hot, so to speak. He read it to the director of the youth theater, and he discreetly praised the imagery. He read it to his art teacher, who replied that Tymofiy was certainly good, but that it would better for him if his classmates didn't know about it. When he read to his family, and said that it was him, unbalanced, with shaken nerves and spoiled metabolism, who had written the poem, extraordinary and sensual, they did not believe it.

"Are you kidding?" they said. "You didn't write it."

At the same time, a black cloud hung over Tymofiy; he closed himself off, walled himself in, like an Orthodox elder in a monastery, and it was impossible to reach him. He was angry at his parents, but not because of their distrust, he looked for other reasons and found them easily. He was angry at his dad because of his helplessness, laziness, and constant unoriginal excuses, which he had seen through for a long time and which annoyed him even more than his father's cynical inaction. He was angry with his mother, who could not keep her head above water; creditors called almost every day, interest grew, she saved on soap and on public transport, while his father would spend the last of their money on, say, a can of Keta caviar. Later, Olha would say that at that time she thought of hanging herself with her tights. Or turning herself into a mental hospital. At least they fed you there. Badly, but regularly. But these were just a few of the many reasons for his despair and this new feeling that he, too, was in this harness of responsibility.

One day he was sitting in the kitchen under the window near a turned-on burner on the stove, rewriting a poem from a draft into a notebook. Felix came in for a cigarette. Sober, and therefore thoughtful and collected. With glasses, a sports magazine, and a pencil. He was filling in the tables. Just then Dynamo had lost to Newcastle, losing their first place slot and getting knocked out of the tournament.

"What are you writing, Sergeant?" he asked.

"And what do you want?"

"I was asking," Felix replied, concentrating on shading the empty cells with his pencil.

"I'm writing, that's all."

"Poems?" he asked dryly.

"Poems," Tymofiy came to life.

"Would you like to read them?" Felix asked.

Felix was still engrossed in the tables, checked and unchecked. But he abruptly put down the magazine, raised his glasses, looked seriously at the boy, as if to say, Go on, I'm listening.

"Do you actually want to listen, or did you just say that?" Tymofiy asked.

"Sergeant!" Felix looked at Tymofiy sharply and attentively. The translucent shadow of the laundry that always hung in the kitchen spread over his dry face, scraped and scratched to pink suede.

He took the last cigarette out of a red pack and crushed it. Tymofiy flipped through his notebook searching for something suitable.

"Give me a match," Felix interrupted him.

Tymofiy grabbed matches from the windowsill and threw them to Felix.

"Are you listening?" Tymofiy asked.

"Go ahead," Felix said, struck a match, lit it. The smoke rose to the ceiling. Tymofiy began to read. And when he finished, he continued to look down at his notebook, afraid to raise his head. Felix applauded slowly and silently, barely touching his palms. He moved the cigarette to the corner of his lips.

"*Świetnie*,[34] Sergeant! You wrote it yourself?"

"I did."

"You got any more?"

"Yes, a few."

"Go ahead. While I smoke."

And while he smoked, Tymofiy read a few more. Felix nodded his head approvingly, clapping his hands inaudibly after each one. Then he put out the cigarette, stood up, grabbed the magazine, and stopped.

"I used to write poems too," he admitted, sitting down again.

"About Stalin?" Tymofiy asked mockingly.

"Why about Stalin?" Felix was surprised. "About different things. When I was an officer, something came over me. I started writing. But I never read them to anyone."

"Were there any bad ones?"

"No, but I don't know. I was a senior lieutenant then, I didn't want people to know. I read one once. Do you know to whom?"

"Stalin?"

"Are you stupid?"

"I'm joking."

"Sofia Rotaru!" Felix said triumphantly.

"Come on."

"I told you, I was a senior lieutenant. In '72. We had a three-hundred-kilometer march then. I was leading, everyone was tired. We ran to some station, and there was a train. Well, I thought, now we'll get a ride, a chance to rest up. We jumped onto the train. I immediately went to first class. I was an officer. I went into the compartment, and there was a woman sitting there. I introduced myself: 'Senior Lieutenant Ignatiev.' She stretched out her hand: 'Sofia.' Well, I had alcohol. So, I poured some for her. And myself. And then I started reading my poems."

"And what did she do?"

"She laughed. She was drunk too. And then I fucked her."

"You did what?" Tymofiy couldn't believe it.

"Well, I didn't know who she was. Then I saw her on TV. By the way, I still write. But not poetry anymore."

"Denunciations?"

"Denunciations, denunciations. I write about Afghanistan."

"Memoirs?"

"A diary."

Felix stood up, slid his glasses down on his nose, and on the way out of the kitchen said, "Okay, Sergeant, come in sometime and read some more."

So, sometimes Tymofiy came in and read. Felix liked everything: he listened attentively, did not ask questions, understood that not everything should be taken literally, and, in fact, not everything should be taken at all. Felix revered all manifestations of creativity. Everything he could not do, he admired and respected. For example, playing the piano. He often asked Tymofiy to play Ogiński. Tymofiy had long since given up on lessons, but he made an exception for Felix. Felix liked that Tymofiy made this exception. Full of sweet arrogance, Tymofiy closed his eyes and played. Three, even four, times in a row, without stopping, flying through the twenty-eighth measure like a night train flying past a flag station. Felix sat petrified on a chair in the hallway, pulling back the heavy velvet curtain slightly. He sat and listened. If he was drunk, he cried and asked Tymofiy to play more, promising to pay. And sometimes he really threw crumpled bills through the crack in the curtain. Tymofiy would pick them up quickly and stuff them in his socks. Olha shouted from the next room, freaked out, asking them to stop. "How long can you play this?" she asked. "You're hysterical, it would be better if you played some waltz, you remember, the one from Gounod's *Faust*." Tymofiy remembered, but he never liked

French composers, except Debussy, of course, so he continued to play the polonaise. He played it so much that he forgot to count, lost the rhythm, sped up, winding and winding circles.

Felix sat and cried, whispering "don't hurry," but carefully, so as not to scare him, so as not to stop him.

And sometimes he just cried. He'd sit there and cry. Drunk, of course. It annoyed the kid and amused him at the same time, like old Soviet comedies. Sometimes Tymofiy did not pay attention to his tears at all—this was a common phenomenon. But even more often he was overcome by curiosity. How deeply can you stick your finger into this wound? What should be the absolute culmination? What is a shell-shocked man capable of in his nightmares? Would he be able to strike? Could he really kill with one blow?

"Is it because of the war?" Tymofiy asked mockingly.

"I'm a bad person," Felix whimpered. He sat, swaying back and forth like a metronome. He put his palms in front of him, yellow, dry, burnt. "I killed with these hands."

"And you should not have killed?" said Tymofiy inquisitively, noticing Felix's heavy look—yellow landscape, pointed stone, bloody mess of uniforms.

"I couldn't. This is not our war. It's not ours, damn it."

"How did you kill?" Tymofiy continued.

"With one blow. I had generals crying in my cellars."

"You tortured them? Why did you torture them?" Tymofiy was getting the hang of it. He dangled a red cloth in front of Felix, picked his wound with sharp dirty nails. Deeper and deeper. To the nerve. Until it released a painful current. Until the fuses blew.

"We did terrible things. We killed people," Felix repeated, as if under hypnosis.

"You killed a lot of people?"

Felix looked at him piercingly, fiercely, as if Tymofiy himself were soaked in the blood of fallen comrades.

"Do you want me to fuck you, you three-faced bastard, or do

you want to live?" he said firmly.

"Come on! Try it!" Tymofiy got him excited. "You're a bastard!"

"Who are you? Who the fuck are you?" Felix screamed and slammed his fist into the wall with all his might, as if it were hot asphalt. Then he slowly raised his hand to his eyes, looked meaningfully at his bloody fingers.

"To hell with this war."

He sobbed, wiping the blood with a towel, reached into the plate of cabbage with his fingers, grabbed a handful, put it in his mouth. The cabbage hung from his chin, fell on his chest, on his cigarette-stained sweatpants. He chewed it silently, tears flowed down his face, lingering in his stubble. He tried to stand up, could not manage it, fell, hitting his head on the table. He stood up, dazed and furious, making formidable animal sounds.

I did it, Tymofiy thought. Felix growled a long, low roar as he assumed a fighting stance, slowly clenching his bloody fingers into a fist. Tymofiy watched his reaction, his fluid movements, with the cruel curiosity of an executioner, looked at his predatory fangs, at his gray emaciated face, at his short gray hair, looked into his wet and cloudy eyes, full of grief and oblivion. Felix continued to growl. At some point he turned around and hit the kitchen door. Thick greenish glass shattered, Felix's wrist was injured. He sat down meekly, lit a cigarette, staring intently at the blood pooling on the gray linoleum under his hand.

"Wrap it up," Tymofiy said, disgusted.

Felix, already calm, indifferent, waved his hand, signaling it would heal by itself. He sat, moving his jaw as if chewing dry earth.

Lida, with tightly clenched teeth and a cold hard look, flew into the kitchen. For a moment, she was deciding what to grab first: Felix's bloody wrist or the glass scattered on the floor like diamonds in a jewelry store. Finally, she began to collect the glass.

"Go to your room," she ordered her grandson.

"Let him sit!" Felix said, muffled. "Let him see!" He turned his eyes to his fist. "How I am afraid of blood! Donnerwetter. Look!"

"I've seen enough," Tymofiy said and went into his room.

In these moments, Tymofiy hated him. A dull and sickening hatred that had been germinating ever since Felix had taken away his faith in fairy tales and Uncle Boba, uprooted it like an old rotten stump, leaving a black pit of disappointment and feces on the towel. He hated him to tears. He hated him for his weakness, for his fatigue, for the fact that the surrounding reality pressed from all sides, trampled and strangled him, and here he was with his damaged head, with his war, bruised knuckles, vodka, blood, crying, with all this moisture that was squeezed out of him as if from fresh cheese. All his moans and curses, all the dirt he left in the kitchen. Whatever was in the kitchen was also in Tymofiy's life.

◇ ◇ ◇

Desperate, Olha found herself selling cosmetics. This allowed her to gradually pay off her husband's debts. She resigned from the daycare, having finally quarreled with Prokofieva, and devoted herself entirely to a quiet sales business. From time to time, ugly women in cheap fur coats came to their apartment, sat in these special deep chairs, and listened to long and sophisticated lectures about foundations, massage oils, and cuticle sticks. The intoxicated shouts from behind the wall added a special poignancy to these consultations. The women in fur coats looked around, confused and embarrassed.

"The neighbor is an Afghan vet," Olha made an excuse.

Sometimes the Afghan vet neighbor would crawl out of his bunker and peek through the curtain into the living room with a confused, toothless smile.

"*Cholera jasna!*"[35] he would exclaim when he saw women in fur coats. And then he would disappear, humbly showing his yellow palms.

"A Pole," Olha said, pretending confusion was a piquant feature.

However, the local clientele turned out to be sluggish and indecisive, so after a few months, Olha, overcoming her provincial fears of the capital, moved to Kyiv, rented an office in the city center, sewed herself a suit, and ordered business cards from a printer. She lived in Voskresenka[36] with her aunt, Lida's sister, in a dark stuffy room overlooking the tree-lined concrete buildings outside the Avrora movie theater. She invited Lyosha to live with her, offering a full-fledged family migration to the capital. Lyosha refused to go, saying that Kyiv scared him: you do as you want, and I'll go skiing. He set off again, still hoping for success, but no one cared, no one was interested anymore. Olha just shrugged her shoulders. There hadn't been respect or love between them for a long time.

Tymofiy remained in Lida's care. He was twelve, and unknown horizons were opening up before him.

◊ ◊ ◊

In the spring there was more light and that feeling of pleasant anxiety, with which one clearly comprehends the fullness of life. With the first March thaws, Tymofiy jumped out into the yard, splashing and screaming as if in a swimming pool. The boys from the surrounding buildings, pale and sickly after a long winter of frosts and piercing fogs, rejoiced madly at the sun and the fresh east wind blowing off the Dnipro, huddled together in noisy, threatening gangs, and went in search of adventures. Usually, the adventures began immediately outside the yard. They were twelve or thirteen years old, free, and unyielding in their principles but still open to learning about the world and themselves in it. They were aware of their poverty, but with a clear conviction that it was temporary, that all this would pass soon, imperceptibly, once they grew up a little. Every family had their skeletons. They did not even have to be hidden in closets; everyone knew everything about everyone. This fact made the feeling of freedom even more intoxicating.

They had known each other since childhood. They would run outside, dazed by the expansive space, happy. In the past, Tymofiy had rarely participated in yard games and gatherings, all his free time was filled with obligations: music, theater, some completely unnecessary clubs, attended lazily and reluctantly. But finally, he renounced it all. There was no more music, no more theater, no more English. He abandoned everything, brushed off all that growth like a dried-up scab, exposing pink flesh—let it be overgrown with new experiences. He kept for himself only Shlosser, to whom he went not to study but rather to rest, to escape all the insignificant and burdensome things that had begun to fill his life. Shlosser received Tymofiy humbly, continued to feed him nuts as he had, listening and giving simple advice disguised as fierce homegrown wisdom.

"To pull out wheatgrass by the root," he said, "you have to pull it long and slowly, otherwise you will tear off only the top, while the roots of evil will remain in the soil."

After these meetings, Tymofiy returned to his yard, reflecting on Shlosser's dictums. Then he would carefully consider his companions, wondering which of them is wheatgrass and which is worth pulling long and hard?

In general, they were not evil children. Sometimes unduly aggressive, sometimes mean and envious, but not evil. All their anger remained with their parents, who were unable to keep the ground steady underneath their feet or find any point to life. Yet, their parents pushed their frail bodies to safety.

They climbed around the neighborhood and the surrounding factories, wandering into workshops and warehouses, exploring rooftops and the banks of the Dnipro. They found a genuine *Stalker*-like atmosphere on abandoned barges and boats, broken test tubes with chemical contents spilled on the grounds of a tile plant, and in apple orchards, reckless hares ensnared in traps placed by local guards. And there were funerals. This was a special kind of pastime. People died often and quickly, and their deaths became surprisingly routine. To die young was the norm, many didn't even live long enough to get wasted properly. Almost every week there was a coffin in someone's entryway. Sometimes, old people lay in the coffins—and someone would say meaningfully: "the person lived a full life." When a very young face peeked out of the coffin, someone would say with indifferent sadness: "he did not even get to live." Tymofiy was fascinated by all these magical and eerie rituals, by the woozy musicians with trumpets, by the priest wrapped in vestments like a refugee in a blanket, by the people standing around the body, united in a single cause. It seemed to him that these people carried on in quick rhythm all the time, pausing only to look at the coffins, and only then feeling the joyous fullness of their lives.

During one such occurrence, Tymofiy and the boys stood about twenty meters away, not daring to venture any closer and yet not moving away. Spring rain was dripping from the black trees, it was gray and mournful, dark and elastic clouds hung so low over the yard that you could jump and grab them. And then, in the crowd that was bustling around the dead man, Tymofiy noticed Felix. He was dressed in sweatpants and a Dubok jacket, had on a blue-and-red ski hat, a cigarette between his teeth. It was not even smoldering, just sticking out like a reminder to stop, rest, have a smoke. The crowd parted for him, giving way as if he, not the wax mannequin with Soviet coins on his eyes, was the occasion's honoree. Felix rearranged the stools, moved the coffin, adjusted the deceased's clothes, wrapped an embroidered cloth around someone's hand, greeted someone, called over someone else to help with the lid and wreaths.

"It's Felix!" Tymofiy joyfully exclaimed to the boys.

"Well, yes," someone said, "Felix. He always comes to funerals."

"Why?" Tymofiy was surprised.

"Well, why are you here?" one of the friends answered, lowering his voice. "Death is such an incomprehensible thing, from which it is difficult to take your eyes off. Death is such a clot . . ."

"Don't bullshit me," the other interrupted. "They serve alcohol at funerals, that's all. He does all the dirty work. Now he's fixing the wreaths, then he'll carry the coffin, then he'll dig the grave."

"And then they will pour him a drink . . ." the third one said dreamily.

"Well done," the first one said. "We need people like him."

"He's like a guide . . . to the kingdom of the dead."

At this time Felix noticed Tymofiy, raised his hand, and said softly but clearly: "Sergeant."

"Sergeant?" the boys repeated.

"Don't ask."

"You have fun with him?" they asked.

"Sort of," Tymofiy agreed miserably. "You bet."

Black spring rain was falling heavily on the ground, turning it to mud. From behind the leaning willows that stood densely along the road, trembling trucks rolled, bouncing sonorously over the potholes. The smell of fried lard drifted through an open window on the first floor. The space was enveloped in mournful silence. In the neighboring yard someone was diligently and rhythmically beating rugs. Something amazing and terrible began to happen, something that Tymofiy wanted to hide from, not to witness, not to remember later. Felix got into a fight with a potbellied man wearing a leather jacket and a similar leather cap on his big red head. At first, the man, his hypertensive eyes bulging, yelled, "Hey, you!" and pushed Felix in the back. Felix reacted sluggishly, moving his shoulder and saying something half-heartedly. The man began to push Felix harder, as if chasing him away, saying, "Go away, go to other dead people, and leave this one to us, he is ours, our dead man." Then Felix turned around, grabbed the man by the jacket and began to push him out, saying that there was no need to divide the dead, that they were all common, collective, so to speak, so go away, you dog. Reinforcements came up, two similarly potbellied men in brown synthetic-sheepskin coats. The three of them pressed against Felix, as if in an elevator.

"Okay, guys," Felix said quietly. "Calm down, guys."

However, the guys did not calm down. They pushed Felix with their bellies. And, once again, the crowd parted, again, making way for Felix.

"Donnerwetter!" Felix shouted with forced necessity. He elbowed a leather-clad belly in, punched one of the sheepskin coats, then another. The one in the leather jacket fell to the asphalt, tried to get up, then Felix immobilized him with a straight blow from above. The two in sheepskin coats tasted blood on their lips and, full of rage, moved at Felix. Felix backed away.

"Vadym! Look out! Vadym is here!" came a call from the crowd.

Felix turned his head to make sure that behind him was indeed Vadym, pale and petrified, with coins in his eyes and his jaw tied as if he had a toothache, lying there motionless. And while Felix was looking at the deceased in amazement, he received a good blow to the head from one of the men in a sheepskin coat, and fell into the coffin and onto Vadym. The coffin slipped off the stool and overturned with the bodies. Coins clinked and rolled across the ground. The crowd started shouting. Everyone began to surround Felix, and Vadym, who was hanging helplessly from the fallen coffin like a rag doll. Felix jumped to his feet, quickly put the two men in sheepskin coats on the ground with the edge of his palm, and dashed across the yard, breaking the icy mud with his boots. He ran into a backing up Zhiguli, rested his hands on it, slowed down, turned around, and ran along the building in the direction of an abandoned boiler room.

Shouts of "Felix! Felix!" rang out from the crowd.

But Felix was already turning around corner, causing the pigeons to disperse in every direction.

Impressed by the chaos, Tymofiy could not even move. Vadym did not move either. The crowd rushed to put him back into the coffin. Two men in sheepskin coats with bruises on their swollen red faces also stood up, spitting bloody saliva. The one in the leather jacket still lay meekly on the asphalt. Blood dripped from his cracked eyebrow, his leg was twisted, stiffly pointing in the direction in which Felix had disappeared. Next to him lay a worn brown boot with a zipper.

In the evening, the cops came to Lida's. Two in front and one behind. To their side was the man in the leather jacket. His face covered with bruises, persistent resentment in his eyes, lips wet from excitement. He stood impatiently looking out from behind the cops. When he saw Tymofiy, who came out to get a look at the visitors, he started pointing his finger, saying, "This one was there!" But Lida denied everything: No, he has not lived here for a long time. I do not know where. No, he does not have a phone. Want to check the apartment? Go check your own, you dogs. Yes, you heard me right. Any other questions?

Lida had never been afraid of anything.

Finally, the cops left, but the guy in the leather jacket kept walking around the neighborhood with his helpers, looking for Felix. They did not find him. Nobody knew where he was. Felix had disappeared again. He even left his briefcase. And the ceremonial coat of the Obersturmbannführer.

And two months later, it was Tymofiy who disappeared.

◇ ◇ ◇

He got a friend. Rodion. They had known each other since early childhood, grew up on the same playground, but had not been friends then. They went to different schools. Tymofiy began to appear in his company more often. They got to know each other better. They visited each other, skipping school. Common interests, cigarettes and stolen beer from the grocery store. They even tried to form a band: Rodion had a powerful alto. They wandered around the district, into the darkest corners. They went to the city center, hung out in the central market, in arcades, where they played for all their pocket money. They were looking for adventures and created them themselves.

Rodion's parents had been separated for many years. Rodion lived with his father, an elderly man with a trimmed yellow mustache. The old man loved his son, but he was too lazy to bring him up. He neglected normal nutrition, ignored his son's schooling and had not appeared there for years. But he had, however, generously shared with his son simple boyish wisdom about courage, honor, and friendship. The father had worked at the chemical plant all his life, and now he worked there part-time in one of the plant's few remaining workshops. He believed that the factory would be revived, naively placing his faith in its corrupt directors.

Rodion's relationship with his mother did not work out. In the early nineties she became involved with a former cop, who gradually became an alcoholic and behaved more like an ex-convict. And he would get her drunk too. They were often seen in the area between the private houses and the *sovkhoz*.[37] Crazed and apathetic, they wandered around the backyards, collecting scrap metal, wastepaper, bottles. The cop worked on the loading dock at a grocery store. She worked for some time as a bus driver, which is why Rodion did not like to take public transportation, but she quit eventually.

Rodion did not respect the old man and did not love his mother. After all, how can you love someone you hardly know? They communicated occasionally, mostly during her spells of sentimental aggravation. She would come to school or meet him in the neighborhood, skinny, wilted, like a capelin fish, with yellow sunken cheeks, wearing a red dog-fur coat and a white knitted beret with a magpie aigrette, throw her arms around him, and assure him that soon everything would be different, that soon she would take him away, and they would become a real family. Rodion steadfastly waited for her to pull away from him with her smell of sour beer. He answered all her questions with only a *yes* or a *no* and turned his head away in disgust at all displays of affection.

He was a child of the streets. And there he felt free and confident, as if these dusty playgrounds and basements smelling of dampness and cats were his home—safe, marked, meaningful.

No wonder Tymofiy was drawn to Rodion. With too much care and supervision at home, he wanted to run away to God knows where, to escape these walls that seemed to close in on him more and more each day. He wanted to be free. He was attracted by the concrete fences of factories, the broken glass of streets, and the coolness of city gardens.

Someone from their group whispered to him that Rodion was not the best choice for a best friend, far from it, he was possibly the worst. He never had any friends at all. And you know why? Because he is mean and evil. And you will see that one day. Tymofiy laughed, said it was envy—the usual stupid envy of a real male friendship.

It was the second half of April. Warmed up by a game, the boys ran on the asphalt patch, knocking one another down, knocking knees and elbows. Tymofiy and Rodion ran too. Everyone took off their jackets. The sun hid in the branches of the boarding school's apple trees, ill-fatedly slipped behind the buildings, melted into the green hill, and the boys' shadows grew quickly. Apricots blossomed, scattering white petals. Someone ran to the fountain to drink water, someone showed up on a bicycle and sat on it, watching the game, spitting seed husks. Someone went across the road to smoke in the pavilion of a kindergarten. On the soccer field nearby, the older boys were chasing a ball into a goal. Near the central building, old women in Soviet training suits were hanging from monkey bars.

And then, amidst this chaotically shuffling crowd, Rodion, stopping and dramatically spreading his arms, shouted: "My knife disappeared! The Swiss Army one!"

The game came to a halt. Everyone freaked out. The sun was still hanging, not yet having had time to slide behind the hill, the bees froze over their blossoms, the older boys stopped the ball and looked around at the nervousness.

"I put it in my jacket pocket before the game," Rodion explained. "And now it's gone. Someone stole my knife! The Swiss Army knife!"

Everyone started looking for it at once. They searched through the low spring grass on both sides of the playground, guessed where it could have fallen, said that the knife was important, yes, without a knife, you couldn't go anywhere. For a kid, a knife is as necessary as a watch or, say, a baseball cap, it is an invariable attribute of a gentleman and a real neighborhood dandy. Tymofiy also searched, tried to reconstruct in his head the trajectory of his friend's movements to calculate where the knife could have fallen.

"It isn't there," Rodion said. "It was in my jacket."

And, he stressed, it had been stolen, so stop looking. Then he went resolutely to Tymofiy's jacket and reached into the pocket.

"Here!" Rodion said triumphantly, holding up the folding knife. "He stole it!"

Everyone stopped, fell silent, looked at the knife with relief, which turned out to be not so Swiss. And then in a moment, there was a ruckus, everyone started shouting, waving their hands, pointing fingers at Tymofiy, shouting curses.

Tymofiy did not have time to say anything in his defense, he stood, opening his mouth in confusion, backing up, looking for something to lean on, finding nothing but an insidious emptiness.

He was surrounded by accusations, not only of stealing Rodion's knife but of all the thefts that had happened over the past few years. Someone swung a leg at him.

"It wasn't me," Tymofiy said quietly, his mouth dry.

"Fuck off!" they shouted.

"Go away, you rat!"

"Rat! Rat!"

"He did it," a tall guy from the distant housing projects intervened. He was the first to bring criminal talk to their team. "You're a cheap thief. Pinching from your mates is lousy, and you're gonna pay."

"Bitch!" Rodion shouted louder than anyone else. "Bitch!" he spat.

"You got busted," one of the older ones said calmly.

There was no point in arguing. The crowd stood in front of Tymofiy. Sincere in its fury, merciless, thirsty for spectacle and blood, united by its conviction. Tymofiy turned around and left. Insults and accusations were hurled at his back. He jumped over the netting that fenced off the playground from the road and hobbled home. What a pity, he thought. Everything was just beginning. A new life, fun and free. First cigarettes, first beer, adventures together, crazy, brave.

In that short-lived new life, he had hid from the devastation and disappointment, rejoiced in the sun and the feeling of brotherhood. There he had discovered a different world, magical and charming, where nothing was demanded and everything was given. And there, in front of the whole playground . . . Without a trial, any chance of acquittal, with insidious and dismal directness. Lost like a dumbass. No way to clean it up.

It didn't even hurt at first. It was just strange. Who would want to set me up like that? he thought. Well, it was clear who. Later, when he realized that he had no friends at all, he became annoyed. But he did not want to cry. Why bother crying? he thought. He did not want to live.

The story with the knife quickly spread around the district and reached Tymofiy's new school.

He told Shlosser the story. Shlosser clicked with thin purple lips and advised him to change his place of residence. At first, Tymofiy thought that this was some kind of allegory, the image of a homespun philosophy, but the serious expression on Shlosser's face testified to the literal meaning of his words.

"Maybe I should move in with you?" Tymofiy suggested sarcastically.

Schlosser did not know how to answer, said nothing, only poured Tymofiy a handful of roasted almonds.

And so, having barely finished the seventh grade, Tymofiy ran away. He gathered all his notebooks with rhyming scribbles, diaries, a volume of Balmont's[38] poems from the period of the first emigration, and on the second of June he was on a bus headed to the summer cottage. Happy that it was possible to escape and already dejected by the inevitable need to return.

For the second year in a row, Lida was taking care of the summer cottage, conscientiously planting the garden, looking after it, and harvesting.

There was no one in the city apartment. Lyosha lived at the service station where he worked, Olha had moved to the capital for good. Felix was somewhere in exile. Half the neighborhood was looking for him to talk about the overturned coffin. And, in any case, who would have left Tymofiy with him?

PART TWO

~~~~

Who Are You?

"Ivasyk. Everyone calls me that."

"And your patronymic?" Tymofiy asked, knowing that Ivasyk was at least three times his age.

"Telesyk."[39]

"Sure," replied Tymofiy.

"What's with your hair?" asked Ivasyk. "Some new fashion?"

They were walking through the courtyards, toward the channel. Ivasyk spoke quietly, posed questions. Tymofiy struggled to hear him but nodded emphatically, so that he would not have to keep asking.

"Yeah, totally."

Ivasyk seemed satisfied with the answers.

The fluttering of dragonflies and buzzing of butterflies, mixed with Ivasyk's amicable cursing, amplified the perfect atmosphere of the July afternoon.

It had not rained in three weeks, the temperature hit forty degrees Celsius. The village wells had dried up, and water had to be brought in tankers from the town center. The channel dried up too; all the carp died, and a pungent, sugary smell enveloped everything in the vicinity. The corn tassels rustled, spreading warmth and sleepiness, the lupine ran along the path in green waves. The dried-out stems pricked their bare feet. Here and there, hunched-over figures loomed in the backyards. The heat was buzzing, and Ivasyk mumbled something quietly, sweat pouring down his face.

Tymofiy was just happy to have someone to talk to. To him, Ivasyk even seemed like an interesting and promising friend. Tymofiy had a few other acquaintances of the same age from his hometown, and those kids from Murmansk, whose parents brought them here for the entire summer to improve their health. Surprising as it might sound, all of Murmansk moved to central Ukraine for the summer months, and with them came new music and new trends, carried along by the sailors from faraway ports. Summer residents did not shy away from these northern gifts and generously shared them with the locals. Still, friendship between the boys from Murmansk and the locals was not feasible. Even their body language was lost on each other. Ethnic clashes were inevitable.

That hot summer not a single would-be friend of Tymofiy came to the village. There was Ivan, but he had set out with his grandfather and their beehives to the banks of the Ros. They lived like two exiles on their motorboat, the *Kolkhida*. They cooked fish soup over a flame, tended to the beehives, and argued.

Only the locals remained. One day in the village center, while waiting for the kvas that was usually brought from the city in a yellow tanker, Tymofiy ran into Maryana. For a moment, he imagined it might not be a bad idea to take her for a stroll. He went so far as to greet her, but Maryana looked at him with pronounced disgust, as if she had just seen the corpse of a hedgehog under a raspberry bush. Tymofiy noticed a bunch of blackheads between her brows, an abundance of tiny pimples on her chin, made a face, and looked away.

At first, he zipped around on his bike and sat with his fishing rod by the channel. But soon enough the bike broke and the channel dried out. He roamed around the village without purpose, looking for entertainment, or lay on a cot under the grapevines; out of hopelessness, he read old Soviet short stories about pioneers and stuffed himself with white bread and strawberry jam. He gained weight and let his hair grow. He looked like George Fisher. Lida vanished into the woods or the backyard, cooked enough food for a few days at a time—a big bowl of borsht or kasha—to avoid more tedious chores. Occasionally, she would make *varenyky* or bake a rhubarb pie to pamper Tymofiy. For the most part, though, she didn't bother. And that's how they lived through this stifling, hopeless summer.

One day Lida sent Tymofiy to get some bread in the center of town. That's when he met Ivasyk, right before the lunch hour. Ivasyk was carrying a sizable piece of glass, his hands covered with cuts, both old and fresh. Blood ran down his wrists, dripping onto the melting asphalt and boiling immediately. As soon as he saw Tymofiy, Ivasyk asked for his help bringing the glass to the coffee shop.

"Sonny," said a small pink mouth lost on a large, watery face, "this thing is gargantuan, I won't manage myself."

Tymofiy hesitated.

"I'll get you *gelatko*."

Tymofiy had no money; gelatko was obviously desirable. He took off his T-shirt, wrapped his hand, and they successfully got the glass to the cool, spacious hall of the Yelizaveta coffee shop.

"They had a christening here yesterday," whispered Ivasyk. "Go figure . . ."

In the corner, an enormous man in a sweat-soaked shirt counted money for the coffee shop's owner, Mire.

Ivasyk took care of a bunch of little things for Mire: he would glaze windows, fix furniture, solder grating for the kiosk, or dig a hole for the swimming pool. Mire paid Ivasyk in diesel or vodka.

"I don't give a fuck," Ivasyk announced.

"Right," Tymofiy agreed.

Tymofiy did not get his gelatko; however, Ivasyk promised to buy him an entire kilo in exchange for his help with something else.

"Don't piss your pants yet," he said, cleaning the cuts on his hands with goosegrass. "Ivasyk. Everyone calls me that."

By the College of Agriculture, they came up close to a pine tree, the one that had fallen last year during the storm. Ivasyk fished a half-liter jar from under the piled-up branches, shook off the sand, and kissed it.

"Do you drink?"

Tymofiy did not drink.

"I do," he lied.

"Let's have it, then. Cheers!"

Tymofiy took a few sips, started coughing, and instantly got tipsy, feeling the warmth spread through his body. Could it really get any warmer? he thought.

"I'm already drunk," Tymofiy announced.

"Do you have a bike?"

"It broke. Something off with the axle."

"Let's have a look," Ivasyk offered.

They wandered through the courtyards again. Ivasyk sprinkled his speech with curses, like grains sown for the New Year, licked his bloodied wrist, and spat out the dried blood. Tymofiy silently pondered his drunken state and thought about the fact that he couldn't let Lida see him like this.

Finally, they reached the lot. Tymofiy jumped over the fence and approached the rear of the shed where his broken bike was. He dragged it over to Ivasyk, who waited by the birch tree, some twenty meters away. It became clear they would need some tools as well.

"Why do you need a bike, anyway?" Tymofiy inquired.

"Gotta go see Nestor."

Tymofiy's imagination immediately conjured an illustration of a monk wearing an old Byzantine robe, hunched over calligraphic swirls.[40]

"And who is Nestor?" he asked.

"Nestor Ivanovych," Ivasyk explained.

Aha, Tymofiy thought. Now I get it. Telesyk, Nestor—it's all crystal clear. Why am I even asking?

It took Ivasyk just fifteen minutes to fix the bike.

"Fucking axle," he grunted with a sense of dissatisfaction. He slapped Tymofiy on the shoulder with his puffy hand, presenting a fat, squished horsefly. "You really don't know your ass from your elbow, huh? Here, have some more."

He held forth the practically empty jar. Tymofiy took a sip. Ivasyk took the jar back, extracted the few remaining drops, tossed it into the sunflowers nearby, mounted the bike, and took off. After about three yards he came to a halt and turned.

"Get on the back, let's go see Nestor."

"Me too?"

"You too," Ivasyk uttered firmly. "I'll stay there but you can go wherever you want. I owe you gelatko. Did you know that the Cherkasy region has the most fertile soil on the planet?"

Tymofiy nodded—obviously, who didn't?

Ivasyk rode carefully, as if keeping Tymofiy safe for some super important future project. Tymofiy got the hiccups. The road swirled in front of his eyes, like a viper in the reeds. He felt elated: feelings of euphoria and nausea flooded him and then abated, like waves on the Dnipro. The sun burned mercilessly. Ivasyk sang.

Nestor lived in Shelepukhy, a neighboring village to which Tymofiy often dashed to pick up witch hazel. After a while, they approached a grayish wooden fence that looked like it had survived since the times of the Ukrainian National Republic.[41]

"Nestor!" called Ivasyk.

They entered a courtyard covered with knotweed that had grown dry under the hellish sun.

Nestor crawled out of a shingled hut with an earthen stoop wrapped around it. Asiatic features, a broken nose, and a multitude of scars all over his body. A faded but noticeable tattoo on his shoulder.

"Who the hell is this?" Nestor greeted them, pulling down his pants. He began to piss off the porch, aiming straight at a celluloid baby doll that had been left by God knows whom in this forsaken courtyard.

"Some city boy," Ivasyk introduced Tymofiy. "He'll be leaving any moment now."

Tymofiy stood there, trying to get a closer look at Nestor through the cloudy haze in front of his eyes. Smiling, Ivasyk glanced at Tymofiy.

"Perhaps he is not leaving."

Nestor did not invite them inside. They sat under the walnut tree by a doghouse with a chain attached to it.

"Where is your dog?" asked Tymofiy, trying to reduce the tension.

"I killed it," Nestor said calmly, lighting a cigarette. "What's with your dreadlocks?"

"It's a new fashion," Ivasyk answered for Tymofiy.

"I used to have them too," Nestor said viciously.

Ivasyk and Nestor started drinking and poured a shot for Tymofiy.

"Drink away, kiddo," Ivasyk encouraged him, stretching out his wide face in a kind of harmless, pinkish smile.

Tymofiy did not want to, but he drank anyway.

Then he drank some more. At some point, everything went blurry. An obsessive question stuck in his head: can one's tongue sweat? He tried to get up but, feeling knocked down by what he drank, sank back into the grass. He looked at Nestor, at Ivasyk, and could not figure out how he had gotten himself into this mess. The gelatko was probably to blame.

That's when the guests arrived.

The courtyard filled with people who were drinking in a peculiar way, as if they just stepped out of paintings by Shulzhenko.[42] They broke the entrance gate, knocked over the doghouse, and, possessed by some wild joy, they cackled and kept on drinking. A woman wearing a dirty brown dress, with cuts on her legs and deep dents in her cheeks, was relieving herself by the fence. It smelled of wormseed and excrement.

After a while, the sun went down, and damp twilight enveloped the village. The broken gate squeaked ceaselessly, and hoarse female laughter came from the house. A neighbor stopped by, sober and grumpy, wearing shorts and a striped robe. He waved his arms, as if doing aerobics, pointed his finger at Tymofiy, argued with Nestor and Ivasyk. They chuckled. Later, there was a bonfire, the doghouse burned, and some guy stepped into a fresh dump with his bare feet.

"Get me home!" Tymofiy begged Ivasyk.

"Go to hell!" Ivasyk chuckled, pushing Tymofiy onto the wet grass.

"Please!" Tymofiy whined.

"We still have to roast Tolik," Nestor said calmly, as if this were a nonnegotiable and Tymofiy must stay. "Toliiiik!" he screamed into the starry sky, his black mouth agape.

Luckily, Tymofiy had no memory of roasting Tolik.

He woke up just as the east began turning gray. The courtyard was empty, a sinuous puff of smoke hovered over the firepit. A nibbled waxing crescent sailed through the sky. Tymofiy rose to his feet, trying to understand where he was and in what direction he should walk to find some familiar signposts at least. He left the courtyard, his thoughts still cloudy, thinking that the tongue definitely does not sweat, walked along the muddy road to the end of street, and navigated himself toward a dark meadow covered with sticky, damp fog. The meadow separated two villages; the residents used it as a pasture for the cattle, and beyond it lay territory that looked more familiar, a discernible, lifesaving landscape. It was cold and he was dying for a sip of water. His headache was unbearable. Tymofiy set out through the pasture, using an old willow tree with dried-out branches that stretched toward the dark sky as an orientation point. Halfway across, he realized, with regret, that he had left his bike at Nestor's. He sat on the grass still wet with dew and started crying.

This whole thing would cost him a pretty penny. Olha came, burned out and exhausted, looking like Linda Hamilton, and promised horrible punishments awaiting Tymofiy upon his return to the city. She had long conversations with Lida, who begged her to stay with the kid for a few weeks, but she had work, clients, she just moved to a new office, she really couldn't take her son back right now.

Tymofiy stayed for a few more weeks. But they did not let him go anywhere. Not even to get some bread at the city center.

"You totaled your bike, right?" Lida spoke angrily, brushing the sweat off her short curly hair. "You want to total your head too?"

Tymofiy grinned. He tried to imagine what it would be like to total one's head. He laughed.

"I know where it is. At Ivasyk's."

"And where is Ivasyk?"

And then a neighbor, Afanasiy, a former schoolteacher of geography and biology, came to help. He assured them that he knew this pig Ivasyk, his whereabouts, and could definitely find him.

Days passed, though, and Afanasiy, a white-skinned fatso with gray seaweed-like hair under his armpits, failed to locate Ivasyk.

"I bet he didn't even look," Tymofiy said. "Asshole. I can do it myself."

"It's not important now," Lida said. "You're not going anywhere."

And so he remained in the house for the most part—hiding from the heat, reading uninteresting books filled with red-bannered victories, watching the World Cup, dying of boredom.

Tymofiy was rooting for the Brazilians. Well, at first he had been rooting for the Italians (Del Piero, Baggio, Inzaghi, Pagliuca), but they lost to the French in the quarter finals. That's why, during the final, he was forced to go against the French and root for the Brazilians. The young and furious Zidane scored a double, and then Petit scored as well, although that did not change anything, really. One way or another, Tymofiy sat in front of the black-and-white Vesna and prayed that the electricity would not go off, something that in those times, in the villages, happened almost daily. This was his first World Cup championship. He could not miss the finals. Toward the end it became clear that the Brazilians were going to lose, and still Tymofiy was hopeful. One can always hope for something in soccer. Until the end.

That was when he heard an odd squealing from outside. He could not tell whether it sounded happy or worried. Men's voices. Laughter. Lida's responses in tense whisper. It was not clear—was she happy or not? Then she started yelling.

"Why the hell did you come? Go back where they kept pouring for you!"

Tymofiy ran to the window but could not make anything out behind the thick grapevines that stretched from the kitchen to the house. It was almost nightfall, and the street lanterns were not bright enough to illuminate the whole scene. He saw some movement. Fast, abrupt, as if someone was dancing. Finally, his eyes got used to the partial darkness and were able to discern the blue-and-white stripes of a sailor's shirt.

The summer cottage was an exclusion zone for Felix. The cottage belonged to Lyosha, who got it from his parents, who were not particularly fond of Felix. Lyosha couldn't care less about the pastoral views. He was just too lazy to sell the property. It wasn't as if he could make any money from it, plus it wouldn't be easy to find buyers for this early-Soviet shack, its soil utterly impoverished by drought. That's why Lida was taking care of the place. But Felix was trespassing. He was not allowed here, oh no.

Somehow, Felix had infiltrated the zone. He was dancing, or whatever you want to call it. And Lida, standing with her sturdy Ardennes-horse legs wide apart, was yelling.

"I don't want to see your face, you piece of shit! And you even dragged along one of your loser friends!"

Said Belqola blew the final whistle on the TV. Tymofiy jumped out into the hall, stumbled on the porch, put on his sneakers, and went outside. Lida was stomping from the gate toward the house, while Felix, excited, wriggled behind her. Some guy—also wearing a striped sailor's shirt, gray-haired, dark—walked gingerly behind Felix. Tymofiy recognized these narrow eyes and flattened nose, the quiet gait and the faded body of an asthenic. Nestor.

"Sarge!" Felix yelled in his false basso. He approached Tymofiy, sizing him up inquisitively. "What's up with your dreadlocks?"

"I asked him the same thing," Nestor said.

Felix glanced at Nestor, surprised.

"Sweetie," Felix turned to Lida. "*Nu*, Lidok! This is Sasha! Nu?" Not feeling Lida's support, he turned to Tymofiy. "My Sashka. Aide-de-camp!"

"Those were the times," Nestor observed with melancholy. "Oleksandr Yuriyovych," he stretched out his hand.

Tymofiy shook it.

"To you he is Oleksandr Yuriyovych. To me, Nestor Ivanovych. Do you know why Nestor? He had the same dreadlocks when he was young. Same as you. Halfway across Afghanistan, we . . . I left . . . and he kept on beating the shit out of . . . while that dude, you know who I mean, kiddo?"

"That guy called Fagot?"

"Nu, this was closer to the pullout."

"Yeah, we pulled out all right. We were already back in the USSR. It was one of ours who did him in."

They entered the summer kitchen. Felix, wearing peculiar shorts and his usual striped shirt that made him look like a sea scout, was swinging his arms and hugging Lida. She made a face and pushed him away, but still set the table.

Tymofiy collapsed on the bed. Felix and Nestor sat by the table.

"You can stay the night, but tomorrow—get lost," Lida warned. "How did you even find us?" she blurted out.

"Counterintelligence!" Felix sounded victorious. "I know how to interrogate people. They told me. I am visiting Nestor. Your village is nearby, so it was not hard to locate."

"I bet you'll find your way home," Lida said acrimoniously.

"Lida! Nu!"

As if from nowhere, Nestor pulled out a bottle, put it on the table, and glanced at Tymofiy.

"Hey kiddo, wanna toast?" he burst out laughing. "The purest *sharop*."[43]

He looked somewhat fresher than he had during their first meeting. Shabby but clean clothes. He was reserved, even shy, but there was a noticeable anger simmering underneath his slow feline movements. Some sort of Asian brutality. He scared Tymofiy. Clearly, Lida was scared of him as well.

They started drinking. Nestor and Felix spoke loudly, slipping into laughter, eating with their hands, stuffing themselves. Tymofiy was expecting the worst. Just a bit more, he thought, two more shots.

"Just a bit longer, Lilulidze," Felix said, as if reading Tymofiy's mind. "Then we'll be gone."

Another drink.

"I'm off to bed," Lida said calmly. "You guys finish up and be on your way. Are you coming?" she turned to Tymofiy.

"I'll keep an eye on them," he said.

"Right, I bet you will."

The bottle was empty, but Nestor took out another one. Poured, drank. Poured again. Poked his cut fingers into the bowl of potatoes. He was grinning and constantly turning around, as if this tight space could hold someone else, behind his back. Felix looked petrified, glanced at Nestor blankly, moved his head unwittingly. They smoked, ashing into their palms, then stuck those palms into the bowl of potatoes. Again, they poured, drank. At first, they kept silent, then started talking. Tymofiy was rapidly sinking into slumber. From his murky drowsiness, he surfaced from time to time, listening to the conversations and recalling how his father had sat at this table four years ago, just after his return from the Slovak prison. How perfect the happiness seemed, and how joyful the sun was, and now Felix was sitting here with this incredibly scary guy, who had grayish cracked heels and the flat nose of a Neanderthal, and they talked, endlessly moving their drunken lips. How many similar conversations had he heard? Dozens and dozens of frenzied and heavy, even feverish, conversations. They talked about Field Marshal Ustinov[44] and the idiot Gromyko,[45] about people who were no longer alive, about the eternal Captain Boria and his cut-out heart, about Ivan and his legs—the only remains that they were able to send to his wife. They talked a lot about legs. How odd it is that we still have them, how strange. Perhaps we would have become different people without legs. Fuck, definitely, we would have been different without them. Just think about Krasnopysky, if he had his legs intact, would he have become a general?! They talked about toxic pain, about the faith they had abandoned somewhere in a bunker near Bagram airfield, about the mountains and pride; they recalled locations and observation towers stained with blood and military courage, and after a bit, they switched to humming and howling. Felix was not drinking anymore. He buried his face in his palms, whimpering, whispering something obscure through his fingers, something horrid, something that evoked a feeling of otherworldliness. Of afterlife, dry and cold.

"They are wiretapping us!" Nestor cried out suddenly. "Petrovych! They are wiretapping us."

Felix slowly raised his head, looking at Nestor with cloudy eyes.

"They are wiretapping us," repeated Nestor.

"Tapping?" Felix struggled to speak.

Nestor abruptly turned toward Tymofiy, pinned him down with his penetrating gaze, and started hissing.

"This one is wiretapping," he said, his angry eyes fixated on Tymofiy. His yellow temples began to move. He rose from his chair, and then froze.

"Sit down!" barked Felix.

"They are wiretapping!" Nestor hissed again. "This bitch is wiretapping us."

"Yes, wiretapping. Let them do it. We are not scared of anything," Felix mumbled.

"Bitch! They planted him!" Nestor screamed.

With one precise jump, he was by the bed, leaning on top of Tymofiy with his bone-dry body. The smell of old sweat and onions. Tymofiy squealed. Nestor pushed him with his bony elbow, landed on his shoulder, then grabbed his throat. The last thing Tymofiy managed to catch sight of were his nails—wide, uncut, and cracked.

After a brief moment, he started to feel as if he were drifting somewhere, definitely not into sleep. Falling asleep feels calm and tender, like taking a warm bath, while this sensation was reminiscent of something cold, like being cut with glass. Instantly, everything went white, and through this cold whiteness, through the snowy gloom Tymofiy heard a thump, as if someone was jumping up and down, barefoot, on unplowed soil. The pain didn't subside, and yet Tymofiy was able to discern the outlines of a cupboard and a stove; he moved his unfocused gaze to the right and saw Felix, who was sitting on top of Nestor, power-fully hammering him with his fists. He beat Nestor for what seemed like an eternity, tearing the skin on his face, leaving dents in his ribcage, leveling his already flattened nose. Finally, Felix calmed down. He sat there, spitting at Nestor, moving his head, growling dryly; this dry sound poured from his throat, like rust crumbling off an old, decommissioned tanker. Then he fell silent, even stopped breathing. As if he had just remembered something, he grabbed Nestor's hand, held it between his fingers, listened, exhaled heavily. He rose to his feet, shaking and looking at his fists tensely, watching blood drip from an almost transparent Nestor.

"He'll live," Felix said. "Hey, let me crash here."

The kid got up, freeing up the bed.

"And what about him?" Tymofiy nodded in the direction of the body with the face all smeared, as if it were made of playdough.

"Fuck him. Leave him there."

Tymofiy stepped over the body, drank some water, and went out. His neck hurt, there was a dull pain in his shoulder, and a ringing in his ears, as if someone were leaning on the doorbell.

The next morning, Tymofiy woke up before his grandma. He was already exhausted from the heat; pink sheetlike wrinkles ran across his cheeks. He wandered, dragging himself outside to the kitchen. A cheery-looking Felix was sitting at the table, finishing off yesterday's potatoes, munching and slurping. It smelled of dirty clothes and digested alcohol. Nestor was nowhere in sight.

"Where is Nestor Ivanovych?" the kid asked.

"To you, he is Oleksandr Yuriyovych. He went home."

"He managed to get up? Oleksandr Yuriyovych, that is."

"He managed to drink up." Felix motioned toward an empty bottle. "How are you?"

"Neck hurts," Tymofiy confessed. "Shoulder too."

"At first, I thought about sticking a knife between his shoulder blades. It's good . . ." Felix went silent, tossing the last dry potato into his mouth. He fished the last cigarette from a pack and lit it, his mouth stuffed with food.

"What do you mean, good?" Tymofiy asked.

"Good that I didn't do it," Felix mumbled, still chewing. "Otherwise, we would be digging a hole for Nestor. Where do you bury aide-de-camps around here?"

"Behind the shed."

Felix grunted.

"He said that he pawned your bike."

"So what?"

"It came to nothing. Like everything in his life."

"Got it," Tymofiy sighed, wiping his face after washing up.

He glanced at the spot where Nestor had lain last night. A trace of wetness remained on the wooden floor. It looked as if Felix had cleaned the blood with a rag. Felix caught Tymofiy's glance.

"Not a peep to your granny."

"Clear," agreed Tymofiy.

"Sarge," Felix announced solemnly. "I am promoting you. From now on, you are a Cornet!"

"A what?" Tymofiy made a face.

"Cornet, psiakrew!" Felix became agitated.

"Yessir," Tymofiy agreed, sorrowfully, and walked out of the kitchen.

Felix left that day. After a prolonged argument with Lida, he looked disheveled and sad. He was away for two days, then showed up again, black and unshaven, resembling an old skipper whose vessel had been sold to cover the Department of the Navy's debt. No joy in his smile, a repugnant look, his sailor's shirt soiled with blood, food, grass, and mud. He stood by the gate and looked at the kid and Lida, not uttering a single word. Then he turned around and left, again in silence.

"What a nutcase," Lida said.

Felix and Nestor wandered through the villages, drank, got

into fights with combine operators and agronomists, visited Nestor's friends, continued drinking at their houses, scaring the owners and their neighbors, burned someone's shed, slaughtered someone's turkey. Later, they went back to Nestor's, fainted from fatigue and drink, slept in, and set off to drink and break the bones of the locals yet again.

A few days later, the cops practically drove onto the porch in their Lada. Scratching the fence with their car, they backed up, grazed the bench, came to a halt. Two squat guys, little fellows in civilian clothes, idly crawled out from the car. In the same lazy manner, they walked around the backyard, flopped on the bench, protecting their cropped haircuts from the sun with black folders. They inquired about Nestor—who he was with, what he drank. Nothing was asked about Felix. It turned out that Nestor stabbed someone and was now himself in the hospital. His kidneys had failed, his lungs were filled with fluid.

"Is he gonna die?" Lida asked.

"Definitely," answered one of the little fellows. "Maybe not right at this moment."

"But soon," the other added. "He is so fucking annoying."

Lida told them only lies—yes, Nestor had stopped by, but only because he thought they sold moonshine here.

"Is it not sold here?" the cops clarified, slyly.

"No, it is not!" Lida sounded angry.

"Pity. Summer residents, then?

"Summer residents."

The little fellows drank some water, plucked raspberries off the bushes, and left. Tymofiy remembered how diligently Felix had pounded at Nestor's chest, as if wanting to break it and get to the heart, the black one—no doubt, it would be black, splurges of pus and the smell of rotten meat—he could have torn it out and swallowed it, right there, washing it down with vodka.

Two days passed, and Felix came again. Dirty but sober. Stationing himself by the gate, he stood there staring at the pinnate leaves, looking for familiar figures. Once he saw Lida and Tymofiy, he walked in, sailing by the porch like a cloud, stopped by the summer kitchen, silently took some cans of meat, a packet of corn grain, and a bottle of cooking oil from his sack-like bag.

"Cornet, who took your bike?" he asked while walking back to the gate.

"Ivasyk," Tymofiy lied, stunned.

"I won't be coming anymore," Felix articulated, sounding distant and irritated, and he disappeared, or rather dissolved into the white radiance of the July sun.

A week went by, perhaps more. The rain that day lingered, felt heavy, depressing. The sky sank into the earth, filling everything with the watery, tart smell of dampness. Tymofiy was in the house, torturing the TV remote with persistent flipping between the two pitiful channels. From the national to the regional and back. That's when he heard a familiar but forgotten voice. As if from a different life, as if years had passed.

"Lady of the house!" the sound came from outside. "Shall we settle?"

Tymofiy remained inside. He decided to observe everything from the window. Enough of these local tramps. How long could he tolerate these bums with their red puffy faces and dirty fingernails? Why did they cling to him? Did they think he was one of them? Their flesh and blood? He was not like them. Tymofiy became pensive. Where were the quiet rural intelligentsia, naive artists, bards of the native land, those who submitted the glorious georgics to the regional press? Where were the local librarians who publish literary newspapers by themselves? Where was any sort of clergy, a shabby priest wearing his ironed formal pants, admonishing the believers to tell only the truth and teaching about love?

"Lady of the house!" the voice boomed from just below the window. Hoarse, spent, cheery.

Ivasyk, his neck covered in dark bandages, his left leg limping, pushed his black Ukraina bike and rang the chrome bell. Lida, girdled in an apron stained with tomato, jumped out of the summer kitchen.

"It was my fault. I am offering to settle," yelled Ivasyk.

Ivasyk and Lida exchanged a few words that Tymofiy could not make out, and then Lida started swinging her towel, as if she was going after the flies on the windowsill. Ivasyk mumbled something indistinctly, some not-particularly-convincing justifications, and then conceded all of Lida's accusations. He squirmed, patiently enduring the beating with the white waffle-weave towel, and tried to lean his bike against the wooden poles that protruded from the ground to support the heavy bunches of grapes. Finally, having made sure the bike wouldn't fall, he backed up, stepped on the flowerbed, crushed the flowers, apologized, and gave a thumbs up signaling that everything was all right.

"Everything is okay, lady of the house! Ivasyk—that's what they call me. Everything is all right!"

And this is how Tymofiy became the owner of a new Ukraina bike.

◊   ◊   ◊

In August, Tymofiy returned to the city. He was stuck at home, taking the garbage out early in the morning to avoid his former friends, who still called him a thief and a rat. He stared at the TV screen until late at night, looking for adult films. From time to time, Olha called, shattering the muted silence of his existence with a powerful reminder of a different world. He always imagined that she was calling from a payphone on some crowded street filled with abundant sunlight, dizzying hustle and bustle, bright colors, fussy pigeons, yelling merchants, and clerks engrossed in their important metropolitan affairs. And even more—dust, fountains, kites, and, of course, cars stuck in traffic, honking and honking, and above it all, the evergreen chestnut trees shivering in the gusts of eastern wind, casting a thick, caring shadow. But Olha was calling from a quiet and dark apartment in Voskresenka, or an equally quiet office, and there were no fountains, to say nothing of kites, around her. She was quite reserved when asking her son how he was: Is he reading books? Is he watching too much TV? He wasn't reading much, except for the volumes of Symbolist poetry stacked on the shelves, most of which had been published in late Soviet times. The TV was on practically all the time. He countered all of his mother's questions with allegations.

"I am not wearing those crappy shoes!" Tymofiy screamed, his spit all over the receiver. "You don't get it."

Olha did get it, but remained silent. This got Tymofiy even more worked up.

"And I'm not wearing the jacket either!"

"The crappy jacket," Olha added quietly.

"Yes, crappy! I look like a bum! Nobody looks like that! This makes me sick!"

"All of us are sick," Olha answered calmly. Her words would terrify him, so he would go back to the previous topic of conversation and lie, with naivete, saying that he didn't care for TV, and as for the books . . . His gaze would roam around the bookshelf and zoom in on something age appropriate, like Marko Vovchok[46] or Garin-Mikhailovsky.

And then school started. Tymofiy got transferred to a different class again. It was as if he were a member of the penalty battalion that was being sent to death. Hitting rock bottom. Keeping company with losers and scum. The new group was completely staffed by some handpicked jerks boasting criminal inclinations. This was a strange age; his peers had the urge to destroy, break, and humiliate. They were taking the piss to the fullest. He was a prime target, especially because of his long hair, which he refused to cut.

One September morning, Felix peeked into Tymofiy's room (his parents' former bedroom which he had turned into a teenager's den).

"Cornet." Felix looked at Tymofiy in a serious and focused manner. "Follow me!"

"Where to?" Tymofiy was surprised. "I have school."

"You're gonna skip it," Felix sounded firm. "We have a special op."

"What is it this time?" Tymofiy asked lazily.

"Stand down, enough with the questions. Are you coming?"

"Let's do it," Tymofiy agreed. Anything was better than school.

"Ten o'clock in the foyer. At ease, Cornet."

They left the apartment at ten o'clock sharp. Lida had gone to visit her son, Tymofiy's uncle, so there was no one overseeing Tymofiy's schedule. He and Felix walked to the bus stop, squinting their eyes in the bright light, and shouting over the gusts of September wind.

"Where are we going, really?" Tymofiy asked.

"To the funeral."

"Oh no," he groaned and stood in the middle of a street.

"It's not what you think."

"You gonna knock down the casket again?"

"Cornet, it's you who I am going to knock down right now." Felix slapped Tymofiy lightly, but it resonated. "It's Nestor's funeral."

"Aide-de-camp?" Tymofiy asked.

"Aide-de-camp."

"Super. He almost strangled me, and now I have to drag myself to his funeral."

"You have to say goodbye."

"Go ahead then, do it," Tymofiy shot back.

"It was me who drove him into the grave. He might have lived longer."

"Felix, I don't want to." Tymofiy sounded serious and tired. He looked back in the direction of his house.

"Don't fuck with me, Cornet. You knew him."

"It would have been better if I had not."

"But you did. You wanted a decent bike, right? Nestor took care of it. And I drove him into his grave," Felix repeated. He added, after a moment of silence, "Such a dickhead, that guy." He grew pensive. "I have no pity for him. I know these dickheads through and through. I can see them from a mile away. I've seen so many of them, it's just sickening . . . And I am exactly like them."

Empty stools stood by the entrance to the gray four-story panel building, surrounded by hefty acacia trees. Still green in September, the courtyard was generously filled with sunlight. A ginger cat, with his tail up, rubbed its back against the legs of the stools. A Christian Orthodox yearning hovered over everything, and there was nowhere to hide. Despite the sun and greenery, the day was saturated with darkness, ineffaceable and omnipresent.

"Should I go up as well?" Tymofiy asked.

"Let's go together," Felix ordered.

In a freshly whitewashed foyer on the second floor, by a wooden trestle left by the painters, leaning against the wall, stood a casket. It was black and tall, like a morning shadow.

Some folks stood right there, just a few of them: two corpulent guys wearing black sandals and a Dubok camouflage with pins from the Council of the Veterans, Hrysha the Saboteur dressed in a sleek gray suit without a tie, a woman in her fifties, a priest. Felix squeezed himself through them, peeked inside the apartment, which smelled of damp earth. Then he walked inside, stumbled over the threshold, cursed, and started a conversation. Tymofiy was left standing in the stairwell. Hrysha was chewing gum. The woman in her fifties—probably a neighbor—was relating the old wolf's complicated fate to the priest, in great detail. That's exactly what she said: *the old wolf with a complicated fate.* The priest nodded emphatically.

Yeah right, Tymofiy thought to himself, the old wolf. More like the jackal who tried to strangle me on that stuffy night in July. The old jackal, brutal and mad, broken and neglected, like the old Soviet-era merry-go-round in Jubilee Park.

Like Felix, Nestor had been discharged from the military in '89 for health reasons. Shell-shocked, he wandered around the neighborhood in his overcoat, regardless of the season. He even wore it at the beach. A Red Star medal dangled from his key ring. Scarred face, broken nose—flattened, pressed into the skull—pale, almost bluish body, a faded undershirt. Nestor went binge drinking, fought constantly, he challenged the local precinct officer, and often fainted in the middle of a street. He scared kids and adults alike.

They called him Nestor Ivanovych because in the seventies he had a haircut exactly like Nestor Makhno[47] in that famous photo from 1919. He even resembled him in temperament. Like Makhno, on the battlefield, neither bullet, nor saber, nor land-mine could take him out. An anti-tank guided missile almost got him in the borderlands of Tajikistan, when their formation was leaving Afghanistan. They had been mistakenly identified as an enemy unit.

As a result of shell shock and alcoholism, Nestor lost it. He could not recognize his mom; he beat her, the neighbors, and the precinct officer. He was especially cruel to his neighbors. Nobody really got him, and he could not understand why they didn't get him, and so he was constantly looking for a pretext to start a fight. They would lock him up in the precinct, interrogate him, let him go half-breathing, or rather, half-dead. And he would drink even more, meet his fellow comrades, get involved in criminal affairs; apparently, he had even killed someone. That's when he was given a plot of land with an old hut, probably built back in the times of Makhno, some sixty-five kilometers away from Cher-kasy. This place was Nestor's personal Valaam,[48] where he battled wicked spirits, suffered, and was overcome with melancholy and desperate loneliness. At first, he tried to go easy on the booze, growing strawberries and handing them over to the state. He had a garden, so in April he would tap the birch trees, distill the juice in August, and drink in winter. As the successor to the USSR, Russia was responsible for all the war crimes he had committed. Therefore, Nestor had a decent pension, and the head of the village council would bring him firewood and coal.

In other words, it was not feasible for him to drink less. He found some questionable friends. Hookers visited from the neighboring villages. Nestor Ivanovych drank an awful lot, without mercy, pouring all his fervor and nomadic passion into his binges. When delirious, he had visions of angels and fantastical animals, blue bears, black roosters, golden doves, and hungry white foxes who hunted mice and moles. Enormous desert lizards crawled in his dreams, he was tormented by hellish thirst, an Antonov-12[49] was evacuating the 200s,[50] a *hafiz* was chanting the verses of Quran in his hideous falsetto, a barefoot *bachata*[51] traded American *choowingam* for buckwheat, and Sharbat Gula stared at him eerily from a magazine cover. In his dreams and visions, he saw Lieutenant Colonel Ignatiev, who yelled, "Nestor, you bitch, watch how you stand in front of an officer!" to which Nestor replied, "Bitch, Petrovych, look at yourself, you fucking *gereushnyk*."[52] Time and again, he saw the parks and community gardens of his native Cherkasy, fresh and cozy, transformed into the exhausted desert, dry and red, like the blood on the sleeves of his uniform. Sometimes, he would see fiery birds rising up in the sky, burning to the ground the nearby pine forests and cornfields with their wings, turning the calm water of the Kremenchuk Reservoir into a fish soup, which tired sailors of Dnipro barges and tugboats feasted on.

And so it happened that one stuffy night in July, laying on the broken, patched-up folding bed after a weeklong binge—filthy, surrounded by miasma and fat flies—Nestor Ivanovych realized that his hope for any kind of life was dead even before his discharge, and there was nothing else left for him in this world but to give his soul to God. Of course, who knows if he would even accept it. It's unlikely that God loves cruel and evil people. Even less likely that he fancies the sick and unfortunate, the forsaken and cursed. Nestor Ivanovych asked his mother to bring him to the city. He wanted to die with dignity, watching pipes exhale smoke, pigeons parade themselves on cornices, and blue light emanate from TV screens. While dying, he wanted to hear the noise of children on the street and neighbors' whispering from behind the wall, random cars honking, and the sound of the water boiling in the kitchen. He wished to be buried as a human being, so that stray dogs would not feast on his body, and peregrine falcons would not peck out his eyes, and foresters would not pass around his bones as tchotchkes . . .

"They are going to carry away the body any minute now," said a woman wearing thick makeup, with a cloven nose-tip, peeping out of the apartment.

Tymofiy decided not to stay and watch, not to listen to this sacred whispering and dreary rustling of feet by the casket.

"He did not have a bowel movement for four days," the woman in her fifties said quietly. "And once he died . . ."

"Let's skip that part." The priest interrupted her. "Here, you carry the portrait." He touched Tymofiy's shoulder.

Tymofiy looked up, glancing fearfully at the disheveled, poodle-like priest, and tried to swallow the deadly disgust; he ended up inhaling too much air, feeling a burp rising in his throat. He produced a deep sound resembling a trombone, grimaced, and ran downstairs stomping his feet, feeling himself blush. He decided to wait out the funeral in the neighboring courtyard. So he sat in the shadow of a rowan tree, trying to discern the mottle of the funeral wreaths and the pitch black of shawls through the dense greenery.

When everything was over, the *pazik*[53] drove off, wheezing and spitting. Those who planned to go back to the heavy stuffiness of the kitchen and continue cooking the cabbage soup and kasha were abandoned by the building entrance. That's when Tymofiy went inside the building hallway, idly looking at those who were still there, searching for Felix.

◇ ◇ ◇

Tymofiy dropped out of childhood without noticing it, as if it were a dream. He spent a year at home being sick, stubbornly, as if on a mission.

Lyosha worked at a car service station and stayed there; it was more convenient for him that way. At the end of the day, it was more convenient for everyone. He saw Tymofiy infrequently. It was possible that Lyosha was not particularly interested in handling a teenager who was constantly down with bronchitis, and when he wasn't sick, was flunking classes and wandering around the city center. So Lyosha was not really part of his son's life, apart from the occasional visit to the school to get the next dose of complaints about Tymofiy's academic performance and attendance. Lyosha would stand and stare blankly, shaking his head as if it were he who had flunked classes. Clearly, Lyosha's reckless attitude toward his family was the result of some psychological pain. Or laziness. Or everything altogether, plus his natural indifference. He was far from young, and life was rushing by like an empty freight train—fast and loud. His hair turned gray, he had tooth decay, and he felt sleepy. It seemed that cigarettes were the only thing keeping him afloat. He smoked them with zeal, greedily. Especially in the mornings, with strong, thick coffee. He exhaled smoke, bending his head down, taking big sips, then inhaled with such force that almost a third of the cigarette smoldered away. His son's academic performance was the last thing on his mind.

In the meantime, Tymofiy completely bailed on his studies and sat in front of the TV, watching every single program offered on all five available channels. Sometimes he turned to his books, but reading wasn't going well. He spent more time listening to music. He didn't have that many of his own recordings, mostly Ukrainian pop music and a bit of rap, so he had to be content with his dad's cassette collection brought from Russia or Poland in the early nineties. These were all pirated copies and mostly old rock, new wave, heavy metal.

It was Lida who took care of his upbringing. There was not much to do, though—Tymofiy spent that whole year in a vegetative state, having lost faith in himself and humanity. He stared blankly at the screen or hid between the heavy Feniks headphones from the eighties that still worked reliably. Lida cooked and, when necessary, helped to bring down Tymofiy's fever; she brought warm bread in from an industrial bakery before lunch, as well as traces of snow on the collar of her winter jacket.

Until late fall, when frost covered the ground and the trees, she traveled from the city to the countryside on the weekends. That was when Tymofiy wouldn't even bother to leave his bed, except to wander into the kitchen to warm up the borsht that had been cooked on Friday.

That year, Felix hardly ever stopped by. Tymofiy did not care. First and foremost, he was interested in food. Felix would almost never bring food, and even if he did, he would eat it himself. Lida once inquired whether he would like to provide part of his pension to cover their needs. His daughter was already grown and could take care of herself, while Lida and Tymofiy were hardly able to afford potatoes. Felix's face flushed red, swelling from a sort of anger mixed with insult, and he said that an officer's daughter could indulge in whatever she cared for, while rednecks were free to eat dirt if they so desired.

Gold and leather, Tymofiy recalled at that moment. Like a gypsy.

He visited Shlosser just a few times that year. He would arrive and wait in the foyer for him to finish teaching his students; he would listen to their drills and observe their progress with some envy. They had all started together, and now . . .

The pupils would leave their classrooms and wave hello to Tymofiy, smiling at him with that patronizing grimace all the straight-A students wore, while simultaneously looking somewhat melancholic, as if they were carrying not music cases in their hands, but refugee suitcases. Without fail, they would turn around, as if they were casting a farewell glance not on the pitiful long-haired figure but on a city just abandoned, bombs already falling. Tymofiy hastened to the auditorium, which was still filled with the resonance of the recently played music. He greeted Shlosser, sat down on a chair without taking his coat off, and felt tears swelling in his eyes—tears of shame and indignation.

Shlosser allowed Tymofiy to pour his heart out. While listening, he rearranged the music books or glued the bridge of someone's guitar. Then he would treat Tymofiy to some tea and say something nice and encouraging, something that would make Tymofiy want to hug him and start crying directly into Shlosser's brown zippered sweater. One time, however, when Tymofiy was done with his usual whining, Shlosser went deep into philosophical musings in lieu of saying something kind and supportive. His eyes glittered with dangerous light; he put his thermos on the piano lid and walked to the window.

"You know, I think you're a poppy." Shlosser spoke with the back of his head facing Tymofiy, who could see only the nervous twitching of the fingers on the hands Shlosser folded behind his back. "The poppy is a plant," he continued. "And it is not at all red. Or, it is red for only a few days. In fact, the poppy is black and white. Or rather, white and black. You, Tymofiychyk, are a poppy. If you cut it down, the stem will release a white juice beloved by addicts. But we aren't talking about them. This milky white juice, opium, turns black later on. It gets oxidized, or whatever it's called. You are a poppy, or rather, the poppy's juice. Some would say you are white, but in reality you are black."

He finished, turned around, and approached Tymofiy.

"Some nuts?" he asked, his eyes still glittering.

"What nuts?" Tymofiy was unsure.

"Nuts, nuts. Would you like some?"

"No."

Tymofiy got up and walked toward the door.

"Think about what I told you," came Shlosser's gentle voice. "When you stop by next time, I'll tell you something interesting about guitar fingering."

That same evening, while falling asleep, Tymofiy kept thinking about his genuinely black nature. He thought and thought until he fell asleep. And in the morning, he decided he wouldn't be going to Shlosser's anymore.

◇ ◇ ◇

One evening toward the end of a long and insatiable winter, the front door opened and in came Lyosha. Two duffle bags hanging from his shoulders, plus a shopping bag filled with sausages, cans, fruits, and various colorful packages.

"Buddy!" he yelled. "Dig in!"

They sat in the kitchen. Lyosha told Tymofiy about some douchebags, how because of them he had to stay with Lida for a while, how everything was their fault, all this mess, cholera and plague.

"All of this is because of human greed, buddy, that's why. I'll stay here in the meantime. You don't mind?" Lyosha did not so much ask permission as confirm his intentions. "And your *maman* doesn't mind," he continued. "She'll have peace of mind if I stay here with you."

"Fine with me," Tymofiy said indifferently, stuffing himself with bread and Nutella.

He ate in silence, smearing thick layers of paste on the white bread, washing it down with yogurt, and peeling an orange at the same time.

"Let's go get you a haircut?" Lyosha offered. "You look like a rooster."

"Sure," agreed Tymofiy. "Actually, you're the rooster."

"Whatever. How's school?"

"No idea. You got money?"

"How much?"

"In general. Do you have money? I need sneakers, jeans."

"What about your mom?"

"What about you?" Tymofiy anxiously scooped up a banana and a few oranges from the table. "You'll sleep in the living room."

Tymofiy walked out of the kitchen. As he passed Lida's room, he heard some drunken babbling.

"To hell with this war," Tymofiy hissed. He was good at imitating Felix's voice now. He sat in the armchair and turned the TV on.

Lyosha would head out somewhere in the morning, driving someone's car—a white CEAT—and would usually return by the evening. He dragged home a new coffee grinder and a toaster but had yet to use them. He walked around the apartment in his old blue fleece robe, girded with the golden wide-tasseled curtain rope, and smoked, filling up the two metal ashtrays with Marlboro and Camel labels. He was reserved when saying hello to Lida, and greeted Felix silently with only a nod. With Tymofiy he spoke very little. What was there to talk about, really? The boy had lost his wits, always angry, gloomy, and silent, always sitting in front of a TV and skipping school. At least he had cut his hair.

Tymofiy suspected that his dad was getting money from somewhere, but that he probably wasn't working. Files full of documents were laying on the piano: car registration, some receipts, agreements, seals; Tymofiy went through all of it but still couldn't figure anything out. Only that someone had given Lyosha permission to drive the car. At the end of the day, Tymofiy didn't care, and Lyosha continued to live as he pleased—he disappeared, sometimes didn't come home at night. Other times, he would come home and bring food. From time to time, someone would call Lyosha, and he would stand with the receiver in his hand, nodding silently, occasionally sighing, and then he would lose his temper and hurl threats, which was unlike him. But soon enough he would calm down, fall silent, and start nodding again. Once in a while, he would appear drunk. He would hover over Tymofiy telling him about his new life, saying that everything would change soon: the main thing is that those douchebags get what they deserve, which would surely happen, 'cause human greed, buddy, always gets punished. On top of that, he talked— pretentiously and cynically—about a certain auntie Inna, who would undoubtedly become Tymofiy's new mom, and how Olha deserved the title of the First Lady Cuckoo Bird; can you imagine that she dropped her son, her husband, everything really, and went away? And where to? That's right! Since they were on the subject, if one ran away, one should really go to Germany, that's where one should flee, get out of this city before it suffocates under its own ruins. Everything is different in Germany. The roads, the food, the clothes, even the air is different—they know how to live, those fascists. Lyosha had been there, and he'd go again, for good. Wanna go to Leipzig? Or Rostock? He used to go there. And how about Cologne? He hadn't been there yet.

Tymofiy listened to all this but took it as Lyosha's usual betting on zero. He was especially amused by the part about auntie Inna.

"How do you feel about the fact that Mom is still paying back your debt?" he asked once, sarcastically, looking his father right in the eye. He had the cloudy, dark eyes of a political prisoner who had gotten used to the murky light but now, finally freed to the light-filled vastness, had lost his sight.

"Your mom and I have our own agreements."

"Such as?"

"I am supporting you."

"You?" Tymofiy snorted.

"Let it go," Lyosha said. "You'll see."

In spring, the ice broke. Tymofiy would go to the river and watch the barges sailing southeast. The water came closer, carrying bulging black logs, dry reeds, and empty dark-green bottles. That's where he often escaped from school, walked on the beach, looking for coins in the damp sand to spend on cookies and lemonade.

Once the days grew warmer, he would wander through the city center again. He roamed around, studying his native Cherkasy, spending a lot of time sitting in the community garden behind the administrative buildings, hiding beneath the vast crown of a willow tree with thick vines that plunged deep into the ground. Tymofiy would get home late. He would hang out on the late-night bus; there was so much sorrowful dreaminess in it, so much love for his city and its people that, sometimes, he would purposefully wait for evening to come before heading home under the streetlamps. He would take his spot in the front seat without fail, right behind the driver.

On one of those days, festivities were taking place in the city. The town hall would organize celebrations, with or without reason—on the first of April, the first of May, or May 9.[54] The Day of the City was even celebrated twice a year. The drunken and restless populace roamed the city center. From a stage on the dirty and featureless square by the House of Commerce, Tymofiy could hear the cheering of a young and jaded emcee, encouraging everyone to raise their hands higher. Local rock bands were performing. There would be fireworks too.

Behind the Ukraina movie theater, three guys in jackets were kicking some granddad. He was yelling fiercely about his criminal past and promised revenge. Girls were screaming. The sound of broken glass echoed repeatedly.

Tymofiy was enjoying the evening. He peeked behind the stage, where some skinny women—backup dancers—were changing in plain sight and without fear. He stood in the line to get ice cream scooped by a chubby woman with big tits. She wore a traditional Ukrainian costume and generously piled the ice cream onto a waffle cone. For a while, he observed two shabby bums, who converged in an amusing and ugly fight.

Pushing his way through the crowd, Tymofiy noticed a group of teens swarming under the pine trees. They did not look aggressive. They were basically like him, only they had beer. One girl was standing among them; she was in heavy white sneakers, a skirt and a pink jacket, with knee socks on her thin legs. She was puffing a cigarette. She had glitter around her eyes and was wearing blue lipstick. From time to time, one of the guys brought a bottle to her mouth. She swallowed hungrily, spitting out the excess, then laughed, inhaled deeply, and let the smoke out, her mouth wide open.

Tymofiy approached the group.

"Hey," he said. "Just saying hi," he added awkwardly.

The girl stared at him for a few seconds, without blinking, then made a squeaky noise and gave Tymofiy a hug.

"You've become such a jelly belly!" she yelled cheerfully. "Seriously, a jelly belly!"

Toma smelled of coconut aerosol deodorant and cigarettes. Her dry, thin hair was up in a short ponytail. She was wearing tiny sparkling silver earrings each in the shape of the Eiffel Tower. She felt like a stranger and yet Tymofiy did not want to let go of her.

"This is Tymofiy, we used to go to the same school," she explained to her guys. "You don't go there anymore either, right?"

Tymofiy shook his head.

"It was practically an old folks' home," she articulated with disgust.

The guys moved to shake hands with Tymofiy. One of them—with fair reddish hair, transparent eyelashes, and gelatinous skin—took a small bottle out of his backpack and passed it to Tymofiy.

"Dzhudik," he introduced himself.

"Ihor."

"Nastia."

And so they got acquainted. Tymofiy cast a piercing gaze at the guy named Ihor. He was skinny, with a prominent nose, a scar visible on his softly outlined chin. Tymofiy shifted his eyes to Toma, gulped the contents of the bottle, and asked for a cigarette.

"Jelly Belly, you smoke too?"

Tymofiy lit a cigarette, inhaled too quickly, and tears came streaming from his eyes. He inhaled some more and his legs went out. Semitransparent Dzhudik, big-nosed Ihor, and Nastia went blurry, like watercolors. Toma was holding Tymofiy under his arm, and for some reason could not stop laughing. She was tipsy and thus light and joyful; she flirted with Tymofiy and he liked that. He felt tipsy too; he was laughing a lot and out of place.

Then Dzhudik started scrounging up cash from all of them, for beer. Tymofiy fished a few hryvnias in change from his pocket, exactly enough for two bottles. He dropped the coins into Dzhudik's red palm, leaving himself only five kopecks to get home. Dzhudik blended into the crowd. Ihor and Nastia were making out, and Toma, having been left alone with Tymofiy, became instantly serious.

"So, what's up?" she asked.

"Not much," Tymofiy answered.

"Sure." Toma sounded distant. "Been here long?"

"A few hours," Tymofiy answered.

"Us too. Gonna watch the fireworks, and then go to Nastia's.

Her folks are in Odesa," she said, looking toward her friend. "Nastia! Jelly Belly's coming with us, okay? I haven't seen him in, like, forever."

Nastia, a brunette of medium height, with a thick unibrow and black Eastern eyes, let go of Ihor, her lips still wet, and shrugged.

"Super!" Toma got excited.

A few moments later, Dzhudik came running, the contents of his backpack clinking promisingly. The host on stage, shaking the mic anxiously, announced that the fireworks would start in fifteen minutes. The guys lit their cigarettes.

Tymofiy started feeling the effect of the beer. Though he hated to leave Toma, he had to step away.

"I'm gonna pay a visit to the backyard," he announced.

"To take a leak?" asked Dzhudik. "Do it here. It's just us."

Moron, Tymofiy thought. He snuck out of the square, crossed the boulevard, ran into the dark entryway of a gloomy five-story building, and squeezed himself between the garage and a concrete fence. It smelled of damp and waste oil, like in the auto shop where his father used to work. Right at that moment he heard a bang. Tymofiy could not see the fireworks, only the red and green lights illuminating the yard. He tried walking faster. Some people entered the courtyard, probably also in search of a cozy spot, and then headed toward the garages. Tymofiy passed them by the swings. Someone hurled a comment at his back. Or maybe he misheard it, but at a time and place like that, you had to be ready for anything. He decided not to react, left in a rush, and ran toward the pine trees. The host continued thanking people from the stage, listing sponsors, naming representatives of the authorities, and entrepreneurs. The organizers started dismantling the stage; the crowd disappeared into the nearby courtyards to continue celebrating. There was nobody under the pine trees. A few empty beer bottles with cigarette butts inside them were scattered around. Tymofiy rushed past the movie theater, toward the

Dnipro. He ran at a breakneck speed, pushing the people around him, trying hard to spot Toma's pink puffer. He turned back, advancing along Khreshchatyk, by the old two-story buildings toward Slava Square. The street kept disappearing into darkness, empty and resonating like a hospital hallway. He ran back to the concrete square. No one. He walked past the white box of the movie theater again, then stopped, stood there, and looked around, cursing at himself for not listening to Dzhudik's advice. Tymofiy resumed walking and collided with a group of teenagers. They beckoned him, rudely. Tymofiy ignored them, rushed by the art musuem toward the Teacher's House building, feeling danger at his back. Passing by the marble edifice with the tiled-mosaic facade, he could hear whistling and stomping. He sped up, passing through some more backyards, ran onto the grounds of a preschool, and jumped into the closest pavilion. He laid low, with knees bent, feeling like his heart could jump out of his chest any moment. The heavy beating in his ribcage resonated in his temples. Tymofiy was breathing heavily, choking on his dry saliva, and feeling nauseated.

He spent some thirty minutes at the pavilion, listening to the rustling outside and recalling the screams of the geezer, whom the black jackets had been bashing some hundred yards away. Tymofiy could have been in his place. Clearly, it would have been him had he not run away. On top of the anxiety, he felt a lump of quiet joy in his throat as he thought about Toma. It was calming to think about her, and he wanted to keep thinking about her. Especially in his tipsy state.

Finally, Tymofiy climbed over the fence and walked to Lenin Street, hurriedly, past Shcherbyna House,[55] the Puppet Theater, and the Hungarian House. In a few minutes he was already at a bus stop, naively waiting for transportation. It was late, and the buses were no longer operating; just one, bearing a plywood sign that read To the Depot, crawled by like a sleepy green caterpillar. Tymofiy stood for a long while, with his head down, until it became clear that it'd be faster to walk. He dragged himself toward his neighborhood, turning back periodically in hopes of catching the last bus. Whatever, he thought, if I walk at my usual pace, it'll take about forty minutes.

In an hour, Tymofiy stood at his door.

He woke up late the next morning. It was Sunday. There was no school, so he could sleep in. Lyosha was rhythmically snoring in the living room, with curtains drawn. He could sleep until lunch, undisturbed by the industrial noise outside or the ringing phone. He slept as if he were about to die, curled up, his arms between his knees. This was typical of late. And once he woke up, he looked anxious and bullied, walked around the apartment quietly and briskly, like a leopard locked in a cage, running to the bathroom every half hour. Sometimes, he would stand still in the middle of the room and listen to the sounds coming from the street.

Tymofiy snuck into the hall. A velvet curtain was hanging between the living room and the hall, symbolically marking the political divisions within the apartment. In the darkness, he ran his fingers across his dad's leather jacket, which smelled intensely of cigarettes and the car. Tymofiy stuck his arm in the jacket, fishing out a few bills and holding them up to the light. Two twenties and a five. Too much, he thought, and put the twenties back.

He got dressed quickly and rushed out to the street; it felt chilly and joyful outside, as it should in the spring. He went around the building and, walking lightly and confidently, treaded toward the supermarket. Actually, the supermarket was no longer there; in its place stood an empty concrete building with dusty windows. Garbage, which had been absorbing sunlight and moisture for years, piled up between the bars and the glass. In a section of what had been the supermarket there was a bar, a hair salon, and a law office—the only lively spot in the building. Grannies sat out front from the early morning on, selling cigarettes, sunflower seeds, and chewing gum, all the stuff that was so desirable to the pupils of the neighboring School No. 125. Tymofiy approached a chubby woman wearing a beige dress and gray sweater. She had steel teeth in a dark mouth. Her name was Ada, and she knew Felix. "Fat-ass Ada, that old gypsy bitch, selling meat all her life," Felix would say. Tymofiy bought a pack of cigarettes and two sticks of Double-mint, stashing the rest of the money for later. From the grannies' location, he turned left and found himself in the suburbs. In a couple of yards, his favorite lane, tightly packed with tiny brick houses, came into sight. There, between the branchy fruit trees, by his classmate Usik's house, Tymofiy came to a stop and lit a cig-arette. It felt light and good, as if he were sailing on an inflatable raft, floating on languid saltwater. He finished smoking, threw the butt into the bushes, and immediately stuffed a piece of gum into his mouth.

At home, Tymofiy dialed Toma's number. He knew it by heart.

"Jelly Belly!" Toma sounded full of joy. "You're not offended that I call you that?"

"I was looking for you guys, yesterday."

"We waited for you for a bit, then went to Nastia's."

"The Georgian chick?"

"Idiot. She's from Kishinev."

"Got it. See you sometime?"

"Tomorrow after school is okay. We're meeting on Gagarin Street, by the Fortune Teller. You know where that is?"

"Yeah, sure. Down there, by the slope. When?"

"Around three," said Toma. "Have some dough on you," she added, emphatically.

Tymofiy remembered the location all too well. He had been mugged there, lost his watch.

"Listen," he insisted after a pause. "Don't call me Jelly Belly."

"Okay, Jelly Belly," Toma laughed and hung up.

Lyosha woke up. Still sleepy, his right cheek slightly swollen, disheveled gray spikes on his head, he anxiously paced around the apartment.

"Who were you talking to?" he asked.

"A girlfriend."

"A girlfriend." Lyosha became pensive. "You have a *girlfriend?* Huh. If someone calls and asks for me, tell them I'm not here. But say, 'No longer with us.'"

"What do you mean, *no longer with us?* Like you're dead?"

"You heard me, right? Come on, don't let me down."

"You are not here. You are no longer with us." Tymofiy was serious.

"Good."

"And if they come over?"

"They won't."

"How about money?" Tymofiy asked directly.

"How much?"

"How much do you think I need for a girlfriend?"

Lyosha said nothing. Instead, he squeezed past the curtain into the hall, then returned with a twenty in his hand.

"This works?"

"Sure," Tymofiy smiled.

Someone called Lyosha twice that day. Different voices. Tymofiy kept saying, obediently, that his dad was "no longer with us." The first time, a certain Ruslan sent his greetings. Second—someone called Midget. That's exactly what he said: *greetings from Midget.*

Tymofiy passed the greetings to Lyosha, who got somber, looked down, his face becoming darker and heavier. Still, he thanked Tymofiy.

Around seven, while they were watching TV, the bell rang. Lyosha froze, like a dragonfly in the August air. Tymofiy glanced at him, inquisitively. Lyosha sobbed quietly, wrinkling his nose like a child.

"We aren't here," he said.

"But the light's on, they must have seen it," Tymofiy objected. "Then open the door." Lyosha laid low. "Go on then, open it." The bell rang again.

Lyosha rushed toward Tymofiy's room, formerly his bedroom, where there was an enormous wardrobe, a wedding present. The doors squeaked. Tymofiy heard his dad getting in, stomping on the vacuum cleaner box, the rustle of the plastic bags. Silence.

Tymofiy opened the door. Outside, Felix stood in his ceremonial coat, blinking the moist eyes of a madman. He was wobbling. A briefcase tucked under his arm.

"Lida?" Felix asked.

"Not here. At the summer cottage."

"I am headed to the bunker to get my papers."

Tymofiy let him pass. Felix was treading military-style toward Lida's room, loudly signaling his entrance with cheery cursing. He closed the door behind him. Lyosha crawled out of the wardrobe.

"You said they won't come," Tymofiy said.

"Who the hell knows?" Lyosha seemed lost.

"Shit happens. Maybe I should make a bed for you over there?"

"Buddy, zip it!" Lyosha was angry.

"Dad, it's you who got us into this mess, not me."

Lyosha grimaced and nodded his head, stepped out into the kitchen, and lit a cigarette. Felix rampaged through the bunker, rustling papers and cursing. Then he fell silent. Tymofiy cracked the door open. Felix, fully clothed, in his heavy boots and coat, was sleeping in the armchair with his mouth agape.

"What a pig," muttered Tymofiy, who went to the kitchen to drink some water, and again collapsed on the sofa watching TV.

The next day, at 3 p.m. sharp, he was standing by the Fortune Teller, a store that sold household chemicals, and gazing at the fresh greenery of the bushes covering the hills. A smell of rot came off the Dnipro. It was last year's grass washed up onto the sandy beach. He had been familiar with this smell since childhood. In the spring, this was the smell of the streets in his neighborhood. Tymofiy liked the smell; it reminded him of his early childhood, the times when he would walk with his grandma along the banks, straying into the woods that stretched over the Dnipro cliffs, descending into the dark-blue hollows where the air was buzzing with insects, then walking on sand again, past the old barges and hulks at the roadstead, tugs and sections of the metal pontoons, then finding themselves by the water again. Fishermen stood in the reeds. Each one had three or four spinnerbaits, while simple fishing rods were used for catching carps. Fishponds were swarming, and scows carrying sand floated on the horizon. Large gulls were flying just above the water, quacking loudly, diving in for prey.

Tymofiy inhaled deeply, then exhaled slowly. He remembered he still had cigarettes in the pocket of his jacket, from yesterday. He smoked one. He liked it, feeling the zero-gravity smoke in his lungs and the almost weightless cigarette between his fingers. There was something about control in this process, a fierce confidence in one's actions. Even emotions could be controlled. For Tymofiy, this revelation harbored a certain unfathomable power that had evaded him until now.

He waited for over an hour, but nobody came. He thought of stopping by Toma's but felt embarrassed. At last, he headed home, walking along the Dnipro and catching pale rays of sun on his face. He turned right by the port and got on a bus.

At home, Lyosha and Felix were stationed in the kitchen. They sat across from each other, with their heads down, as if observing a chessboard. Instead of a board, an ashtray overflowing with cigarette butts sat on the table between them.

"Getting wasted?" laughed Tymofiy.

"Get lost!" Felix waved him off.

Lyosha winked, as if saying, Come on, buddy, leave us alone.

Tymofiy was surprised to see them congregating and sober; it was extremely suspicious. He didn't know how to react and felt embarrassed, so he called them Tweedledee and Tweedledum, and disappeared into his room. The old man was smoking in the apartment again, Tymofiy thought to himself. He locked the door of his room and lit one too. He was sitting on the chair, swinging back and forth with his legs against the windowsill, slowly exhaling the smoke into the ventilation opening. After that he called Toma. Her mom picked the phone, her voice dry like an executive assistant's, and informed Tymofiy that Toma was out and would be back later.

Tymofiy got angry. Filled with impatience and irritation, he put on an excessively worn-out cassette of *The Fat of the Land*,[56] turned the volume up to the max, and flung himself on the sofa. After about a minute, Felix stormed in.

"Turn it off!" he barked.

"Get lost!" Tymofiy shrugged.

"It's distracting, Cornet." Felix sounded more agreeable now. His face displayed a particular kind of confusion that had a tendency to morph into a wild grimace of rage. At the moment, though, Felix just stood there and looked at Tymofiy with sad, moist eyes, resembling a melancholic gibbon. Tymofiy recalled the first time he saw this expression. It was one of their first encounters. Tymofiy was five. He was getting ready for daycare. Well, they were getting him ready. Devoid of any sense of responsibility, he wandered around the apartment for a while, unable to find his long johns or sweater, went back to his toys, and just dragged out the time until the very end. That morning was reminiscent of a black-and-white film about the war—mushy and bleak, with heavy, depressing light. It probably was late fall or early winter. There was no snow yet but one had to dress warmly. Gray morning anguish was in the air.

Felix was standing in the foyer. Tall, with hair cut short or even possibly shaved, with his tiny confused eyes. He looked at Tymofiy and tried hard to shake his hand.

"Give me your paw," he kept saying. "Nu! Your paw!"

Tymofiy adamantly refused to stretch out his paw, turned around, wept, hid his face in soft throw pillows, simply trying to stay afloat in the everyday, in a delicate equilibrium unable to handle the intrusion of anything new. Just him, long johns, sweater, and the grayness outside the fifth-floor window. Back then Tymofiy did not know who this man was, what he was doing in their apartment, or why Tymofiy had to shake his hand. Whether because Tymofiy did not extend his paw or because of the general messiness of his own life, Felix's face reflected an animalistic confusion bordering on some sort of profound, biblical sorrow.

"Fine," Tymofiy agreed, getting up from the sofa and turning down the volume. Perhaps he did it because of Felix's look, or perhaps because of all the sober seriousness Felix could convey with his requests. Tymofiy collapsed on the bed, covering his head with a blanket.

An hour later, the phone rang. It was Toma.

"Sorry." There was softness in her voice. "Our plans changed. See you tomorrow?"

"Tomorrow," Tymofiy repeated feebly.

"Same time. Okay?"

"Okay, okay," Tymofiy repeated. He had doubts and felt sweaty, worked up.

"Are you mocking me?" he asked.

"Not at all. You know, I was glad to see you."

"And me too, you know."

She burst out laughing, and he got angry again. But then he got a hold of himself and said that he would definitely come. Same time. He'd be there. He would not miss it. Even if his legs were broken, if it came to that. Of course, he skipped mentioning that part but he thought it all the same.

Before going to bed, Tymofiy diligently did twenty push-ups.

He got sweaty and felt out of breath but fell asleep happy with himself.

◇ ◇ ◇

In the morning, Lyosha woke him up.

"Hey man, get up!"

Tymofiy thought he was still dreaming, chewing on his lips in that sweet, warm state he would have given anything to stay in. But Lyosha kept on tapping Tymofiy's shoulder and whispering with his hoarse voice, "Man, come on!" Tymofiy struggled to open his eyes. He saw the dark outline of his dad, then glanced at the clock, lethargically. Six o'clock in the morning.

"What the f . . . ?"

"Come on, you're going to the summer cottage."

"Why on earth?"

"Come on, get up. I'll give you some dough. Buy something for yourself. Like sneakers. Just get yourself to the cottage first."

Tymofiy got up, reached for his pants, then stopped.

Felix peeked into the room.

"Cornet!" he growled.

"What the hell is going on here?" Tymofiy lost it, throwing withering glances at his old man, then at Felix.

"To the cottage . . . Georgie the Sack will drive you . . . to the station . . . Georgie . . ." Lyosha was blabbering.

Tymofiy started to get that something unpleasant had happened, something from which he was being protected. He remembered the kitchen séance last night, all those phone calls, the anxiety that had been hovering over Lyosha like a storm cloud—scary, rattling, flashy, finally breaking open.

"Everything okay?" Tymofiy asked Lyosha. "Everything's gonna be okay?"

"Sure, sure. Let's go. Don't drag it out."

Tymofiy got to packing—T-shirt, socks, deodorant.

"How long?"

"A few days. I'll come get you," Lyosha said.

"Yeah, right. Like last year? When I waited for two months."

"Move it." Lyosha started shoveling some briefs and notebooks into his son's backpack. For some reason, he also grabbed an old Soviet flashlight and a compass in a black plastic case from the table and tossed them in. Then he fished three twenties from his jacket pocket. "Here you go."

Tymofiy took the money. Three twenties. He had never had that much money in his life.

Out on the street, by the entrance door stood the Zhiguli belonging to Georgie the Sack, a former classmate of Lyosha's. He used to be known as Georgie the Wool Sack, since he had hair all over his body, then he became just Georgie the Sack. In the early nineties, he was involved in some fishy affairs, none of them particularly profitable, hanging around the vegetable warehouse just for show, as well as at the canteen selling *pelmeni* on Podolynskyi Street. Georgie the Sack constantly got into fights, passionately swung his switchblade, but later, when his father—a stocky bearded guy with clouded eyes—was discharged from the mental hospital, Georgie calmed down. He took care of his disturbed father, buried him, got married, started fishing, and bought the old Zhiguli, which he then used to deliver fish to the market. And now this guy was supposed to drive Tymofiy. Lyosha let his son into the back seat and tossed his backpack inside behind him. He was stone-faced, as if paralyzed; only a hint of a smile, painful and sad, appeared on his face.

"Here you go." He pushed another twenty into Tymofiy's hands.

"You gave me enough of those already."

"Yeah? Take it anyway."

Then Lyosha turned toward Georgie the Sack.

"Go to Ilyina's."

"Lyeshania," said Georgie the Sack with emphasis. "Take care, Lyeshania."

"Georgie boy!" Lyosha was at a loss for words.

Georgie boy stepped on the gas. The Zhiguli took off. The inside of the car smelled of the Dnipro.

The city was empty. Especially on Ilyin Street, which was filled with private houses. The stumpy structures flashed by, along with lanes, green fences, and fixtures. Through the bare fruit trees, one could make out the four high-rises—the student housing that stretched along Thälmann Street. This was a socially challenged neighborhood, a hotbed of everyday criminal activity, filled with the tenacious smells of petrol and beer. From Riabokon to Dobrovolskyi streets, the houses were packed tightly, side by side, and still there were more auto shops and tire fitting stations, even a hairdresser. The dilapidated playground in front of the student housing, a daycare center, a rusty fire tower rising from the garden—the latter a reminder of the imminent decline and palpable death that saturated the sweet air of the neighborhood. Further on, a few neat houses, the bottle-redemption kiosk, the dark-turquoise brewery, and quiet, empty Verbovetskyi Street. The houses ran all the way to Chekhov Street, with the red bricks of the maternity hospital visible right behind. It was an edifice of pain and fear, a formidable fortress, where life starts and hope ends.

The heavy gray sky folded itself tightly around the Zhiguli, pressing it toward the wet road. They passed the flea market where Felix had bought Tymofiy the watch. Still two blocks left until the station. The car rumbled. Georgie the Sack was going at high speed, running red lights, and looking back at Tymofiy from time to time.

"Everything's okay," he kept saying. "Everything's under control."

"Okay," agreed Tymofiy. He was finally wide awake, aware that something radically new was taking place. Only in the movies would someone be taken to a summer cottage to escape possible death.

"I'll get you on the train, you'll go to your granny's," Georgie the Sack said, approaching the station. "It's strawberry season."

Strawberries in April? Tymofiy thought to himself. But he decided not to argue.

They came to a stop. Georgie the Sack, amiable and big, with his grayish-brown convex nose, ran inside the white glazed-brick station building and bought a ticket. Twelve minutes until departure.

"Should I get you a Snickers? Are you hungry?"

"Thank you. I'll eat those strawberries when we get to the cottage," Tymofiy replied.

"Strawberries in April? You're kidding, right? I'll get you something."

He walked away from the kiosk—it turned out to be locked. A rusty-blue coffee shop was right nearby, its windows decorated with Christmas lights. Georgie the Sack pulled the yellow varnished doors open and disappeared inside. An old pazik with a sticker on its windshield rolled into the third platform. The sticker featured a tank with the American flag. The driver crawled from his seat; he was, as expected, plump and silent. He circled around the bus, pensively scrutinizing the back wheels, lit a cigarette, and cursed. Georgie the Sack was walking back from the coffee shop, heading to the platform. He held a hot dog in his hand as if they were at a soccer match. Mayonnaise dripped on the wet ground.

"Here you are." He passed the hot dog to Tymofiy. "This is our platform, right? And here is your bus. Making a stop at Moshny.[57] That's right. Okay, take care. Don't worry about your old man."

"Thanks," said Tymofiy. He snuck onto the bus and sat in the back, on a soft and cold seat with pieces of old, brittle foam sticking out in all directions. He bit into his hot dog and, as if on autopilot, pinched off a piece of foam.

A couple sat in front of him—an old guy wearing a shabby Soviet overcoat, his head shaved, and a woman in a blue jacket, not so youthful either, but still robust and sturdy, like fruit bread. Probably the guy's daughter, he thought. They were engrossed in a disgusting, uninteresting process of nesting, taking their sweet time rearranging their numerous bags, and once settled, they started arguing.

"Didn't I ask for a green one? It would have been *idealissimo*! Why didn't you listen to me? Come on, you look ancient," the woman said.

"I *am* ancient," the old guy replied in a surprising basso.

"Now you're gonna become a mummy."

"I'm already a mummy anyway."

"Did you take your pills?" the woman asked and, without waiting for a response, spit on her finger and started wiping the old guy's face with it.

Watching this scene made Tymofiy sick. He even stopped chewing.

In a few moments, the half-empty pazik took off. It was cold and scary. Though more cold than scary. The bus rolled out, lethargically, onto the main street filled with unhurried, sleepy pedestrians. It went for a few blocks, then made a turn near Tymofiy's old school, passing by the muddied cemetery and gloomy backyards of private houses, where bare trees stood among the concrete slabs and flowerbeds. The bus then set out toward the highway. At the edge of town, near the regional hospital, it had to pick up the remaining passengers, and so they stopped under the pine trees, chuffing. Tymofiy glanced at the driver, who was leaning against the steering wheel, tapping his purple fingers on the dashboard. Tymofiy moved his eyes toward the pine trees. They were crooked and tall, with their lower branches cut, while the crowns on top remained quite dense. Typical pine trees that grow in the suburbs, by the cottages that were demolished long ago and forgotten, their lace valances only to be found on pre-Soviet postcards. Then he looked at the old women skidding with their bundles and flimsy dollies, struggling to get on the bus. Tymofiy glanced at the bald geezer and his chunky female companion. His eyes fixed on the pine trees again. He remembered the dry, light forest near the cottage, Maryana with mosquito bites on her legs, the smell of her sweat, her flats. Then he remembered Toma.

To hell with your summer cottage, Tymofiy thought, abruptly jumping to his feet. He ran into some lady who was trying to squeeze herself onto the bus while carrying a giant white contractor bag. He apologized and ran outside. Everything went fuzzy. He saw Lyosha in his mind's eye, or to be precise, Lyosha's eyes—cloudy and overcast, anxious. Lyosha was smiling, baring his gray decaying teeth. To hell with your summer cottage.

Tymofiy crossed the street, got on a bus, and headed downtown. He got off in the city center, near the House of Commerce. The streets were packed, it was noisy. Something heavy and thorny was pressing at him from the inside; the unkind adventure that he had committed himself to was nagging and eating at him. Had he not been told to go to the summer cottage, to sit it out, to wait until it was all settled, and then someone would pick him up? And even if things didn't settle, and he wouldn't be picked up, he could just hide, read about Ren and Zavhorodniy,[58] watch the news, or simply sleep for days on end . . .

He got to the square in front of the movie house, threw a penetrating glance at the pine trees under which he had met Toma and the guys so recently, then approached the phone booths nestled together like penguins. He inserted a card, fished a notebook from his backpack, found the number, remembered that he knew it by heart, and dialed.

Toma picked up the phone. She was still sleepy and struggled to talk, yawning all the while.

"It's me," Tymofiy said.

"Jelly Belly."

"I'm in trouble," he informed her.

"What the hell? Really?"

"My pop's in trouble," Tymofiy clarified. "They sent me to the summer cottage. I ran away. Need a place to crash."

"Crash where?" Toma wasn't getting it.

"Someplace," Tymofiy repeated.

"Mom's getting out of here in an hour. Let's meet by the Fortune Teller. We can go to my place later."

"The Fortune Teller it is," Tymofiy agreed.

In just fifteen minutes, he was already hanging around the closed shop. Toma showed up at half past eight. She was wearing the same pink jacket and lipstick. Her hair was a mess. She looked sleepy, angry, determined.

"Jelly Belly, what's up?" she asked once she had approached.

"I don't know," Tymofiy said. "Smoke?"

"Not here."

They walked closer to the shrubs that covered the slopes and took a seat on some concrete slabs in the thicket of a young maple tree, near an abandoned house. They smoked and studied one another in silence. Toma did not know what to ask. Tymofiy did not know what to say. Finally, he told her what he knew.

Again there was silence, and they sat in the thicket for a full hour, counting the minutes until they could go to Toma's place. Tymofiy dug the bottle caps out of the rammed-in black earth with the toe of his sneakers. Toma filed her nails. Just after nine, they headed toward Toma's building, measuring the soccer field with their hurried steps.

The apartment smelled of coffee and cigarettes.

Rolls of fabric were scattered around the rooms, a sewing

machine stood in the living-room, patterns, fashion magazines, and spools of thread were piled up on the dark-yellow sofas and armchairs. A porcelain deer, with his formidable head raised, soared over the TV. Relatively new wallpaper was curling at the seams. A voluminous ginger-colored curtain covered the window. The mess prevailed, but there was no sense of poverty.

They sat in the kitchen, which turned out to be surprisingly spacious and clean, almost sterile. Toma made coffee, took sausage and cheese out from the fridge.

"Do you know, by any chance, where I can crash for the night?" asked Tymofiy. "I'm sort of on the run."

"Definitely not here," she said. "If that's what you're getting at."

"That's definitely not what I was getting at. I just asked. You mentioned that your friend's parents were away in Odesa."

"Not an option. She's with Ihor."

"Oh, okay . . ."

"A hotel, maybe?" she proposed. "You'd need money, though."

"That I have," Tymofiy informed her. "A hundred."

Toma raised her eyebrows.

"Don't worry about it," Tymofiy sounded like he was guilty of something. "What about the hotel?" he asked.

"It's the Cherkasy, by the Lenin monument. Basically an old folks' home. We celebrated Ihor's birthday there, in December. Had to pay extra to get in."

"I know it. How is the owner's St. Bernard?"

"It's a hole in the wall, not a hotel. As if it had been in a war. And Sophie died, the neighbors poisoned her."

"I don't give a shit," Tymofiy snapped. "I mean, about the hotel, not about Sophie. Sophie? Such a weird name for a dog. By the way, in case you care, I am so glad to see you. You are so beautiful."

"Don't start." Toma sounded like an adult, which felt unpleasant. "But I am interested," she added silently, moving only her lips.

Tymofiy stared out the window, looking at the trees swaying in the gusts of spring wind, scratching one another with their prickly branches, as if fighting for space, the right to stand their ground until the sanitation workers would come and cut them down. He looked tired, sleepy. That's exactly the kind of gaze one should reserve for looking at the trees. Toma was sitting opposite him. She was wearing white jeans and a casual blue top, looking like a young C.C. Catch. Tymofiy looked at her, noticed the tears swelling in his eyes, tried hard to restrain himself, and finished his too-sweet, strong coffee. Then he got up and went to the living room, collapsed on the sofa between the spools of thread and stacks of magazines, and fell asleep.

Toma woke him up after the sun had already traveled to the other end of town.

"Jelly Belly, get up!" She tapped him on the shoulder.

This was the second time that day he'd been woken up like that. Tymofiy got up. He had dreamed about something bright and sparkly, something that resembled a table lamp and which had a rotating film cylinder inside. From that cylinder, brown-purple blobs of light spread around the room. The dream was gentle and warm, being pulled out of it felt jarring and violent.

"Let's go. My mom'll be here soon."

"Let's go," Tymofiy agreed, still floating in the cozy sparkling warmth of his dream. Staggering, he threw on his shoes and jacket. "Would be nice to grab something to eat," he added, already standing in the hall.

Unexpectedly, they stopped at McDonald's. Toma ordered a bit more than she could manage to finish. Tymofiy ordered two hamburgers, a Coke, and fries. They ate in silence, chewing with focused attention. Tymofiy noticed that everything around them was filled with magic—some unreal substance. His world lacked this kind of light, food, and smell, as well as its measured, practical clatter. This episode was about other people—those who could afford to dine at McDonald's.

"It's my first time here," he confessed.

"I've been here before, with my boyfriend," Toma said, vigorously chewing her sandwich.

"You have a boyfriend?"

"My ex. He's such a jerk."

"Got it."

"You don't get anything." Toma pretended to be offended. "Look at yourself! You don't even have a place for the night."

"I'll figure it out."

"Yeah, right. You should have gone to the cottage."

They finished eating and hurried outside, heading toward the darkening streets, noisy and windy. This boulevard would be a great place for taking walks under the chestnut trees, drinking light beer from a dark bottle. You would just keep walking, until you ran into that black, brass lump of a monument, that hurdy-gurdy bard from the epic poem,[59] standing on the ugly square that was transformed into a market, leading to your neighborhood. Then you might approach the lanes hiding in the dark depths of apartment blocks, walking past the workshops, until you see the building with all its windows lit, without fail, teasing you with coziness and warmth. And then, feeling gentle and tipsy, you would climb the stairs to your apartment, walk into the kitchen, scoop something hot and filling from a pot on the stove, and collapse on your bed.

"I'm gonna do the talking," Toma said, walking into the hotel. "Otherwise, you'll ruin it."

"Thanks, Mom."

Toma shrugged.

At the entrance to the lacquered plywood booth, behind thick glass, sat a woman with a young face and gray hair. She resembled a hamster in a cage. She was unfriendly; puffing up her cheeks, she kept asking why they needed a room, whether there would be any issues, and if so, who would take care of them. Toma promised there wouldn't be any. This young man is here for team training, and she is on his team. He needs a place to stay. The coach has been binge drinking. In the end, they settled for thirty hryvnias. Twenty for the room, ten to avoid further questions.

The room stank of bleach and was furnished with cheap plastic pieces. The brown linoleum was covered with rusty stains. The bathroom door had probably been painted over three times—tiles black at the seams, yellowed sink. The wallpaper looked like it had been done before Cherkasy's 700th Jubilee.[60] But the windows looked out onto the boulevard.

"This will do," observed Toma. "Let's have a drink?"

"Sure," Tymofiy agreed, cautiously taking a seat on the soft bed covered with a sticky greenish cloth. "Should I go out and get something?"

"I'll go," Toma offered, disappearing instantly.

The sun was going down somewhere in Sosnivka, illuminating the swollen, bud-covered trees with its last rays of purple. The trolley made a strained, screeching sound. Passersby were chatting under the windows. Tymofiy sat on the bed. A tenacious weight spread across his body. Something was squeezing his throat, something inanimate, mechanical, and thus heartless and unrelenting, like a locksmith's press soiled with grease and metal shavings. He tried to get rid of the sensation, drawing in long breaths, but the pressure in his chest and throat only increased. He wanted to go home, and even more than that, to see his mom.

This was his first time in a hotel. How will I sleep here? he thought. How do people sleep at hotels? In this dirt and soot, among the traces of someone else's stay? Among the smells, which make you want to jump out the window or slice open your veins. Had someone done that in this very room? The thought was eerie, and Tymofiy got up to check on the door lock. There was none from the inside, only a latch. Like in the latrine. Okay, at least something. He came close to the window and pushed back a transparent curtain, then tried opening the window. The glass in the frame cracked, the plaster crumbled. He left the window alone, went to the dressing table, saw his reflection, and ran his hand along the glass. Fatigue and tension made his eyes tear. Tymofiy sat on the bed. He kept sitting there, staring at the wallpaper.

Toma returned a quarter of an hour later. She took out a pack of chips and a bottle of transparent red fluid from inside her coat.

"Cranberry!" she cried with excitement, put the bottle on the dressing table, freed herself from her jacket, and collapsed on the bed. Immediately, she got up in disgust and balled up the sticky cloth, exposing bedding of dubious whiteness.

"Something strong?" asked Tymofiy.

"A juice," Toma said. "You'll love it. And don't you stare at me with your leopard gaze!"

"We don't have glasses," said Tymofiy.

Toma grabbed and opened the bottle, took a few sips, then passed it to Tymofiy. He took a few sips as well.

"Some juice this is," he commented.

"Told you so!"

Toma kept on drinking. With a jerk, she tore open the bag and chips flew around the room like candies. For some time, they just sat there in silence, chewing and sipping the so-called juice.

They got tipsy pretty fast. Toma was walking around, waltzing, complaining about the lack of music. Tymofiy, feeling dejected, peered into the penetrating darkness of the city. Indeed, the room felt empty without music. Plus, this city, so cruel and large, with all its pale lights flowing along the avenues and boulevards. And even this hotel . . . How many times had he walked past it, peeking into the nearby pastry shop with the basement entrance? These tiny balconies and window frames made this particular building one of the most elegant in the city. Who knew that it hid such sorrow and emptiness inside, that the rooms were meant for sadness, bottomless and dark, like a coal mine?

"Can I sleep here?" Toma asked. "With you?"

"What about your mom?" Tymofiy sounded on edge.

"What about your mom?" Toma mocked him in a low voice. "What about her? She thinks I'm at Nastia's."

"Go ahead." Tymofiy pretended to sound indifferent, but immediately felt a thumping in his temples, blood rushing up to his face.

His mood improved with the "cranberry juice." He took a few more sips to hold on to the feeling of euphoria, to stop from falling into the black pit with its tightly soldered exit.

Three times they stepped out onto the shared balcony, facing Lenin Square, for a smoke. This place had been called Cathedral Square, Market Square, Cathedral-Mykolayiv Square, then Cathedral again, and then back to Market, and at one point Central Square. Now it was Lenin Square. Before the war, a cathedral stood here. During the all-night vigil, people circled around it carrying crosses and banners, stopping by its western gates and singing, "*Christ is risen from the dead, trampling down death by death, and upon those in the tombs bestowing life.*" And now Ilyich stood there, having supposedly risen from the dead, and after all this time, he was still very much alive. And incidentally, he is also in the tomb, Tymofiy thought, rapidly inhaling cigarette smoke. Suddenly, he remembered how, just a few years ago, he used to be fascinated by reading the Bible and going to church, and how the good-looking older woman, Ilona, a friend of Olha and Lida, had brought him to the vigil. He had been dying to get some sleep, and even more, to get something to eat. And then some granny at the service, secretly chewing a pie stuffed with pâté, treated him to a piece. Later on, Ilona completely lost it with her religious shenanigans and cut off all of her relationships.

The cathedral had been destroyed back in 1945.

Frozen through, they returned to the room, took a few more sips from the bottle, and started jumping on the bed, which squeaked like an old, seriously arthritic patient. They stood by the window for a while, in silence, enjoying the weightlessness of their drunken state, taking in the city that looked so sick and tired, like a grown-up oppressed by debt and unemployment.

At some point, Toma took off her blouse, leaving only her black bra on.

"Is this better?" she asked.

Tymofiy said nothing, merely noting to himself the remarkable variability of his life experience. Toma started singing something in English. Tymofiy knew the lyrics but could not remember the singer. Sheryl Crow? Meredith Brooks? They stood by the window and sang, pausing only for a sip of cranberry juice.

"I'm gonna show you something," Toma said, unclasping her bra.

Tymofiy froze. He gasped, feeling the rhythmic flow of blood pulsating in his head.

"Mine are bigger," he joked, coming to his senses.

"Moron." Toma was offended. "It's like nothing's changed, you were and still are an idiot. I was in love with you from first grade on."

"And then?"

"And then I wasn't. Get under the sheets."

Tymofiy hesitated. Unsure of what to do, he squeezed himself between the bed and the window and just stood there looking at Toma, who kept singing and dancing. When she raised her arms, her breasts would almost disappear; her ribs, illuminated by the streetlights, glistened like the keys of a grand piano in a concert hall. Her arms were skinny, her clavicles stuck out, while her shoulder blades seemed to almost cut through the pale skin. Just skin and bones, Tymofiy thought. He was still standing by the bed, numb and lost in doubt, observing her clumsy dance.

"We're adults, let's do it!" Toma cried out and started taking off her jeans.

Tymofiy got himself out of his jeans but kept his hoodie on. He was uncomfortable with taking it off, so he hurried to get under the sheets.

"Do you know why I loved you?"

Tymofiy raised his eyebrows.

"I won't tell you!"

For some time, Toma kept on dancing, wearing just her panties and socks, the remaining alcohol sloshing in the bottle that she grasped in her hand. For a moment, Tymofiy closed his eyes, feeling that his world has lost balance. Everything around him was flickering and foaming, like a frothy sea at night. Or as if someone put him on a merry-go-round and forgot to fasten the belt. Had the hotel ripped from its foundation and started circling over the city? Higher and higher, gliding over the parks and high-rises, around the TV transmission tower, touching the tops of pine trees? It flew toward the dam, circled around the sandy island and dark backwaters, turned around, hitting the giant wheel, and headed south toward the industrial quarter, flying over Azot, Khimvolokno, Avrora,[61] scratching the old brick chimneys and gabled slate roofs with its foundation. The hotel climbed higher and higher, until, where the city once was, there remained just a tiny silver dot in the dark-blue murkiness of the universe. Right then he felt Toma's cold palm sliding down.

"Hair, darling," Toma whispered. "Last time you were still a boy."

Tymofiy opened his eyes. The hotel stood firmly on the ground. Some people were having a loud fight, right under their windows. The first voice, male, high-pitched, was hysterically arguing that everything was paid for, while other coarse voices insisted that firstly, the prices on the menu differed from those on the check. And secondly, they were supposed to split the check, and then what? What now?

Exactly, Tymofiy thought. What now? He was certain that the fight under the windows had something to do with him.

What now? he asked himself, and, unable to find an answer, he retreated, becoming aware of Toma's hand still touching his skin. The thoughts did not listen to him and roamed someplace outside of his head. And even his head, it seemed, was separate from his unruly, heavy body. At last, his hand landed on top of her pointy nipples. His hand slid down. She turned her back toward him; he touched her timidly, sensing the rhythmic tensing and softening of her body. He was panting, constantly swallowing his saliva. Faintheartedly, he ran his hand lower, tracing the sharp curves and steep caves, his fingers getting stuck in something hot and wet.

"And?" Toma's voice came out muffled.

Tymofiy moved closer to her, feeling a light and gentle current running through his body. There was a smell of warm skin, shampoo, alcohol, and carelessly laundered bedsheets. The scents made his head spin even more. The hotel took off from the ground again, carrying him farther and farther away from the city, somewhere westward, past the vast green mountains, the countries with black spiky spires and smooth highways, spacious meadows with green silky grass, cities erected out of Ligurian marble, and gloomy rocks inhabited by freedom-loving Basques. Approaching the ocean, the limitless azure and bottomless white sky, the warm stream carrying all the ardor and love, hastily moving to the North Pole . . .

"You came inside me?" Toma suddenly asked, bringing everything to a halt.

It felt as if Tymofiy had resurfaced from a warm bath into which he had submerged his entire body, sitting there until he ran out of breath.

"I don't have sperm yet." He sounded embarrassed.

Toma abruptly turned her face to him. She ran her hand through his hair, pausing with her fingers near his eye.

"You are still a boy," she said gently. "A little boy. Go to sleep, Jelly Belly."

Tymofiy had a hard time waking up the next morning. He felt thirsty and feverish, and his eyes hurt, as if someone was pressing them from the inside. Toma stood by the window, already dressed, even wearing her jacket.

"I'm off to school." Her voice was cold. "Can't miss it."

"Seriously?" Tymofiy lifted himself, propping up his head with a pillow.

"If you want, I can ask Dzhudik to drop by."

"No. I don't like him."

"Up to you," Toma said, dryly. "Got any money left? For one more night?"

"Dunno." Tymofiy reached out for his jeans.

"Okay, call me then."

She headed to the door and lifted the latch. The door closed tightly behind her; the curtains fluttered in the draft. Tymofiy got up, dragged himself to the window, quivering like a buoy in water. His head hurt. He was ecstatic about last night. Yesterday in its entirety, however, was terrifying. What should he do now? He drank some tap water, got into the filthy bathtub, and turned on the faucet. For about twenty minutes, he sat under the warm stream, not daring to move. Finally, he got out, dried himself, got dressed, and counted the money. Forty hryvnias left.

Outside, the city dwellers went about their daily affairs. They ran and ran, like zebras along a wide runway someplace in Africa. A gray, thick silk screen enwrapped the city. It was drizzling. The streetlight blinked idly at the crossroad.

Tymofiy sat on the bed in his jacket, staring blankly at the gray light streaming from the window and hastily processing everything—all the words uttered in the last few days, his old man's odd behavior, all the strange calls and eerie greetings from the Midget, coming from the black phone receiver, browless Dzhudik, Ihor with his prominent nose, Nastia with her thick brow, horrifying Russian music about delicate flowers and sweet names—the music coming from the neighbor's window—all this dreary dreg that he was living in and was unable to overcome. He was trying to solder all these fragments into one consistent story, like a movie with a clear and comprehensible script. Nothing would stick together, though. Instead, it was all crumbling and falling apart. And because of all this, he decided to go home. He was dying to get back home. They couldn't kill him there, right? He left the hotel in a hurry, quickly crossed the boulevard, and jumped onto the minibus. Once inside the half-empty vehicle, he started thinking about his dad—his frightened eyes filled with fear rather than shame, his unusual, perplexed fussiness that made Tymofiy feel contempt. In spite of it all, he wanted to hide Lyosha in a matchbox, as if his dad were a beetle terrified by the unknown. Even Felix had been uncharacteristically reserved. Usually when sober, he would crack jokes or at least project a calming sense of lightness. But this last time he had seemed like someone else— clear eyed, jaw clenched, his movements measured. Tymofiy felt as if this were happening to someone else—it was not him leaving the hotel and going home, having just endured a night of adulthood. He felt as if he had played the first two quarters of a game, the rules of which nobody had bothered to explain. He tried looking back, to comprehend the surrounding space, see the people around him, take in the minute details of their clothing, the interior of the bus, listen to the engine, to the chat between the driver and conductor, or the rustling of plastic in the hands of a woman in the back seat. If it hadn't been you, none of this would have happened. This is happening to *you*. It is you who is heading home from the hotel, and yours is the adult night. Nobody will ever take it from you.

Tymofiy got off at the artisans' workshops, passed the fence of the brick plant and an expanse dotted with elder bushes, walked around the remains of the outdoor play-hut made of metal rods torn from a bus stop. He trudged through the backyard, stumbled over the domino table, passed a poplar, and paused for a bit by the entrance to his building, as if trying to recall something important, a password without which he would not be able to enter. Finally, he pushed open the door, stepped into the foyer, and rushed upstairs to his floor. Burning with despair, he realized that, in his haste, he had forgotten his keys yesterday morning. He buzzed the door, obstinately, for a long time. Maybe they're asleep? But he already knew that the apartment was empty. There was nowhere to go. He slid down the door, landing on the dirty, frayed doormat, and rested his hands on it as if he were doomed. He felt something hard, lifted the greenish rag and almost burst with joy. There, on the cold concrete, lay a key.

He took off his clothes and got into bed, where he stayed until lunchtime. He was overloaded with hangover, exhaustion, emotional fatigue, sensations of the surreal and the absurd. He recalled the hotel, the night, the purported cranberry juice, Ilyich and the striking aerial tour of the city. He felt guilty for not making the bed in the hotel room. Within a quarter of an hour, Tymofiy was asleep, and upon waking up his entire body hurt—something was weighing on him, on the inside, some dark matter was pressing hard and strangling him. He forced himself to get out of bed, paced around the apartment for a long time, turned on the TV without sound. He thought of Toma, called her, and told her that he was home, alone, and did not know where everyone had disappeared to.

He was so nervous that his arms cramped up. There was nothing in the fridge, apart from a dried-out sausage. He ran to the store to buy pelmeni and yogurt. He swallowed his food without chewing and felt better. Then he sat in the kitchen for a long time and unconsciously watched the budding branches swinging in the wind, scratching the windows and zinc cornices. Somewhere further, past the daycare and near the boarding school for the children with scoliosis, big birds were nestling close to one another, sitting on black oaks strangled with mistletoe. From time to time, the birds flew from one tree to another. Tymofiy remembered he had cigarettes and went to the bathroom for a smoke. Then he turned off the TV and put on a pirated Western Thunder[62] tape of the Beatles. Listening to "Sgt. Pepper's Lonely Hearts Club Band," he dozed off in a chair.

He woke up when it was dark. At first, he could not figure out where he was or whether tomorrow had already arrived. It hadn't, and yet it was already late. Time to call it a night. The apartment was filled with heavy silence and inexplicable fear. Tymofiy turned on the light, got his diaries from a few years back, the ones that were sitting on a shelf above his writing desk. He started rereading his notes, smiling at his own naivete.

He called Toma again and invited her to come by. She refused. He wanted to talk about what had happened yesterday, while she diligently avoided the conversation, joking around and, when necessary, telling him to shut up. Finally, she lost her patience and became patronizing, almost crude, and asked that he never mention that night at the hotel again. When he suggested that they move in together, she hung up. Before that, though, she called him silly.

Tymofiy put the tape with the Dire Straits album *Brothers in Arms* into the player, then spent a long time going through his mom's papers. Among the notebooks on history and literary theory, going back to her college days, he found watercolors. The dominant themes were rain and sadness. Leaves and umbrellas, evening and loneliness, violet tears on thick granular paper. All of it made him burst out crying, all the childlike powerlessness, all the teenage fear and loneliness poured out from him. He remembered feeling the same way two years ago—the same kind of uselessness, hopeless and sticky.

Nobody returned to the apartment that night. Felix came the next day, around lunchtime.

In the morning, the homeroom teacher called, attempting to determine why Tymofiy had missed school for the last two weeks. Tymofiy pretended to be sick. The teacher rumbled incredulously, and finally asked for Olha's phone number in Kyiv. Tymofiy lied, saying that he didn't know it, but that he would ask his mother when she called next. That's why, when the door opened unexpectedly, he thought for a moment that the homeroom teacher had gotten into the apartment, wearing her long gray raincoat. This, on the other hand, appeared to be the black ceremonial coat of the Obersturmbannführer.

"Cornet!" Felix sounded outraged. "Why are you here?"

He was not drunk but the sparkles in his eyes, as well as his pink swollen lips, all pointed to last night's drinking escapade.

"Just 'cause." Tymofiy sounded calm.

"An order was issued!" Felix screamed somewhat unconvincingly. "For you to go to the cottage!"

"I had my own plans," Tymofiy muttered, irritated.

"Donnerwetter!" Felix cursed. "Are you stupid or something?"

Tymofiy decided not to reply to this one, asking instead where Lyosha was and what was really going on. And the key . . . why did Felix have the key to the apartment?

"This is Lyosha's key. And mine."

"You have your own key?"

"I left mine for you under the doormat. Just in case . . ."

Felix paced around the apartment, headed to the bedside table with Lyosha's belongings but then paused and collapsed into the armchair, with his coat still on. Sighing, he looked at Tymofiy with darkened eyes.

"Listen up," he said. Then he fell silent. He stayed that way for almost a minute. Another sigh.

Tymofiy kept looking at him, scared of learning something unpleasant, scary, something he was not ready to hear.

"Lyoshka is in the hospital," Felix finally uttered, referring to Tymofiy's father with uncharacteristic tenderness.

In a daze, Tymofiy listened to the story and could not believe what he heard. It sounded like an action movie. He struggled to process what had happened to his dad, though to be fair, he should have expected it.

"These people are evil," said Felix. "I never liked them and always gave them a good pounding. But this time it didn't work. Okay. Let's get his stuff. His mom, your grandma, is there now. She's scared to death, as if she's never seen anything like it."

"I mean, he's her son," Tymofiy pointed out.

"Yeah, so what. Ain't able to fix things, no use. He asked for a *fleeska*. It's cold there, at the hospital. No heat."

"This one." Tymofiy pulled out a blue plush sweater from the drawer. "I'll go with you to the hospital."

"Stand down, Cornet. Officially, you are at the cottage with grandma. Stay home, watch TV."

"No, I'm going to the hospital."

"You'd better not. He's not looking great."

"All the more reason to."

Lyosha was lying in the corridor. His brother, Boria, was hustling nearby—a sturdy, tall guy with a long, pointy Adam's apple, a big, dark mouth, and a face that was motionless, chiseled. He flipped posh cars from Germany and knew how to enjoy life; most importantly, he knew how to survive. Tymofiy did not like Boria and was always cautious around him. He emanated a sort of coarseness, almost cruelty.

"They're moving him to the ward in a sec," Boria said, opening wide his cave-like jaws.

This was Hospital No. 3, notorious as a place where people went to die. Usually, to die suffering. The foyer window was facing the brick edifice, with crooked green letters across it spelling "Morgue." Behind the morgue stood a standard panel building, surrounded by a dense cluster of acacia trees. And behind that building, there was another one just like it—gray, bleak, weather-beaten. This was where Nestor had spent his final month. Tymofiy looked down at his dad, who was lying on a bare mattress, motionless, wrapped in his sheets, from under which stuck a transparent yellow tube. Brown spots of dried blood stained the sheets. The old man was silent, hopelessly staring at everyone with a resigned expression. He glanced at his brother first, then Felix, and finally Tymofiy. He paused when looking at Tymofiy, struggling to mutter something but instead gurgled, as if blowing air into a cocktail through a straw.

Lyosha's mother came running, a short and chatty woman with glossy gray locks of hair on a tiny skull. She glanced at Tymofiy with animosity, as if whatever happened to her son was his fault. Her gray eyes sparkled with quiet anger. She did not look at Felix even once. Turning to Boria, she asked him when Lyosha would be transferred to the ward and whether the doctor had already visited.

"They're moving him in a sec," Boria repeated for his mother.

Tymofiy spent a few minutes by Lyosha's bed, passed the fleeska to his grandma, glanced at his uncle with horror, and disappeared in the dark hall of the hospital unit. He walked downstairs, blinded by the bright, ill-timed sunlight, and took out his cigarettes. A minute later, the heavy white doors opened on their hydraulic hinge, and from behind them appeared Felix.

"You're smoking, Cornet?"

"Yeah."

"Yuck."

"And you're binge drinking, remember?" snapped Tymofiy. "How's it look for the boss?"

"Honestly? Shitty. Don't get all glum, though. It'd be one thing if the doctors were any good. But these quacks are only fit to treat horses. They'll let him rot."

"What the hell should we do?"

"Tough it out."

"Fuck that."

"Stand down, Cornet!" shouted Felix. "Go home, stay out of the way. I'll go too. Or maybe just go to the cottage already. Who's gonna keep an eye on you otherwise? Them?" He pointed in the direction of the hospital. "They won't. They've always avoided you . . ."

"I want to see Mom," Tymofiy said, dryly.

"You will, soon. Come on, don't fall apart."

Tymofiy went upstairs to the Intensive Care Unit once more, to speak with his grandma. He said that he would stay home so that she wouldn't worry about him, even though he figured that she wouldn't bother worrying. He nodded to his uncle and glanced at his father, who moaned, tilting his head slightly. His eyes were covered with a cloudy yellow fluid, like pear compote. Saliva was trickling out of his mouth.

A year ago, Tymofiy saw his father's father, Slava, in a similar state after a stroke. Unlike Lyosha, Slava was sturdy, visibly strong, even though he had a sick heart. He had been born in Germany in 1937; his father, an officer in the Air Defense Units, worked with the Germans until 1939. During the war, he headed an aviation unit, and in the aftermath served near Dresden as a lieutenant colonel. Tymofiy's grandfather studied at the local school for six years, but then the family moved to Cherkasy. Slava served his military duty in Zaporizhzhia and got married there. From time to time, he taught Tymofiy certain things, as is expected of a decent grandfather—how to use a fretsaw or a lathe, for instance. Or the history of naval warfare. He spent his entire life playing with soldering irons, reeking of resin and old magazines; he built model ships, concocted homemade liqueurs, and ate borsht cooked with nettle leaves. Despite all this, Tymofiy felt that he was unwanted in that family, and in time he reached the sad conclusion that he was uninteresting to his grandpa as well. For the sake of his son and daughter-in-law, Slava would bring his grandson to work (he led a ship-modeling club), take him fishing, or sit him down in the workshop—a retrofitted chicken coop. Then he would turn on Radio Mayak and tell stories about diodes and resistors, but all of this he would do reluctantly, and at half strength.

Grandpa had a stroke right in the workshop—a narrow space stuffed with various tools and appliances. Tymofiy went to the hospital a few times. Once, he visited him at home. Grandpa Slava was pouring Fanta with his shrunken arm, getting excited by the bubbles, like an infant, and that's exactly how he behaved— munching with his drooling mouth and looking, with an eerie smile, toward the ceiling. Tymofiy stood in the pass-through dining room with the low, uneven ceiling, a tiny window facing the dark garden, and a brass barometer on the wall. He stood and looked at his grandpa, feeling despondent. Just a short while ago he had taught Tymofiy how to cast a spinning rod, and now he was sitting there with a diaper on—pale, bald, like a white button mushroom.

He stopped visiting Grandpa. Olha did not let him come to the funeral.

She arrived on the second day after her husband's death.

She had lost even more weight. Her exhausted face showed traces of unending daily struggle. She bore the weight of a rented apartment and office; she had already paid back the debts, but now, it seemed, had other troubles. Part of the money went to Lida, on Tymofiy's behalf. While in Kyiv, Olha had fallen deep into esoteric teachings, and constantly tried to share her discoveries. She said it all helped her to keep on living, that it was saving her, and that it wasn't even about God, though she was a believer and occasionally stopped by church. These conversations irritated Tymofiy, and he brushed her off. He no longer believed in God, much less in this new-age crap. Lida, on the contrary, listened attentively and with interest. Since her daughter had moved away, their relationship had improved, grown even more tender.

Tymofiy walked around the apartment, taking note of the traces of his father. The stereo, two duffle bags stuffed with clothing in the hall, the renovation that had been done in the late eighties, the collection of audio tapes. There was a pile of his things in the mezzanine that he had probably forgotten about—a few rods, a metal fish cage, a black leather bomber jacket with a fur collar, some boxes of tools. In the kitchen was a new toaster and a coffee grinder, which Lyosha had picked up not long ago. In the bathroom, cartons of overseas cigarettes covered the back wall. You still couldn't find these here—Fine 120, Dunhill, Lexington. He used to bring them home and smoke.

From the hospital, they headed to the cemetery. Not many people, mainly the inner circle. A few friends, a few ghosts from the past. Apart from Tymofiy and Lyosha's mother, no one cried. At the end of the day, who else had loved him?

Tymofiy sleepwalked through that day. At any given moment, he could not remember what had taken place just a minute earlier and had no idea what was currently happening. He followed everyone like a puppy. He answered what he was asked, did what he was told. He cuddled with Olha, even though she, too, was in a daze—unable to recognize anyone, to understand anything, and clearly felt like an outsider. Later on, during the wake, Olha got into an argument with her mother-in-law. They kept accusing each other of something insignificant, both of them wound up, tired, shattered. Someone asked for silence, someone insisted on figuring everything out right that moment. And someone else shared a recipe for pork, French style, claiming that the onions should definitely be soaked in milk.

Finally, everyone left.

Tymofiy could not fall asleep for a long time; the image of his old man in the casket would not let him go. He lay in bed, his gaze sliding over the ceiling, studying the geometry of the lights reflected from outside. And when he fell asleep, he dreamed of his father's brother, who stood over Tymofiy and kept opening his huge, dark mouth, in silence.

◊ ◊ ◊

In September, Tymofiy asked to be transferred to a different school. He could not handle the pressure at his current one, and Toma insisted on the transfer as well.

"You have to study," she kept saying. "You are smart. Just study and get your head straight."

She studied the same way she dragged Tymofiy along: with ease, carefully monitoring his successes and helping him with the subjects he was failing. In early September, he had stood in the principal's office, trying to explain that his grades did not reflect his lack of interest in studying. Rather, they reflected the suffering and pain that he had endured at his previous school. The principal, tall and hunched over, with curly hair all over his head and the good-natured face of a functionary, resembled a buffalo. He said that he did not mind offering Tymofiy shelter at his school ("you have good grades only in History and English"); however, certain head teachers would hardly welcome another problematic student. "We have quite a few of them, the problematic ones, and we can't kill them to free up some space. Unless they kill themselves, of course."

Sure enough, except for one teacher, no one supported the idea of accepting Tymofiy. They nitpicked his report card, as if inspecting a festering wound, they alluded to the overcrowded classes, the directives of the Regional Department of Education, the parents' committee. And that single teacher, whom Tymofiy approached last, seemed to have some kind of guilt complex that made her feel like she owed something to the entire world. All kinds of outcasts flocked under her wing—orphans mercilessly poisoned by life, poor souls whose parents struggled to make ends meet, autistic kids with genuine psychological issues. And so she ended up accepting Tymofiy as well. He looked like a quiet kid without serious problems. Indeed, there were no issues. He settled into his new environment, even made some friends.

During one of the first physical education classes of the new year, Tymofiy's group was dispatched to get the old Soviet textbooks from the school library and bring them to the gym storage, right by the P.E. teacher's office. There were tons of wastepaper there, from before the Soviet Union's collapse—history books, works by Lenin, some eerie ideological ramblings about pioneers, and even manuals that were still used by a few dissident teachers.

Some of Tymofiy's buddies stripped metal at night. They would rummage around the neighborhood and its industrial yards, recklessly peeking inside the dark, abandoned workshops, wandering into the hastily reanimated production lines. They looked for scraps of aluminum, bronze, and brass, cutting it all and bringing it in for recycling. Tymofiy was cautious of cutting metal. He heard many stories about the guards who would catch teenagers and toss their disfigured bodies into the Dnipro, and of those who were electrocuted when carelessly cutting through wires. It was a shitty business, plus you had to go in groups of four or five just to carry all that metal. And then, once you divided the profit, you ended up with something ridiculous, maybe enough kopecks to buy an ice cream. Nobody would be snatching wastepaper, though. Who would even think of stealing paper?

The thought occurred to Tymofiy by accident, when the P.E. teacher mentioned that a trailer would be coming by to pick everything up, and one of the students said something like, "no kidding—you could build a whole other school with that."

Tymofiy asked Felix to be his accomplice. The guy was physically strong, light on his feet, and always penniless. At the time, Felix had a job as a security guard at the D.O.K., Derevoobrobnyi Kombinat, the wood processing facility. He got paid around a hundred and twenty hryvnias a month, just a bit more than Lida's pension, and handed it over to Lida for groceries. He was usually left with just enough hryvnias for cigarettes. He hadn't been drinking for over three months.

One dark October night, they pulled off their first heist. They dragged the paper in sacks, for more than a mile. In one week, they managed to expropriate almost half a ton of wastepaper.

"There's still some left. Let's do it, yeah?" Tymofiy asked.

Felix waved his arms.

"Cornet! It's a game day!"

Soccer was of great importance and could not be argued about. It sometimes happened that Felix would even stop drinking just to be able to watch the game.

"Who is playing?"

"Us and the Russkies."

Even though Tymofiy cooled down after Petit scored, he kept following the home team. The stars of Dynamo Kyiv— Shevchenko, Rebrov, Luzhny. Once he found out that the French and the Russkies would be knocked out if Dynamo won, Tymofiy opted to watch the game.

"The Russkies aren't human," Felix said, turning on the TV.

"Aren't they paying your pension?" Tymofiy observed.

"Let them pay. The Germans paid reparations too. And they, by the way, were human!"

"Right. You would have made an excellent SS officer." Tymofiy gave Felix a sarcastic look.

"I *am* an SS officer. It's just that not everyone knows it."

It had been a few months since the TV's cathode-ray tube broke. The sound was there but instead of a visual, a muddy-green emptiness filled up the screen. One could only guess what was being broadcasted. Really, the sound didn't come through so great either, but Tymofiy managed to get it working through the amplifier attached to the speakers.

"It's like we're back in the fucking USSR," observed Felix. "I used to listen to soccer on the radio. Back then, the broadcaster made comments for those who couldn't watch. And this rookie's gonna moan and groan, like a Silesian frau in a city sacked by the Russkies."

The soccer match was broadcast on Channel One. The whole family watched, or rather, listened—Felix, Lida, Tymofiy.

Felix started smoking from the get-go. He stood by the open balcony door, looking at the sky, chain-smoking. In the first seventy-five minutes he probably smoked a whole pack. And when the Russkies started to pull ahead, he went to the kitchen. Lida followed him. Ukie soccer was uninteresting to her, the Russkies even more so. Tymofiy was left alone in the room. In the eighty-seventh minute, when Shevchenko scored a penalty, he quietly said, "Goal."

Bursting with joy, he ran into the kitchen, saw Felix standing under the vent, and yelled, "Sheva![63] It's a tie!"

"Bullshit," Felix barked.

"I'm telling ya!"

With the cigarette still in his mouth, Felix ran into the room and silently planted himself in the chair. He was ashing into his palm. This was how he sat until the very end of the game, with extinguished cigarettes in his fingers.

When everything was over, when the broadcaster had said all the necessary and unnecessary words and the ads rolled out, Felix got up, stood straight, put his arm on his heart, and started singing the national anthem in his signature false basso. Tymofiy joined him on the eighth measure. Lida ran from the kitchen, looking at them in silence, holding a steaming spoon in her hand. Quietly, practically without a sound, she uttered, "Idiots."

The next day they went to do the paper recycling. For almost half a day, they filled the sacks with books. Luckily, the recycling facility was close by, in the artisan workshop. There, a fat guy with tiny eyes, wearing brown joggers and a low-quality crumpled hoodie, took his time adjusting the weights; first he moved them one way, then another. Tapped on them one more time.

"Don't you fuck with us!" Felix took a step forward.

"Hell," the guy said. "This is, like, nothing." He pulled out a calculator with a long charger. The green digits lit up, and the guy started tapping on it blindly. "Forty-five."

"Give us more!" Felix burst out.

"Won't work."

"Oh yeah?" Felix growled and moved straight toward the guy, flexing his fingers.

"Felix!" Tymofiy caught Felix's dangerously sharp elbow. "Don't."

"Don't?" Felix turned toward Tymofiy. "Did you see how he was tapping those weights?" Felix's voice became cranky, an almost childish whine.

"Felix, don't." Tymofiy sounded firm.

They split the money in half. Felix gave half of his portion to Lida for groceries, while the other half was supposed to cover the expenses for the secret operation.

Felix had been going on and on about this secret operation for a few weeks. Tymofiy had an inkling as to what it was all about. Felix had been abstinent for the last couple of months. Back in May, after a prolonged fight, Lida managed to kick him out of the apartment. For about a week, he stood in the stairwell, as if stuck in an elevator, refusing to leave and banging on the door. He rang the bell and yelled, as if trying to reach a dispatcher. Then he gave up, retreated, and went back to his cabin on Pio- . nerska Street. His wife had left a year ago. Felix lived with his daughter. Well, rather, his daughter lived in the apartment, while

Felix would come visit from time to time, as if just to make sure that everything stayed the same—the maps, a worn-out and faded carpet that belonged to his mother, papers, books, documents, a glass beer-bottle chandelier. During that time, he would just lock himself in the cabin and didn't let his daughter anywhere near him. He drank, smashed the furniture, and called Lida in vain. The only person he could talk to was the boy. Tymofiy knew that Felix was drunk, so he would change his voice and pretend to be either Lida's new husband, or a *dukhan*[64] owner named Akram, or even an SBU[65] general. Felix—either playing along or possibly really believing Tymofiy—would mumble something in response, lose his temper, curse, threaten. In the end, he drank himself into such a state that he was unable to reach for the phone. Again, he wouldn't let his daughter come close. She had to call Hrysha the Saboteur for help. Hrysha, full of enthusiastic resolve, came running. Instantly and expertly, he joined Felix in his drinking binge. After a week, he extricated Felix from his drunken state, without effort or pain.

The July weather was stifling. Lida remained in the city since Lyosha's mother, together with the cave-mouthed Boria, had sold the summer cottage, including the farm animals, without mentioning anything to either Lida or Olha. Boria and his mother came in May, picked some lilacs, and handed the keys over to the new owner, who immediately let the chicks run outside. They did not even bother to remove the former owners' things. Children's books, favorite childhood vinyl records, some other things dear to Tymofiy, all purged. Finally, memories too. Regardless of how dear. Regardless of what childhood had been like . . .

Olha shed bitter tears into the phone receiver while speaking to Tymofiy. She could not understand why they didn't tell her; she would have bought the cottage herself, offered more money—it had been sold for nothing, just like that, out of spite, contrary to everything. Tymofiy kept repeating, "That's okay, Mom, we'll get a new one," even though he knew that it was not really about the cottage but all the sentimental tchotchkes that filled out the summer with their plain, pastoral perfection. But Olha would not calm down, and she hung up the phone without saying goodbye, choked with tears. Lida was not stirred by the news of the cottage being sold. Perhaps she had sensed something; after Lyosha's death, she did not plant anything in the garden. In the city, she would run to the beach—crowded and dirty, like the central market—almost daily. She would walk into the woods filled with mushrooms, herbs, and random masturbators. Sometimes, she would go to her friend's cottage.

One evening in July, Felix came to see Lida. He was sober, wearing a new T-shirt and sunglasses typical of a cop; his sandals, however, were old and worn. The two of them talked, argued, negotiated. Felix's arms were crossed behind his back. Lida held hers crossed over her chest. Finally, they agreed that if Felix were to quit drinking, he'd be allowed to come back. No exceptions. Even if it were someone's birthday, August 2 or February 15. Lida even asked Tymofiy to join this bizarre family intervention. She sat him in the kitchen right in front of her, as if he himself was guilty of something, and asked whether he agreed with these conditions. Tymofiy, by and large, did not care. What could he possibly say? Of course, it was better for Felix not to drink than to drink. But again, Tymofiy didn't really care. In the meantime, Felix stood in the hall and listened to their conversation, then came up to Tymofiy and shook his hand. Tymofiy shrugged.

He didn't care about anything. He struggled to finish the school year. They let him graduate, but just barely. Taking into account his personal situation, he was roundly given all Cs in the main subjects.

And now Felix started talking about the secret operation again. Tymofiy hinted that Felix should be more careful.

"You know how sensitive she is to this stuff. She'll kick you out."

Felix pretended not to understand.

"It's your call," nodded Tymofiy. "She didn't fall in love with your drinking."

◊ ◊ ◊

Tymofiy saved the money he earned from recycling paper. In six months, he managed to put aside over five hundred hryvnias. "Here's Felix's pension," he observed bitterly, leaning over his savings.

Saving money took time. Toma was saving as well, with less success since she constantly bought sweets and cigarettes. She spent change on daily lottery tickets and plastic tchotchkes—hair ties, bangles, pins with symbols of peace and anarchy. In August they had agreed to move in together. Toma had been calling him a dummy for a while, but she obviously wanted it as well. She wanted to taste real adulthood, so that others would call her mature and independent, whispering behind her back during smoke breaks. Their timing was good; some big shots had offered to get Toma's mother a job in the Czech Republic, they needed a seamstress to work for a famous brand. Or rather, they needed someone to manage an entire workshop of Ukrainian seamstresses. Toma's mother agreed and planned to depart in November. And her daughter? Her daughter was an adult, she could take care of herself. Inga, Toma's older sister, would keep an eye on her. And then there was their father—a jerk, naturally, but also an adult. Toma wouldn't go hungry. And as for the rest, Toma had been leading an independent life for a while. Dating guys, spending nights where she pleased; she smelled of wild street scents, a mixture of coconut, cigarette smoke, and insulated pipes. And she was only fourteen. What would be next? The main thing was that she wouldn't end up like Inga, who had not yet turned sixteen when she took off and moved in with that thug. She was happy, in a way, but good luck explaining that to her teachers and neighbors.

Toma mentioned it to Tymofiy rather matter-of-factly. In passing.

"If you want," she said, "you could move into my place. Three rooms. When you start boring me, we'll call it off."

"We won't," Tymofiy said. "We'll need money, though. If I leave Lida, who's gonna feed me?"

"We'll need money," Toma agreed.

They calculated that for a modest cigarette-free life, they would need a hundred and fifty hryvnias per month. Tymofiy did not mention that he and Lida managed to survive on a hundred, between the two of them. By himself, he could have made do with fifty. He was used to living on soybeans and bread with jam.

They had to put together a thousand hryvnias for the two of them, to last until the summer. And after that, during summer vacation, Tymofiy would get a job and make more money—he was physically strong, no longer a child. Plus, Olha would send some money, and so would Toma's mother. The two of them would survive.

After Lyosha's death, Uncle Boria tossed Tymofiy a hundred hryvnias. "Don't lose heart, Tymokha, we'll all be there sooner or later." Keeping it a secret from Lida, Tymofiy also put aside some kopecks from the money that Olha sent. He sold his father's home sound system—source, amplifier, and speakers, for a hundred and twenty hryvnias. But he also bought a Chinese tape player for fifty—he couldn't manage without music. Lida would spare some money, and Tymofiy would cheat some more out of Felix. Plus, paper recycling, and selling his stamp collection. Tymofiy and Felix were hired to dig graves a few times. In late August, Tymofiy transported sand for a neighbor who was building a garage. That's how he reached half a grand. He diligently hid all the bills in a Herzen[66] book. If they cleaned out the apartment, they definitely wouldn't take Herzen. Who needed Herzen? Who needed books at all? So, he stuck all that miserable cash inside volume seven.

This was his chance to break free from that apartment, to live with a woman as if he were thirty, not fourteen. God, Tymofiy thought to himself, what'll happen to me when I'm thirty? What will I be like? What will I be doing? Will I even last that long? Guys like me don't live that long. They die way too early, he kept thinking while falling asleep. Life isn't worth that much fuss. Yeah, definitely better to fizzle out at thirty, he thought, jumping to the upper shelf to check on Herzen. He opened the book—everything was there. He counted the money, counted the weeks left until November.

Tymofiy and Toma would meet in the city. He would arrive haunted by some sort of nagging premonition. She yearned for him, she knew he would understand and support her. He was full of those clever ideas not unusual for a sensitive teenager, and his advice would always lift Toma's mood. She was having difficulties with her old circle of friends. Something wasn't sticking together. The guys got into drinking, adding gossip and judgment into the mix, the abortions and jealousy started, someone jumped off a roof, someone else opened his veins. They drank moonshine, smoked pot, wandered the streets like drunken sailors at port, provoking shock and resentment among passersby. Toma felt an overwhelming loneliness. All this exerted pressure on her—the noise and vanity, pretending to be an independent adult when she didn't even want to. More and more often, she would stay at home, observing rationally that one enters adulthood through different kinds of doors. She became fond of reading, even though previously she'd had no interest in it at all. Most importantly, she became close to her sister. Inga had matured with poise—she worked as an administrator at a shabby but bustling restaurant, settled into the protective shell of everyday life that she had put together for herself. All the placemats, the graters, the comfortable poufs in the hall were part of it. She waited, hopelessly, for her thug to return from prison—he was serving his third term over in Khutory. Inga was kind to Toma, telling her not to do stupid things, to graduate, to get into college, or even better—go overseas. She also tossed Toma some money.

Occasionally, Toma visited Tymofiy to kill time. On those evenings, Felix would practically walk on his tiptoes. Lida constantly tried to feed Toma, calling her Buchenwald, but did not interfere with the personal stuff. At least Toma wasn't involved in anything criminal. The rest was fine by Lida.

They would sit in Tymofiy's room, among the posters of Dolores O'Riordan and the Cure that Tymofiy used to find in Polish teen magazines, on a sofa leaning against the graffiti-covered wall. Under the mystical light of the lampshade painted red, they shared their dreams, naive and full of joy. They talked about the future—the winter they would spend together, the weekend dinners at Inga's restaurant, how Tymofiy would go to the new school and Toma would tutor him, and how later on they would enter college to study history, of course. And no kids. Maybe they'd get a cat and name it Bunin. Or Belle. Or if it's a she-cat, they'd call her Vira Ivanivna Kryzhanivska.[67] They'd pick a name straight off the bookshelf. They talked about everything fourteen-year-olds would want to talk about. Love was the only topic that avoided their direct gaze. They were afraid of it. What's with love anyway, they thought. We're together because we have something to give one another. We have sex, mutual understanding, friendship; we want to live for each other. We're adults. Who needs love?

◊ ◊ ◊

In the spring, Tymofiy asked Felix to show him a few combat techniques. Moved by the request, Felix asked Tymofiy to step out of the room into the hall with him.

"Cornet," said Felix. "Visually, a human body should be divided into two parts. Horizontally. Anywhere you look, you should see two parts—chest, core, back, neck. What do you have right now? Only the dimples on your chin and your ass show that you consist of two parts. The rest of you looks like a trunk. You are a shapeless trunk."

"I thought I was a poppy."

"A poppy?" Felix sounded surprised. "No, a trunk."

"A trunk," Tymofiy repeated with bitterness.

"Yeah, donnerwetter," confirmed Felix. "Now hit this." He pulled Lida's coat from the hanger, rolled it into a *makiwara*, and put it in front of Tymofiy.

Tymofiy punched it.

"You do it like a rookie. Again!"

Tymofiy punched again. Felix sighed and started him with the basics.

He was certain that Tymofiy would give up soon and return to sleeping past ten. For some time, Felix woke Tymofiy up at six, pushed him to go running, then made him exercise on a jungle gym. Tymofiy hung from those bars like a carcass in the meat section. "Let's go. Punch it! Run," yelled Felix. "Punch!" Tymofiy ran and punched. Later he dragged himself to the jungle gym, hanging hopelessly and wallowing in the mess of metal rods, a fish caught in a net. But Tymofiy did not give up. He had a goal—he started to wake up before Felix, jump out into the chilly morning, run to the Dnipro, fall on the wet sand, do push-ups, and take long swims, almost all the way to the fairway. He would come home exhausted, collapse on the sofa—all red and sweaty, energized by the morning breeze. As the evening approached, he would wish for it to be morning again, to break free once more, to run, to connect with the Rocky Balboa inside himself—in his gray training gear on the steps of the Philadelphia Museum of Art.

It was Felix who gave up, or rather, went on a binge. He drank and took off. Tymofiy lost motivation and the desire to pursue his goal; the glimpse of happiness faded, laziness and apathy took hold. For a week after that, Tymofiy bailed entirely. Out of habit, he woke up early but did not run anywhere. He wandered the apartment, made sandwiches, and collapsed on the sofa to watch TV with a sense of humiliating surrender.

One day in early June, Tymofiy and Toma went to the beach. Toma took off her clothes in one swoop, showing her bluish chicken skin, and rushed into the gray water. Tymofiy sat there in his T-shirt, under a willow tree, soaking his feet, unhappy and full of self-hatred. He hated giving up. As usual, he had backed out. He had lost. "Jelly Belly," he kept saying to himself, "a dumb Jelly Belly."

The next morning, he started training again. No self-defense, no fantasies about insidious takeovers by special forces, but still. He would run to the Dnipro and back, go to the boarding school stadium, do push-ups, pull-ups, squats, until the heat rose over the brick buildings and Tymofiy, exhausted by the dry scorching air, would collapse.

In July, when Felix returned and started badgering him again, Tymofiy's strength and motivation returned.

"Let's go, Jelly Belly," he whispered to himself as he ran, "let's go, fuck it." He accelerated, and it felt like his heart was about to jump out of his chest; he gasped for breath, his lungs were filled with needles and broken glass, his body with fire and thickened blood. He came to a stop by the water's edge, feeling the Dnipro slowly seep into his sneakers, his pulse slowing down, allowing him to breathe freely. When his blood started flowing normally again, Tymofiy would have a runner's high, and he'd push himself to do a few more miles along the beach, in a half-conscious state.

His young body was happy to comply and began changing. He had to splurge on some new clothing.

In early August, having just returned from a run—still hot, in wet swimming trunks, Felix and Tymofiy sat in the living room, waiting for Lida to make them breakfast. She'd been in the kitchen a long time, periodically producing loud rattling noises with pans and plates, as if conducting the percussion section of an orchestra. The smell of roasted onions penetrated the room. Sunlight, refracted by the tulle curtains, jumped all over the patterned wallpaper, which had long ago been torn in places, splashed with wine and Coca-Cola, faded, written on with a pen: phone numbers, medication names, fragments of homework assignments. Still, Tymofiy never grew weary of examining those walls, teasing human contours and animal grimaces out of its colorful curvatures.

Lida entered the living room. She was hot, her hair wet from sweat and kitchen fumes.

"Felix," she said, "Yurka called you."

"Yurka?" Felix was surprised. "How did that one find me?"

"Call him back," Lida said.

Mumbling curses, Felix went to the phone, and hovered over the dial as he struggled to recall the number.

"It's Felix!" That was all he said. He stood holding the black receiver against his ear, silently, listening to the rumbling voice on the other end. He stood there forever, just listening, not interrupting. At the end, Felix said "aha," hung up, and muttered something quietly, intently, looking out somewhere through the translucent tulle, through the window and the distant greenery of the neighborhood.

"Mom passed away."

Lyudmyla was over eighty, she had been struggling to walk, her legs hurt, but after Old Petro's passing, she managed to take care of herself and Yurka. Yurka was drinking irregularly but passionately, diving into steep, bottomless binges during which he drank a lot, finishing a few bottles of wine each day. He sat on his bed, drinking and singing. In a high-pitched tenor, he sang pieces from the choir of his childhood: "White Chestnut Trees," "Mist over the Valley," "Hutsulka Ksenia." In those moments, Lyudmyla did not bother him, cautious of traumatizing Yurka for whatever reason. She called Felix, occasionally, asking him to step in, to talk to Yurka. If Felix was sober, he would come and slap Yurka across his face, yell, call him a stupid cow and a bitch. Felix would kick the furniture and tear his brother's sheets off the bed. Yurka made feeble attempts to protect his face with his arms, and kept on sobbing, promising to sleep himself sober and quit drinking. Yurka was scared shitless of his brother, hated him, called him a fascist when he wasn't around. Still, he was always submissive and obedient. Sometimes, Yurka would actually stop drinking for a few months, go back to the market where he had a gig as a loader, and give the money to his mother. In the evenings, he would crawl to his local buddies to roll the dice. The guys disliked Yurka, an uneducated softie. He wasn't thrilled with them either. With special contempt, he called them dickheads.

Lyudmyla died by the apartment door. She was climbing the stairs, wheezing and struggling to breathe—the air was hot and thick, suffocating her and burning her lungs. She pulled out her keys but then sank down to the floor. Her eyes filled with darkness, her body with dull and pervading pain. She died on the spot.

Felix disappeared for a few days. All the work was his to bear. Yurka was scared to even step inside the apartment, saying that it stank of the deceased, even though the body had been taken to the morgue right away. He begged Felix to stay with him for a few days, worried that his mother would visit him at night. Felix stayed, looking after his brother's alcohol intake. Felix was watching himself, too. That's how they ended up sitting around in the stuffy apartment for four days straight. They didn't even go through their mother's belongings.

After his return, Felix remained silent for some time. He wandered around the apartment, humming some plaintive Polish song about the house dear to one's heart. He would sit on the balcony with a notebook, taking his time, drawing, and staring senselessly at the interwoven branches of lush greenery that rose behind the mechanic's shop on the grounds of the cannery. Lida did not engage with him, only served food.

From those times, just one thing stuck in Tymofiy's memory. Felix was sitting on a stool, smoking, scratching his cheek, slurping tea—as usual, it was black as tar, and exceptionally strong. Then he looked up with dull, faded eyes and said, "It's Yurka who killed her." He fell silent, took another sip. "And me."

◇ ◇ ◇

One morning in November, Tymofiy phoned Olha, full of resolve. She asked about his studies at the new school. She wasn't that interested but must have felt obligated to ask. She knew that her son had changed schools, because the new one was closer to home than the one before, but she was not interested in his grades. Who cares about grades? Anyway, Tymofiy's academic performance had improved, especially in the humanities. All those disciplines— history and literature—gladly nested inside him, like autumn snakes in toasty burrows. She then started singing the same old tune about taking Tymofiy to the capital. She had even chosen a school for him—the one with the Stalinist Empire architecture, the judicious teachers, the pedagogical achievements. Tymofiy cut her short.

"Mom," he said. "Listen, Mom. I'm not going. No way am I living in Kyiv."

"Didn't you want to? What are you going to do in your hick town?"

"Well . . ."

"There's nothing to do there but make babies," Olha interrupted him.

"I don't want to have children," Tymofiy said. "Still, I'm not moving. Not this year. Not now. Mom," he said, pensively. "Listen, Mom . . ."

"Here you'll have a chance, but at home?"

"Listen up, Mom! I'm leaving Lida's."

"What d'you mean, leaving?" Olha wasn't getting it.

"I have a girlfriend, and I'm moving in with her."

Olha fell silent, looking for the adequate, ironic words; failing to find them, she started laughing.

"Okay Mom, take care," Tymofiy said, getting nervous, and hung up.

Olha called back a few minutes later, but once Tymofiy heard the single clank before the main ring indicating it was a long-distance call, he knew he wouldn't be picking up.

He presented Lida with a fait accompli as well. He even smiled while talking to her. Lida sighed but asked to call Olha, just in case.

"I already did."

"And what did your mom say?"

"She laughed."

"Well, well." Lida sounded dissatisfied. "I can imagine how we're all gonna laugh later on."

Tymofiy packed his things—T-shirts, deodorant, shampoo, tape recorder, textbooks, an extra pair of sneakers. Then, early in the morning one icy and windless Saturday, he sailed off to his new place.

On the bus, Tymofiy began to think that he was doing something irreparable, incorrect. Something weighed down on him, as if maybe this was not what he desired, what he had saved money or prepared for over the last months. In later conversations, his mother had tried, obstinately, to talk him out of it, hysterically insisting that he was still a child, that this nonsense would evaporate immediately as soon as he ran into day-to-day troubles and shared problems, as soon as he smelled the powder, the medications, the scent of ironed diapers. According to her, Tymofiy was under the spell of inexperienced youth, ripe anger, and of course, hormones, all of which were obscuring his true desires.

"Sonny, I wish you would have introduced your girlfriend to us," Olha would say amicably into the receiver. She would lose her temper in a second: "Oh God, please don't do it!" And then, already hearing the short beeps, she'd yell, "And don't you hang up on me! Don't!"

Introduce Toma? Toma, whom Olha had known practically from her birth? Olha would then start calling Toma's mother, and interventions would inevitably follow, in hopes of saving the kids from ill-conceived frivolity. Two mothers would stifle the rebellion and troublemaking out of the kindness of their hearts. They would smother the kids, deprive them of the life-saving oxygen that made their lives meaningful, that painted everything in bright colors. Tymofiy had studied these tricks through and through. One should keep to oneself, live as one pleases, and share only with those one trusts.

Only Felix knew about Toma. At the beginning he tried giving advice, but he quickly gave up.

"If you need something, let me know. Don't ask for money—I won't give you any. I have none."

From time to time, Felix arranged secret operations. Tymofiy had a hunch about these. Maybe Lida did as well, but she kept silent. Felix was the last thing on her mind. She was worried about Tymofiy. She was angry at him for leaving her, and at herself for not being able to do anything to stop it. Finally, she let it go. He would manage.

Tymofiy and Toma slept together, in Toma's bed, in Toma's room. The wallpaper, a reserved light blue, with a thick line running along the room at head level. A gray hexagonal wardrobe, an inconspicuous table by the window, a snake plant with broken leaves on the windowsill. Notebooks, textbooks, and moldy sandwiches wrapped in napkins piled up on the table. A typical Chinese-made chandelier, chrome plastic, hung from the ceiling.

They almost never went to Toma's mother's room and always kept the door half closed. They were reserved and quiet, trying not to draw attention to themselves. Tymofiy would go running in the mornings. He would spend a few minutes standing in front of the door, holding his breath, making sure none of the neighbors were lurking on the staircase. Once sure there were none, he would leap into the resonant concrete of the inner courtyard and set out for a brief run along the frozen beach, stumbling over sleepy fishermen and dog owners. Afterwards, he would head back to the apartment, drink coffee, and eat a few sandwiches like an adult. Then the two of them would walk out together—Toma to her school, while Tymofiy took a minibus to his. He would come home after lunch, grab a quick bite, and sit down to do homework. Toma helped him with science, while Tymofiy told her stories about Stalin. In the evening, they would go to the city center to meet up with friends, or wander into the parks covered with untouched snow and filled with expressive silence. Sitting on the old, wrecked carousels, surrounded by postapocalyptic stage sets, they would get drunk. Otherwise, they would sit in the Jewish cemetery, amid marble and granite headstones and black trunks of hornbeams covered with ice, or on the roof of the abandoned and desolate hotel Turyst, its windows shattered and doors broken long ago. Only empty walls, with the remains of white tiles and dirty-yellow Soviet wallpaper, were still standing. Hidden among the pine trees planted for the fiftieth anniversary of October Revolution Park, by the Ferris wheel, Turyst brought to mind a hotel in the abandoned town of Pripyat. Only instead of the respirators, syringes and vials lay scattered among the broken bricks and destroyed toilet bowls that lined the long corridors destroyed by *gopniks*,[68] punks, and homeless people. Toma loved dancing on that roof, playing a current hit record as an accompaniment. Tymofiy watched her gazelle-like body, excited by the peach schnapps or whatever else he'd had to drink. He surprised himself. He wondered how he managed to live this way, with this gazelle, who was still a mystery, who hid her emotions so diligently, never crying or yelling. Instead, she played a role only she could understand, following Tymofiy obediently and at the same time leading him confidently. There was a kind of a comic horror to it all, an uncertain, shaky reality that he liked.

Tymofiy was fast getting used to this new life. For the first two weeks, he felt uncomfortable, he was even hesitant about opening the fridge, but then he got used to it. Keeping his promise, he phoned Lida every day in a businesslike manner to let her know that he was doing okay and was not coming home. Sometimes he would talk to Felix, who laughed good-heartedly and promised, for some reason, to give Tymofiy a full dinner set made of concrete as a wedding present. Tymofiy reacted to such humor half-heartedly, saying that Felix wouldn't be invited to the wedding because he would definitely ruin the cake. After all this idle talk, Tymofiy enjoyed thinking about his new adult life, feeling the magical power of handling things, taking care of himself and her. Especially her.

In late December, Toma came down with some sort of virus. She was in bed with a high fever, face pink and hot to the touch; she struggled to swallow or move her dry lips. Tymofiy did not go to school. He requested a house call, washed the floors. While the doctor was examining Toma, Tymofiy hid in Toma's mother's room. Later on, he dashed between pharmacies in the central district with a list of medications. Her lungs were clear for now, but pneumonia was suspected; Toma would need to be kept under observation. And so, Tymofiy sat next to her and observed. He made some concoctions, gave her anti-inflammatory drugs, rubbed her clumsy but well-developed body with a wet towel, kissed her knees and warm belly, making her smile wearily. At night, he monitored her fever, and in the morning prepared new potions of tea and poured all the prescribed fluids into her.

Once Toma recovered and winter break began, Tymofiy came down with fever himself. Right before the holiday season.

Toma's friends were organizing a party. With the help of some acquaintances, they rented an apartment, stocked up on alcohol, canned food, and chicken thighs. They even dragged a stolen Christmas tree from the market.

On December 31, Tymofiy woke up with a deep, nagging cough. Clearly bronchitis. He lay on the sheets soaked with sweat and spilled tea, helplessly moving his limbs, which were numb from fever. Still sleepy, he glanced at the window, through which a painful white light crept.

"What should we do with you?" Toma said. "I even got you a present."

"Do the sick really need gifts?" Tymofiy tried to crack a joke.

"Not funny." She grimaced. "What if you croak here?"

"You should go." Tymofiy sounded calm and deliberate. "Seriously. I'll just lay around. Ribbit-ribbit."

Toma ran around the city for half the day, buying last-minute presents, then watched some traditional New Year's show with Tymofiy. She was anxious, constantly checking her watch. Fireworks exploded outside, excited voices and celebratory screams. In a futile attempt to bring his fever down, Tymofiy stuffed himself with Toma's leftover medications,

"Off you go," he said. "I'm fine."

"Are you sure?"

"Positive." Tymofiy forced a smile.

And so Toma left.

He stared at the TV screen indifferently, late into the night, lacking the energy even to get vertical and put together a sandwich. He remembered how, as a child, he would come down with pneumonia, and when there was no one to look after him, he had to stay home alone for hours. He remembered a lampshade that he worshipped, in the form of Donald Duck with his red umbrella, the shade hanging above Tymofiy's bed. For some reason, he also recalled that back in '89, that lampshade had cost ten rubles, which is why it was even more precious, since ten rubles seemed like a lot of money at the time. Tymofiy had laid in his bed and studied Donald, the witness to his illness, wishing the duck would come to life. Tymofiy wished Donald would jump around the room and talk in his signature quack, which Tymofiy had heard just once, when his father's buddy Alik, the owner of a video store, invited Tymofiy to the stuffy room inside the supermarket one evening. For an hour, Tymofiy sat and watched cartoons alone. And yet, Donald did not walk down the wall, and the bulb inside him went out, and five-year-old Tymofiy sobbed the afternoon away—he was offended, lonely. As soon as he closed his eyes, he would become painfully aware of his own uselessness and the inevitability of death. When frozen Olha, with her cheeks pink, came in the quiet, pale twilight of his room, Tymofiy burst into tears even more, this time in happiness.

Toma probably also had a lamp like his, but it must have broken long ago, or have been hidden someplace in the mezzanine or the basement. At the moment, an inanimate Chinese lamp hung above Tymofiy, shining a dead white light that caused his eyes to tear and the back of his neck to hurt.

Tymofiy fell asleep around eleven but woke up after two in the morning—in a new year, with a high fever. He got up, shaking, walked to the phone, dialed Olha's Kyiv number with his frozen fingers. Feverish, he stood on the cold linoleum, wet from the snow they had tracked in during the day, holding the receiver with his folded palm, waiting. Heavy thoughts of death circled around in his head—more vexing than scary. And this annoyance, this offense blocked all other feelings with the indifference of a black folding screen. What if he had croaked last night, for real, in the first hours of the year 2000? He would be lying on this uneven linoleum, in the middle of the hall, among her shoes, wearing only his boxers and holding the receiver in his hand. Toma would be surprised, wouldn't she? Maybe not. She might step over him and collapse on the sofa to watch cartoons. She still loves cartoons, he thought with bitterness. I would be just lying here until the neighbors smelled my decomposing body and called the cops. Those guys would come in, break the door. And what would she say? "I thought he was sleeping. How could you do this, Jelly Belly? I thought you were asleep, but you were dead, Jelly Belly. You guys are gonna take him away, right? Oh, and his stuff. Go ahead, take his sneakers, textbooks, the notebooks with his scribbles . . ."

Olha did not pick up the phone. Tymofiy dialed home. Lida answered almost instantly, as if she had been waiting for his call.

"Granny," Tymofiy said. "Happy New Year!"

◇ ◇ ◇

For Christmas,[69] Tymofiy went to see Olha. He is really an adult now, she thought to herself. But still as silly as he used to be. For Tymofiy, by contrast, the proximity to his mother helped him soften up, to be able to feel her support, or at least the possibility of it. He slept late, ate an unhurried breakfast, then wandered around his mother's rented second-floor apartment. Then he ambled out of the house and headed for the city center, taking walks through the streets of Kyiv, tinted with yellow twilight. On his third day, he caught himself thinking that he didn't want to go back to Cherkasy. He felt a certain fatigue that he hadn't noticed before. He carried it across his back, speeding up along a stretched-out misty road, steering through the curves, and ending up on the dirty curb; once he stopped, it dawned on him that he wouldn't be able to carry this fatigue any longer. He had to, of course. If only he knew where to go.

Toma and Inga went to the mountains during the school break. Somewhere just over the border. The Tatras? The Sudetes? The girls' father bought the older one a travel package for two. That's how Inga brought her sister along. They met some Germans who paid for their meals and invited them to their hotel rooms. The older one went. Toma, wrapped in her white hotel robe, sat on the king-size bed in her room with an enormous packet of M&M's, watching movies in a language she did not understand.

Toma and Tymofiy returned on the same day. They embraced for a long time, standing in the hall. Tymofiy was in his casual clothes, while Toma was still wearing the frozen ski gear she kept on the whole frigid train ride home. In a few days they went back to school. At first, they tried to keep their usual schedule, so that everything would be as it used to be, but something was off. They were drifting away, like icebergs in the ocean. Tymofiy was engrossed in his own world. He gave up on his running routine and started flunking school.

Toma noticed that their savings were melting away fast. Forget about summer; at this point, surviving until spring would be an issue. She brought up money more and more often, which irritated Tymofiy. It was the last thing he wanted to talk about. Instead, he talked about their relationship, analyzing who invested more, and who was just benefiting. They both threw around a lot of nonsensical accusations about various things: their studies, who cleaned the kitchen and the other rooms, the high cost of clothing and sanitary pads. Toma's mother wouldn't send anything before the next month, and it was doubtful her father would either. Tymofiy would never, ever ask Olha for money, and Lida probably didn't have any. In short, it started with money and it ended with money. Nothing was said about love. They did not even broach the subject, as if it didn't exist and never had.

Naturally, they made up later on, got under the blankets, and stayed there until well into the evening. They fell asleep without having dinner.

One day in February, wandering the dirty streets, Tymofiy ran into Shlosser, whose legs were covered with slush up to the knees while his cheeks displayed an improbable pinkish color. Shlosser shook Tymofiy's hand for a while, asking him how things were, how his family was. Unable to extract a response, he invited Tymofiy to a performance at the musical college. A jazz quartet would be playing on Tuesday night. Shlosser on double bass. Tymofiy agreed.

"I'll be coming with a girl, though," he said.

"A girl?" Shlosser sounded joyful. "Of course, bring her along! Is she good-looking or frozen like a fish? For people like us, beauty is secondary. For us, the most important thing is that there is no emptiness in here," he pointed to his chest. "Does she have something in here?"

"So, can she come?" Tymofiy persisted.

"Bring everyone along!" Shlosser shrugged. "All of them!"

Toma was curious about the famous Shlosser, as well as his double bass: an instrument she had seen, it became clear, only once before in a musical film starring Marilyn Monroe. The couple arrived on time. The half-empty concert hall with its suffocating light made a pleasant impression. New seats, new floors. The beet-colored rugs in the aisles, though old, did not have holes in them. The program was mostly jazz standards, but the arrangements were interesting. Every piece had a solo by one of the musicians, who would go into a cheery medley, fusing compositions and themes. For the most part Toma was bored, but if she recognized any of the melodies, she would get madly excited, slap Tymofiy on his knee, and grin. Shlosser sent sunbeams into

Tymofiy's eyes, and the light reflected back in the metal pegs of his fingerboard. Smiling frantically in the fury of his crazed pizzicato, he rotated the bass on its endpin.

After the concert, all of them gathered in the hall. Tymofiy, feeling embarrassed, introduced Toma to Shlosser, who was wrapping a wool scarf around his neck. Shlosser shook Toma's hand while introducing everyone to the handsome trumpet player, Valera, who energetically slapped Tymofiy on the back and said that representatives of the younger generation must understand music well if they had come to listen to Ukraine's greatest virtuoso. Tymofiy did not comment. Shlosser, having observed Toma attentively, leaned toward Tymofiy and said in a barely audible manner, "Be gentle with her. And honest."

Walking home along the city streets at twilight, under the orange streetlights, Tymofiy thought how wonderful it would be to spend the rest of the evening as lighthearted as he had been right after the concert. In the last weeks, the kitchen fights had been weighing on him. He could not escape them. These petty fights, with maniacal persistence, followed him wherever he went. He would have loved to think and stay silent, instead of yelling without thinking.

At home, they were met with the dirty dishes in the sink. And the messy bed, and some things packed under the bathtub—whose belongings were those? Why should we buy such expensive cookies when the cheap ones are still around? And why can't we keep the fridge closed? Before going to bed, they made up again, cuddling under the blanket. The dishes remained unwashed, the cookies half eaten.

In the morning, they woke up and started arguing all over again—about belongings, laundry, money. Be gentle with her, Tymofiy remembered Shlosser's words from the day before, and decided not to escalate. He put on his clothes in silence and, without any breakfast, hungry, dragged himself to school. Toma went to school as well. She ate first, though. Tymofiy sat in class, thinking about money, chores, and Lida, who had warned him about it all. He remembered Olha, who hysterically and hopelessly tried to prove to him that he couldn't survive like this for long. After school, he took his time walking to the bus stop, poisoning himself with thoughts that he'd rather not think, and waited, digging up a layer of frozen snow with the toe of his boot. He dragged himself home from the bus stop. He stopped by the hill, down which the youngsters were sliding on plastic bags that used to hold ammonium nitrate. For an hour, he wandered along the Dnipro, not daring to step on the thin ice. He started feeling cold and headed back to warmth.

He crossed paths with a woman of about thirty near the entrance to the building. Greasy black hair stuck out from under a green knitted hat. She was wearing black felt boots and a black men's coat with a ripped sleeve.

"I know," she said, pointing her finger somewhere close to Tymofiy's belly, "that you live with Tomka. I hear you sometimes. Through the wall."

She pulled out a dirty kerchief from her pocket and wiped her red, chronically congested nose. Tymofiy looked at her with agitation and disgust. Even through the cold air he could smell her stale clothing and unwashed body.

"Through the wall," she repeated wickedly, as if expecting to hear an excuse. "And you are still children!"

Tymofiy looked at the woman tensely, with disgust—at her cracked fingers with short, dirty nails, her inflamed nose, the spots of yellow pigmentation on gray cheeks, the thin, straight folds on her forehead, the kind one doesn't usually see on a young person's face. His nose caught her warm smell, that of neglect and poverty. He wanted to hit her—her face, with his fist. Out of despair and suffocating boredom. And, of course, out of fear.

"And?" Tymofiy said defiantly.

"And here we are!" the woman said, turned around, and walked along the building. Tymofiy followed her shrinking black figure with his eyes, a heavy and tight lump forming in his throat. It was something rotten, like a piece of meat that had gone bad, shooting up from his stomach. He wanted to run to his apartment, as fast as possible, lock all the doors, crawl under the blanket, and stay there until the thaw, until this fatigue evaporated. Everything that he carried on and on. Carried *on* and *on*! Everything he pulled and dragged, like a Sisyphean dung beetle dragging a big, hairy ball of droppings.

When Tymofiy entered the apartment and heard Toma's breezy chirping, he suddenly became aware of himself, of the fact that he was standing in the hall of someone else's apartment with its own smells that he had not yet grown used to, with its own sounds, so different from the ones he had experienced as a child. Toma was next to him. They were fifteen years old, and they would have to talk about money, again. Or about responsibilities. They would talk for a long time, not knowing when to stop. And then she would dump him. Not today, of course. She would dump him in a month, perhaps in a year. But she would. And then her mother would return. Tymofiy and Toma would wander the streets, walking and talking. What would they discuss once the subject of money became irrelevant? What could they really discuss after half a year of living together? Be honest with her, the gentle voice of a certain Kaniv[70] resident resounded in his head.

Tymofiy dropped into their room, tossing his belongings into a backpack with his frozen fingers—notebooks, textbooks, deodorant, socks.

Toma walked into the room. Standing by the entrance, she watched Tymofiy, looking scared and lost.

"I'm spending the night at Lida's," he said.

"So that's it?" she said morosely, clenching her fists.

"Just one night."

"One night . . ." she repeated. "Don't forget your tape player."

"I just told you, one night."

"Take your fucking tape player with you!" she yelled, sobbing and collapsing into pillows, crumpled T-shirts, crumbs from the sandwiches eaten at night, his book, her magazine. She collapsed into the space that was still warm and cozy, and stayed there.

"I'm just going for one night," Tymofiy repeated quietly.

But he took his tape player with him.

He ran out into the twilight, the chill of the street, and dragged himself by the high-rises, passing fresh piles of snow, jumping over dormant flower beds. He traversed the sports field, walking between the outdoor fitness equipment and soccer goals, reached the road, and went uphill toward the city center. For some time, he roamed the streets, kicking up the stale snow with his boots, his backpack filled with stuff, his tape player tucked in his armpit. Silently, he walked into the apartment, undressed, and closed the door of his room behind him without uttering a single word.

The next day, he did not leave the room. Lida walked to the door just once, to make sure he hadn't done anything stupid. Once she made sure it wasn't the case, she retreated. No questions were asked. He had come back, and that was okay. He would manage.

◇   ◇   ◇

In spring and summer, Felix drank. At times, he would come, stand by the front door, begging to be let in. Lida wouldn't do it. Felix would then disappear for a few weeks, leaving behind a bitter sense of reticence. He would return, occasionally spending the night, pounding the wall, and losing his voice mid-sentence.

"I am an officer!" he shouted.

"I don't give a damn," Lida replied. "You're no officer! You're a piece of shit."

Felix would lose it. He would growl and drool, banging on the furniture with his fists in a futile attempt to emphasize his affiliation with the military.

"You animal!" he shouted. "I was at war!"

"Who were you fighting? You piece of shit! Who? You were swilling vodka while your boys fought."

He swung a blow at her with the side of his palm; she fought back with a baseball bat. Blood from Felix's wrists and elbows sprinkled the doors and the walls. He ran into the hall, screaming and swinging his blood-covered hands, as if fighting flies, then came back to the room, full of resentment and rage. Lida would grab all his belongings, open the entrance door, and toss his clothing, shoes, notebooks, soccer magazines, and cigarettes down the stairs.

"This is where you belong, *Officer!*"

He would hurl the most vulgar obscenities at her, close his eyes, and count to five, run toward the staircase, fall softly and soundlessly, as if made of modeling clay. He would get up and stand there with a lost look on his face, trying to make out how and why he had gotten here. His eyes narrowed, he started crying, repeating the same lines about the war.

This happened over and over for almost a year. Tymofiy was a witness. He did not interfere, but he would occasionally engage, not in the best of moods. He would rush into the room, yelling in his cracking teenage voice. He screamed at Felix, he screamed at Lida—at him for binging, at her for patiently enduring it. How long could one stay calm? How long could one squirm, wipe off the snot, wash Felix's nasty underwear, cook all these smelly mussels, soybeans, and potatoes for him?

"Granny!" Tymofiy yelled. "Granny! I can't take it anymore! Tell him to shut up, just shut him up! This prick needs to sober up."

"Prick?!" Felix grabbed the wardrobe, fell down, and got up again. "You! Shithead! I'm gonna . . ."

"Gonna what? Hit me? Go ahead!"

"I've killed people with one blow!"

"Fuck you, scumbag!

"Who's the scumbag? Chin up, shoulders back before an officer!" Felix would fall again, banging his head and arms, grabbing hold of flowerpots, Lida's purse, or the cable running along the wall. Unable to keep his balance, he would collapse on the floor, crushing stuff, spitting.

"I'll kill you! Donnerwetter!" he growled.

Tymofiy rushed out of the room, as if someone had set it on fire. In his own room, he slammed and locked the doors. He cranked up the volume, black hip-hop or white heavy metal; he screamed and cried out of hopelessness, loneliness, then spent a long time sitting by the phone and calling Olha.

"Mom," he would say. "I can't take this anymore. I can't live with them. I can't eat her cooking."

"Whose cooking? Live with whom?" Olha asked again, knowing very well whom Tymofiy was referring to. Still, she would repeat the question, fearful of hearing the inconvenient and conspicuous truth.

"Lida," Tymofiy explained. "Her food's so oily and spicy. I'd get better food in prison!"

"Be patient," Olha would say.

I've been patient all my life, he thought to himself. And yet, there was nothing to do, so he put up with Felix, with Lida, the both of them. He endured the greasy soup, the deprivation, the loneliness. He endured, locking himself in his room, spraypainting the once-white walls and covering the ceiling with his mother's watercolors. His hatred for the reality outside grew, and so did his self-pity.

Still, at times Tymofiy showed Felix his other side. His face conveyed a message of compassion; he sounded droll and at the same time prudent, using that particularly adult tone so typical of immature teenagers. Tymofiy stacked up stilted banalities regarding

Felix's invaluable experience—difficult, important, gradual. It was not necessary to view this experience as something sacred. Life goes on, and one does not have to look back time and again to feel human, reminding oneself and everyone else about the war experiences. Irritable, Felix would wave Tymofiy away, make a face, and remind him once more of the pain—how it destroys, drives you mad, unhinges you, overpowers you. In a sober state, you might still be able to tolerate it, but when plastered, you can't even control your bladder, let alone the pain . . . These conversations birthed an armistice devoid of mutual understanding. But then Felix would start drinking again, running out to the stairwell and scaring the neighbors, yelling and punching the fuse box with his fists, calling Lida a bitch and Tymofiy scum. What reconciliation? God, give me strength to stay sane! Tymofiy thought.

Olha would come by occasionally, staying for a week or sometimes longer. On those visits Felix would return to his cabin. He would neither show up nor call, trying to avoid a fight, trying not to get on the Iron Lady's nerves—she was irritated enough as it was. Olha brought Tymofiy clothing from the secondhand stores in the capital, or German chocolates from the wholesale market, or sausage, as if there wasn't enough of it in Cherkasy. Lida complained about Tymofiy to Olha. Tymofiy complained about Lida. Both of them complained about the lack of money. For the most part, Olha remained silent. What could she do? She would leave some money, of course, spare some of whatever she'd made as she continued to pay everything back—the interest, the new loans, the old loans, the recurring bills. No end in sight, it seemed. Olha would still bring up the subject of Tymofiy moving in with her, a new school, a new life, the Empire style, and the pedagogical achievements. But something was amiss, would not cohere. Things unraveled like the stitches on a fake Adidas sneaker.

Olha found a guy, though, and by strange coincidence, he was in the military too; he taught at the Academy. The man was too proper, too polite for Tymofiy's taste. When Tymofiy came to Kyiv on school break, the three of them met up. They were sitting at a table in the small kitchen of a one-bedroom flat in Solomyanka.[71] The kitchen was packed with furniture from the fifties, the cabinets were stuffed with the landlord's belongings, a greedy *alte kaker* who always had a tape measure on him, constantly measuring everything. And so, the three of them—Tymofiy, Olha, and her guy—sat around, chewing fish pie baked by Olha, drinking beer. They brought soft drinks for Tymofiy, as if to mock him. The conversation was stilted. Olha kept bragging about Tymofiy like a matchmaker, while the military man kept silent and wiped his lips with a napkin every other minute. The only thing he asked was whether Tymofiy had scoliosis.

Tymofiy still refused to move to Olha's. He was afraid of losing something that he already took for granted and had gotten used to—his native city, familiar sounds, the trails around the neighboring factories, every inch of them known to him, the wild beaches that stretched behind the cement plant, gardens embedded deep in little neighborhoods, overgrown with hemp and thistles, the vast sky that emerged from behind the water reservoir. He held onto the piers hidden in the thickets, hosting scows, barges, and tugboats. He held onto the brick chimneys of the old industrial buildings, the line of stuffy, ramshackle buses that spanned his bedroom window, dragging their clumsy carcasses toward the ring road, where chestnut trees faded from the concrete dust and poisonous red exhaust of the chemical plants. Tymofiy was afraid of letting it all go and never being able to find it again, of uprooting himself from the fertile Cherkasy soil. He had found some new friends, a girl named Anya in particular. A neighbor. She was much older, more experienced. She had spent three years in Canada and came back after the tragic death of her beloved, who was mauled by a polar bear while working in the far north of Manitoba.

For days on end, Tymofiy would hang out with Anya and her friends, all promising alcoholics and failed musicians. He flunked out of school and became a fan of drinking wine. In winter and spring, they would vanish into strange apartments. Rather, it was the occupants who were strange—creative young people just hatched from music schools and community centers, grown men in biker jackets, their greasy hair dyed jet black. They did not know much about good music but were experts on popular drivel. They were woozy ravers, who would flee at the first opportunity to the night clubs in the capital, only to hitchhike back home, penniless, burned out, exhausted by low-quality drugs and lack of sleep. Now Tymofiy knew all of them—who was sleeping with whom, who had broken whose guitar, who had hepatitis, whose father had opened a casino. Almost every evening they could choose from some five apartments where their young adulthood and Tymofiy's youth could be lost.

Tymofiy introduced Anya to Felix, who behaved very politely, practically like a gentleman. Later on, sitting on the balcony at night, Felix lectured Tymofiy in a hushed tone, saying that a woman like this didn't just appear in one's life, it's like winning the lottery, not just a few bucks; you should take good care of her.

"And," Felix added in his raspy voice, "never, ever lie to her! Understood?"

Tymofiy took care of her and, obviously, he never lied.

One day they were drinking wine in Tymofiy's kitchen. Lida was out of town for a few days, Felix was watching TV in his room, but got bored and joined Tymofiy and Anya. Felix sat, laughed a lot, swinging his arms and not drinking much. Then he turned sour and insisted on running to the store for vodka. Anya managed to talk him out of it. Felix got drunk anyway. He held it together until he couldn't anymore, finally losing his grip and bursting into tears. Anya tried to leave but Felix wouldn't let her, growling and blocking her way. She patted his shoulder, gently squinting her almond-shaped eyes, pleading, "Come on, uncle." This informality, however, worked him up even more— he yelled, demanding something only he could understand. To their amusement, he assured Anya that she'd be sleeping here, with Tymofiy, since the boy had no one else to sleep with. Felix then told her that Tymofiy had lived with a girl for a few months but broke it off, his fire extinguished, hence his desperate need for consolation. Finally, Felix sat Anya in front of him and told her everything about Nicaragua, and how he killed his aide-de-camp, and how he sent Ivan's legs to his wife, the only bits that remained. He even shared that his daughter—*just a bit older than you are*—had her heart positioned on the wrong side. Then the tears, manic dashing, banging fists on the wall, bending forks. I bet there aren't any forks left, Tymofiy thought. He bent them all, the fucking Terminator. In the end, Tymofiy dragged Felix into his room, dropped him on the bed, covered him with a blanket, and turned off the lights. He had to swear to Felix, for a good while, that the light hadn't been knocked out by shelling— it could be turned back on anytime. While Tymofiy was busy putting Felix to bed, waiting for him to fall into erratic, hurried sleep, Anya left.

Generally speaking, their relationship was unhealthy. She called Tymofiy "my little one," which on one hand was sweet, but on the other, also crushed his hopes. It seemed that he was in love with her. Still, he was afraid to acknowledge that even to himself. He was loyal and obedient, the way he behaved with all women. He nurtured this loyalty as if it was his primary virtue. For Anya, though, it was not a convincing enough reason to stay together. But together they stayed.

Soon enough, Anya moved in with a boyfriend. Tymofiy didn't even notice when she started seeing someone. He pursued her for some time, calling her, running into her on the street, and sparking conversations. He pressured her. She suggested he get a life. He suggested that she burn in hell. Even Felix talked to Anya, pressuring her, appealing to her conscience: you can't do this to a kid. You're a big girl; don't you get these things? Anya got it entirely but told Felix to get lost too.

That's when the books came in handy. Olha bought Tymofiy a new TV, but he only watched music channels. What else was there to watch? He read a lot. His home library, which for years had been absorbing humidity and collecting dust, suddenly became interesting, essential even. For the most part, it included classical Russian literature, the Silver Age of Russian poetry, editions of Nabokov and Bunin published during perestroika, solid second-tier writers, the American novelists in translation by Rait-Kovaleva.[72] He read insatiably, as if he had found in books the meaning of life, as if everything he desired was sitting right here, on these seven shelves.

Unexpectedly (to himself, anyway), he fell in love with a classmate, and so he started going to school again, returning to his studies, making up for lost time, and catching up with the curriculum. In the evenings he would stay home, occasionally going out with his buddies. He would inevitably get drunk and scream in the faces of passersby, "Chin up, shoulders back before an officer, you punk!" He thought it was funny. Among his companions was a certain Rodion, a robust, wide-shouldered guy with the brick-like firmness of a golem, though his puffy boxer's face showed no anger. Within the gang, he was considered incredibly reckless and not very smart. That was how Tymofiy thought of him, too, as he murmured noncommittally at Rodion's sexual comments. Once, though, unable to curb his curiosity and under the influence of alcohol, Tymofiy posed a blunt question about the knife incident Rodion was always bragging about. Rodion just waved his arm and spat on the ground like a mobster, confessing that he was not even sure why he had done it.

"I was a moron," he said candidly, "I was just fooling around."

The gang, which Tymofiy had joined out of boredom, was wearing on him. Their company was too simplistic and uninteresting, a childish card game in which one was at the mercy of chance, where intelligence and wits played no role. It seemed better to just stay home with books, if possible. He would close the door to his room and watch his new TV set, not letting anyone in, not even Felix, who begged to be let in to watch soccer. It wasn't begging, exactly. Rather, he would lose it, work himself up, demanding access to the television while banging on the door with his feet.

"It's the quarterfinals, bitch! The quarterfinals!" Felix yelled.

"Go fuck yourself with your quarterfinals," Tymofiy yelled back, quietly adding, "I am so fucking tired of this," and then returned to his books, or one of those big journals that Olha brought from Kyiv, which he used to write in, or rather, to dump everything that could be extracted from his sixteen-year-old head: poems, first attempts at writing fiction, private notes, and dirty dreams.

◇ ◇ ◇

Behind the sandy dunes washed by the river, where the last of the cement factory melted into the greenery, stretched a wasteland. It ran along the water for a few miles, all the way to the village. Nobody ever walked there. Sand quarries, stagnant water, piles of building debris, accumulations of reinforced concrete blocks overgrown with propulsive poplars. And to the side, a rotten barn where a custodian had once lived. Not a soul around. Dead field, dead earth.

"Ready?" Felix asked.

Tymofiy nodded. Felix pulled the disassembled rifle from his briefcase.

"Can you put it together?"

"I have no idea how."

In a couple of minutes, Felix handed Tymofiy the compact Kalashnikov model in one piece.

"This one is called a spitter—used by the tankmen. Where are you spraying that thing?"

"Wherever, how about the shed?"

"Sure. We used to light them up when we were kids."

"With a machine gun?"

"Yeah, I'll tell you about it later. Okay, look here. This is the safety. Pull it down. Press harder or you'll end up firing a round. Here's how you do single shots, targeted fire. And here is the round, that's for when you're taking a piss and you need to hold the enemy off. You are fucking them, but not for long and not on target. It's less scary then. Go ahead, show me some single shots."

Tymofiy pulled the trigger. He heard a resonant click and felt a jolt. Again. Something whizzed over the shed.

"Wanna finish the mag?"

"No, that's okay." Tymofiy sounded worried. "I can't really hit it."

"You'll be doing that in the army. Just keep firing."

And so Tymofiy emptied the whole magazine with single shots.

"That's it, huh?" Disappointed, he handed the Kalashnikov back to Felix. "I thought it'd be more interesting."

"More interesting . . ." Felix mumbled, offended. "Go to the shooting range. You can aim at the penguins, knock yourself out."

For a few hours, they wandered around the wasteland and its surroundings, scouting out the groves and ravines. They peeked into a workshop that had been abandoned for a decade, now completely covered with sand, with maple branches shooting through the window frames. They used to mix lime in there. The metal rods of a hoist ran below the roof. The rest of the metal had been torn out. The workshop looked like a swimming pool filled with sand. Later, Felix and Tymofiy climbed to the roof of some rectangular, concrete edifice with its only entrance soldered shut. From there, they looked out at the Dnipro, its surface topped with the remains of white ice. The sad industrial landscape, the washed-out sun sinking beyond the spacious slope dense with acacia trees.

They walked back through the suburbs. Swampy dirt roads, houses hammered into the ground, roofs of slate and tar paper, broken equipment piled up in courtyards. Tymofiy kept asking Felix about the war. Felix replied reluctantly, sounding lethargic. It was obvious that he had grown tired of this month's long walks along the beach. And this intolerable sun, shining the whole day. Blinding, merciless light. Fatigued by layers of clothing and water-logged boots, their winter-burdened bodies were unused to the ultraviolet warmth. Tymofiy and Felix walked up to the Khim-reaktiv factory and continued, dragging themselves down the lane planted with poplars, along the white concrete barrier. Behind the factory, the production workshops buzzed in anguish, whispering three decades of industrial pain into the air.

"You know, I finished writing my book," Felix shared. "I can show it to you. It's about the war, actually."

"And Stalin?" Tymofiy was grinning.

"What does Stalin have to do with it?" Felix sounded surprised. "Psiakrew!" he yelled. "You take me for a moron?"

"I'd like to read it," Tymofiy said, finally.

"Yeah, well . . . We'll see about that."

They walked slowly. They were hungry and tired. Felix smoked. Inter-city buses passed them by, gliding down the wet asphalt. Tymofiy fantasized about the coziness of home, a filling dinner. After that he would collapse on the sofa with a book or turn on a movie, whatever was airing on Saturday night.

From behind the barrier, right where the lane ended, three young men emerged. They were in a hurry, clad in short black jackets. All three were smoking. Two of them Tymofiy knew from his old school; he remembered them graduating. Grimacing, clean-shaven, with faded angry eyes. They had been the school's major agitators. How did they even make it to the eleventh grade? Once they graduated, everyone breathed a sigh of relief. There were others, though, but at least not these two. The Brothers Romanian. That's it, Tymofiy recalled, the Romanians. He'd seen the third guy around the neighborhood a few times. This one was short, with acne and sharp little teeth. Once, Tymofiy had seen him walking a pit bull through the village. His jacket, rolling off the shoulders, stopped at his elbows. A V-neck sweater underneath. Sneakers clearly "borrowed" from an imprudent passerby. His glare was ice cold and militant.

Their paths were set to meet, and having noticed Felix and Tymofiy, the three guys were now facing them directly. They sped up, brazenly, as if late for something. With about ten yards left between them, one of the Romanians yelled in his dry voice, stretching out the vowels, "Haaalt!"

Tymofiy came to a halt, for a second, but Felix pulled him—let's go, why are you stopping? Tymofiy followed. They kept walking in silence.

"Haaalt!" the Romanian yelled, again. A kind of anguished resentment and unbound rage appeared in his face—directed perhaps at Tymofiy and Felix, perhaps at life in general.

They had almost caught up with them, now walking very close. Their facial features were piercing, as if cut and sanded out of wood. Tymofiy realized that all three Romanians were wasted, perhaps strung out. Probably on uppers. It was like something was propelling them to walk into the fire; something was igniting aggression in them, inviting them to hurt others.

Felix stopped suddenly.

"What the hell's your problem?" he yelled. "Who the fuck are you?"

"What's up, pops?!" the sharp-toothed guy screamed, pushing his chest out and brushing it against Felix's. The Romanians were on the move. At that exact moment, Tymofiy managed to glimpse the opaque black of the briefcase as it flashed by his eyes, and the plastic handle left in Felix's hand. One of the Romanians collapsed into a puddle. In an instant, the Obersturmbannführer's ceremonial coat swayed in front of Tymofiy, and he heard a crunching noise, as if someone had broken a ham hock at a festive meal. A few jolts, and the coat started fluttering like the sail of a pirate ship; shoes shuffled against the asphalt. Another crunch. Three bodies were lying in the black water, powerlessly twitching their legs in the dark leaves of yesteryear.

"I asked, *who the hell are you!*" Felix screamed to the bodies.

He stood over them, his legs wide, a dark and frenzied expression on his face, holding the briefcase handle in his hand. He cleared his throat. The Romanians' features were now less piercing; instead, something childlike was coming through, stares of indifference and exhaustion.

"I am going to kill one of you right now," Felix said calmly, coming to his senses. "And then I am going to break the fingers of the other two."

The bodies moaned, protecting their heads with elbows.

"Which one of you fuckers should I kill? *You?*" He kicked one of the bodies.

"Felix, don't," Tymofiy said tensely. "Let's go."

There was no reply. Felix stood over the bodies, breathing heavy, almost wheezing.

"Or maybe you, fucker?" He pushed another one. "Make a choice!"

"Please, Felix. Let's go, Felix!" Tymofiy started screaming.

No reaction.

"Move! Come on, let's go!"

Tymofiy grabbed Felix's coat with his stiffened fingers and pulled, unable to make him move. Then Tymofiy pushed Felix.

"Let's go! Come on!"

"One out of three. Donnerwetter! Am I going to have to choose?"

Tymofiy pulled his hat off, started nervously rubbing his face with it, sensing that something irreversible was about to happen, something he would not be able to process or forgive Felix—nor himself—for. Something that he could never wash off or escape from. "Let's just go, please. Let's just go home."

At this moment, one of the Romanians tried to raise his head, just to prop himself up on his arm. He made an abrupt movement, sticking his arm out unwarily and stretching his torso. Felix leapt on top of the guy, knees first, pressing him into the ground even more, grabbed his throat with one hand, and beat him over the head with the briefcase handle.

Blood gushed from his ears. In the twilight, it appeared black, as if it were watery mud streaming down his temples, under his jawbone, melting into the darkness behind his neck, where a thick chain glistened.

"*Co się stało?*"[73] Felix yelled right into his bloodied ear. "Something hurts?! Oh, it'll pass!"

Felix stood up slowly and stepped to the side, his nostrils gasping greedily for air.

"I'm leaving!" Tymofiy could not take it anymore.

"Take the briefcase with you," Felix said, still not taking his frenzied eyes off the bodies that no longer tried to move or even produce a sound. They just lay there, quiet and black, like dolphins beached on the shore.

Tymofiy grabbed the briefcase with his trembling hands, squeezed himself past the Romanians and the sharp-toothed guy, and ran toward the highway, passing through the meadow planted with round maple trees and stocky lindens. He crossed the road frantically and found himself by the artisanal workshops. Tymofiy stood there for a few minutes, impatiently looking out for Felix, expecting his dark silhouette to emerge from the gloom any moment. Felix's coat, cigarette, blue Adidas pants. Under the coat, the sailor's shirt, blue and white—a constant presence in Tymofiy's life, a nauseating refrain. But Felix, apparently, still stood there in the alley, under the poplars, deciding whom to kill.

Tymofiy headed home. His heart was racing, his eyes felt heavy, as if he was carrying a boulder in his skull. Charged fragments circulated in his head: coat, briefcase, blow. And crack. A soft cracking sound that made his esophagus contract.

At home, he yelled at Lida, sending her outside to pacify Felix, to appease his thirst for murder—if, of course, he hadn't already killed someone. Lida just waved him away—go ahead, figure things out by yourselves. "By ourselves? How? He crushed their bones, he'll kill them, don't you get it? He'll get ten years! And that'll be the end of him, he won't last in prison with his liver."

Tymofiy could not calm down. He ran back out to the street, sprinted to the manufacturing shops but did not go farther. He stood there, looking in the direction of the poplars. He could not make out anything except the trees. Saddened and agitated, he returned home. The briefcase was sitting in the hall. Tymofiy took it to his room, stuck it behind the wardrobe—the same large, black wardrobe where his father had hidden between the boxes and bags. After a bit, he took the briefcase out, opened it, felt the cold metal with his hand, wiped it with a dirty sock to remove any fingerprints, and smiled at his own cleverness. Then he shut the briefcase and hid it in the wardrobe again.

Felix turned up the next morning. Drunken and merry, he stood in the hall. Lida was set to kick him out, furiously growling, anxiously jerking her head, shaking her bulldog jowls. Did we not agree? And just how many of these agreements have we come to? How many promises? How many pledges? And still the same things happen, again and again. This endless refrain trudging on and on, like Ogiński's polonaise—hysterically, arrhythmically, losing grip of its finale in fizzling darkness.

Felix showed an uncharacteristically nasty smile. Yellow grass was sticking out of his torn left shoe. Spring precipitation dripped down the Obersturmbannführer's black ceremonial coat, as if it were a submarine that had just resurfaced from the very bottom of the ocean. He held a brand-new briefcase under his arm. How many of those did he own?

"Let's talk," he ordered, looking at Tymofiy gravely.

Felix turned around and walked out of the apartment. Lida was yelling something at his back—something about a point of no return, a last straw, some puffer coat purchased from Valentyna Hryhorivna for their last penny. She screamed at Tymofiy, ordering him not to go. But would he listen? He dressed himself rapidly and rushed outside, hopping on one leg while slipping his shoes on. Lida hissed something about the puffer coat at Tymofiy's back.

Felix was sitting near the entrance to the building with his legs folded up to his chest, looking gloomy.

"Where's the briefcase?" He jumped at Tymofiy the moment he saw him. "Cornet! At eaaase!"

"What did you do to them?" Tymofiy asked.

"Who?" Felix's face reflected a fake naivete. "Fuck 'em." He waved Tymofiy away. "Where the hell is the briefcase?"

Tymofiy disappeared into the foyer. In a few minutes, he brought the briefcase and handed it to Felix, who checked the weight and finally nodded, satisfied.

"You should come over sometime," Felix said, getting up with some difficulty.

"What did you do to them?" Tymofiy asked again.

Felix said nothing, staggered through the small front garden, chewing on mumbled curses. An unlit cigarette dangled from his mouth. He was holding the new briefcase by the handle. The old one, handle ripped off and disassembled rifle inside, rested under his armpit.

He would never live in their apartment again.

◇ ◇ ◇

On his way to Cherkasy, it dawned on Tymofiy that he had chosen the wrong music for the road—too much percussion and bass guitar. He craved something more sorrowful and tender. This was important to him. Each time he returned to Cherkasy, he felt the influx of a distinct sadness, a whimpering that would well up inside him, taking shape as he approached his destination, as the bus approached the dam. From behind a pond, flat as a skating rink, the city emerged from the mist. The place was completely open to the eye, stretching along the river like a panoramic view of some alpine village on a prewar postcard. As if in a dream, the city lay quiet, from the sandy dunes in the southeast to the pine forests in the north. As far as his insatiable eye could reach, Tymofiy contemplated the urban diorama, the remarkable and weighty signs of his imminent homecoming—the Hill of Glory, the hotel, the university, the ridge of high-rises in the Mytnytsia district, the cranes of the cargo port. Once again, he regretted his choice of music. It suited the new and unknown, not the old.

Tymofiy and the city had grown apart, but it still maintained its grip on him. This was his fourth visit in the last two years. The fourth! Not infrequent, but it wasn't as if he was here all the time. His fellow university students would dart off every weekend, leaving behind the dormitory bunks, and heading in the direction of home-cooked meals and former schoolmates. Their hometowns and villages did not let them go. They probably never would. But what was here for him? What kind of people attracted him, what places? There was new wallpaper up in the living room, a new fridge, and a boiler with a pilot light. Lida had rented Tymofiy's room to some skittish provincial girls who studied at the medical college. They reacted to Tymofiy's arrival like a flock of pigeons being chased from their nests. They were afraid to leave their room, greeting him only sporadically and avoiding eye contact, as if they were illegal workers down at the dockyard.

He did not have any friends, only a few acquaintances. He ran into old ghosts, though he would have preferred not to. The neighbors were dying off and their children were moving into their apartments. That was the best-case scenario. But for the most part, the new inhabitants were those same skittish provincials, yesterday's villagers. Unfamiliar people, adversaries. What about his relatives? They had been distant for a long time, forcefully relocated to the periphery of his attention.

And yet, he was on his way. Pity that the music didn't fit the occasion.

It was autumn, yellow and smoky. Apart from the oily smoke, the air was also saturated with an anxiety that kept increasing, inflating, and filling up all the surrounding cavities. It was especially noticeable in Kyiv. The autumn of 2004, at first glance, differed little from autumns before. But there was this premonition of social explosion that was slowly burning, promising to transform itself into something extraordinary and unprecedented, a cheerful riot to overcome all this absurdity, this Oran plague. Or perhaps it wouldn't. Tymofiy felt, even knew, that he wouldn't be spared when the zeppelin, filled with combustible anxiety, finally exploded. He would be caught in it. All this would take place against the backdrop of his troubled, eccentric relations with reality. Everything was spinning as in a mad zoetrope, simple images whirled around like a carousel—the bloodied and cheerful geezer who couldn't hold his drink; random friends incapable of helping; a beautiful, treacherous woman who had escaped from the uncle, leaving behind languorous despair; parties that spouted a dark plume of embarrassment and hangover; the lonely neighboring woman always walking her dachshund, whom Tymofiy had secretly named Putter. University, smoking room, library. Montesquieu, Weber, Durkheim. Auguste Comte, Henri de Saint-Simon, Georg Simmel. Life was out of tune, like a neglected vintage piano. And now, as if poised to ruin Johannes Kepler's harmony of the world, the piano yields a disgusting, excretal chaos.

He had arrived.

On this misty morning, Tymofiy walked along the boulevard painted in October's sepia palette, peeking into the familiar backyards where he used to hide as a child from the heat and the penetrating eyes of adults. He dove into the chilly secondhand stores as if they were ultramarine grottos. Lightheaded, he wandered sunlit, almost celebratory, streets, freshly noticing the old brick houses that had never before been of interest to him, alongside the whimsical architectural liberties offered by new buildings that mushroomed in place of demolished single-story homes. Empty fountains, neglected stores with something to sell even in times of wicked scarcity. Nobody was going to fix the broken swings in the backyards. Plastic cars parked near the entrances to buildings, glossy supermarkets sprouted across the suburbs, plastic flowers in window boxes. Dead birds. Hushed conversation. Dry cough.

Printing services, notary, funeral home.

Drugstore, convenience store, pet store.

By his old building, Tymofiy ran into Ivan, who was taking out the garbage. Empty bottles clinked in the plastic bag. Ivan was glad to see him, and even touched Tymofiy's forearm with the palm of his hand.

"Come on in! Let's catch up!" Ivan sounded gentle.

"Some other time," Tymofiy replied. "I'm in a rush."

Ivan had gained weight. His fair-skinned, puffy face, unusual for him, betrayed signs of adulthood. He's just finished school, Tymofiy thought, and he's already grown old.

"You're in college?" Ivan asked.

"Sociology," Tymofiy replied.

"Dunno about that stuff."

"And how are you? How're the bees?"

"Grandpa harvests the honey, I sell it. You wanna stop by some-time?"

Tymofiy hesitated. There was nothing to talk about. Should they reminisce about country life? Talk about Stalin? About bees?

"I'm in a hurry," he said, putting on an artificial smile. "Honestly. I gotta go."

As expected, Tymofiy spent two hours at Lida's. They sat in the living room armchairs, facing one another. Tymofiy chatted about his student life, listened idly to his grandmother's complaints about a neighbor, and checked his watch. From time to time, they would fall silent. It annoyed him to notice that with every visit, it was getting increasingly difficult to find common ground for conversation. The Department of Philosophy was not of much interest to many of his folks, even close ones. When the silence had finally stretched out for too long, Tymofiy remembered what he meant to ask. It was something that had bothered him for some time, resurfacing in his memory now and again.

"Granny," he asked, fingering at a hole in his sock, "do you remember where you used to get mangoes from? Remember those mangoes?

"I do," Lida smiled cunningly. "Do you remember that you did not want to peel them?"

"I don't. Where did you get them, anyway?"

"Back then they had already stopped prosecuting sellers of stolen merchandise, and one woman, who married an Indian guy, sold them right near the checkpoint. One for two rubles. Expensive, but you loved them."

"So is that who Uncle Boba was?"

"No, her name was Nelya. Her daughter passed away, only a schoolgirl."

Tymofiy was lost in his thoughts, remembering the yellowish fruits under his pillow. He hadn't tasted one since.

In the evening, he killed time with his old buddies, the musicians. They generously treated him to beer, and finally, at the exact moment that he should have escaped from the smoke-filled kitchen, they invited him to crash for the night. Lie down right here, on a mattress, get a good night's sleep, have some coffee in the morning, and then go wherever. In the meantime, the guys were going to dash out and get more beer. The local stuff was so cheap, so intoxicating. C'mon, Tymokha. Stay.

And he stayed. They made a bed for him. Even though, back in Kyiv, he would normally be getting up at this hour, Tymofiy lay down, exhausted, in his wrinkled clothing, squeezed between the greasy gas stove and kitchen chairs that had grayed from use. His buddies were still there. They were still drinking, singing songs only they knew, toasting, reminiscing. They were brushing cigarette ash off their chests and lamenting that nobody had invited that guy Bodrov.

Tymofiy looked long and hard at the feet of one of his friends—more precisely, his toes. God, a thought flashed through his mind, what's wrong with his toes? Long crooked toes with yellow talons on them, like a sloth's. "They look like hands." Tymofiy said this last part out loud, giggling to himself. It all seemed quite funny to him: *feet like hands.* There was something entertaining about it, a sort of anatomical curiosity, something straight out of the world of Bosch. Tymofiy's buddy got offended and would not let it go.

"Hey, what's your deal with my feet? What's your point?"

"Nothing, I was just joking."

"Get lost then. Go crack jokes someplace else. Look at you, just 'cause you're from Kyiv, you think you can talk shit?"

Tymofiy got up, thanked the guys for their hospitality, collected his belongings—a cell-phone charger and a notebook—put on his jacket, and walked out into the frozen street. He was bitter that his friend had been so easily offended, and annoyed that he had basically been kicked out of the kitchen, even though he hadn't been particularly interested in spending the night between the stove and those long hand-feet. He headed home with a grim, nauseating heaviness in his heart.

On this quiet, murky morning, the door to Tymofiy's room was partially open—the renters had left for the weekend. He peeked inside just to make sure. Nobody. He stood there, examining the floral-patterned duvets with disgust. The girls' belongings irritated him, as well as the smells of their distant provincial towns—cheap perfumes, foot cream bought at street stalls, the shoddy smell of cheaply made shoes. But the most maddening was a heart-shaped glass lamp. It was not just a lamp, it was callous stab in the back, a disgrace to his good memory, treacherously pouncing at him from out of the provincial darkness. Filled-up notebooks and glossy magazines piled up on his desk. Tymofiy checked the closet. A few polyester tops on hangers, but otherwise everything looked the same. All his things were there: faded T-shirts he'd outgrown by the eighth grade, old jeans bought in one of the first second-hand stores in the city, a terrycloth blanket that his father used to wrap Tymofiy in during daily naps, old cassettes, a box with the autographs of famous musicians who used to drop by the Fraternity of Peoples cultural center while on tour. Plus, there was a reel-to-reel player, a vinyl record player missing a needle, a collection of coins from Eastern Bloc countries, books on numismatics, a folder filled with sheet music. Tymofiy stood there, staggering from fatigue and what remained of the cheap beer in his blood-stream. Looking at all these things, he felt sleepy and lost. Why is all this stuff still here? he thought. Why is there a bumper sticker from someone's Moskvich? He and his friends had stolen it in the spring of '97. And what about the old Opel's hubcaps that they found in the landfill? Or all the art he painted when he was fifteen, a record of his sublimation and processing of something? Or the shelves stacked with children's books up to the very top? Why did nobody bother to toss these out? Tymofiy thought. And for fuck's sake, why did they get rid of the piano? But what could he do, really? You forgive your relatives because you haven't seen them in a month, or two, or three. You spent the nights who knows where, with God knows whom, drinking whatever was available; your lungs inhaled all kinds of stuff in the last two years. Now you're here, and the nostalgic smell of the apartment lulls you. You can fall asleep to the jittery rustling of the autumn leaves outside. You will certainly come again, in a month, or two, or in a year. You will come to experience the affection of an apartment that was once your home. The bits of happiness will collide with the pain you feel when you leave the nest. What's the point of all this? All these feelings, the complex of Stepan Radchenko,[74] a stubborn clot preventing the rapid and jolly gushing of blood. Why can't you snap, cut, burn this cursed knot connecting you to the person you were yesterday? Why not sever all relations? No obligation to call your ex-classmates, your former friends, greet your old neighbors. Almost no one is left there from your past, and gone are those with whom you could sit and reminisce, whom you could ask, with stretched syllables, "Do you remember how . . . ?"

Almost no one.

Secondhand store, slot machines, copy shop.

Notary, pharmacy, Romance Emporium.

◇ ◇ ◇

Having woken up late on a sunny morning, the first thing Tymofiy did was to make himself a cup of coffee. Still foggy with a hangover, he added milk that had gone bad. He kept drinking the sour dregs, cringing, and waiting for his breakfast. Lida was producing an energetic clinking sound with the dishes; a dull murmur emerged from the radio. On the street, someone was strenuously yelling, "Petrovych!" The dense black shadow resurfaced teasingly in Tymofiy's memory. From his old things, he fished a velvet-covered notebook, found a phone number written in his childhood handwriting. He walked to the receiver and stopped, feeling indecisive. He stood there, drinking the disgusting coffee, hypnotized by the dial.

Finally, he called.

A young woman picked up the phone. Was it the daughter? Must be.

"I'd like to speak with Felix Petrovych," Tymofiy said.

"One moment."

"One moment," Tymofiy mimicked, whispering. On the other end of the line, the doors were squeaking, there was some rustling and subdued nagging.

"Hello," the same voice said. "He can't talk right now. Who is this?"

Tymofiy hesitated.

"Hello!" The receiver came back to life. "Are you there? Who is this?"

"His grandson," he finally said, sarcastically.

"What the hell d'you mean, grandson?" His daughter didn't get it.

Tymofiy burst out laughing and hung up.

This situation struck him as equally funny and sad.

He poured his unfinished coffee into the toilet.

He had the address; he had been in Felix's backyard numerous times. As a kid, he waited for him by the entrance—next to that posh garage, spacious enough for two cars. He had always looked at the huge red star painted over the door. And now, too—garage, star, yellow birch trees surrounding the building covered with blush-pink tiles. A pair of white round antennae mounted on a wall, pointing to the sky. Scraps of political ads by the entrance. Electronic door lock. Tymofiy waited for a few minutes for someone to let him in. A middle-aged woman came out, looking at Tymofiy with suspicion, but she remained silent, and Tymofiy stepped into the resonant dark of the foyer. What floor was it? Six? Seven? Four! Definitely the fourth floor. He walked up the stairs. There, apartment seventy-two. He ventured to ring the bell. Someone approached quietly, standing tensely behind the doors and cautiously examining Tymofiy through the peephole. The breathing was measured, heavy.

"Who is it?" The voice, familiar from this morning, sounded abrupt.

"I'd like to see Felix Petrovych."

"You're the grandson, right?" Felix's daughter asked.

"That's right," Tymofiy smiled.

Immediately, he heard loud steps and anxious rustling from behind the door.

"Grandson! Cornet! Move! Move, I said."

The door opened. Here he was, Felix. His tired face, a toothless smile, a shapeless blob of an omelet. He happily raised his arms. The daughter's tired, tense face peeked from behind Felix's back, looking at Tymofiy inquisitively. Tymofiy had never seen her before. She was certainly not pretty.

"Let's go to my cabin," Felix ordered. "Straight, straight, then left."

Tymofiy nodded his head toward Felix's daughter, walked straight past the kitchen, then the "museum." He followed a scent—the thick, stale scent of vodka. And finally, they reached the cabin.

The rectangular room was not big—no wallpaper, no carpet; instead, there were bare windows, as if renovations were underway. A sagging, moldering sofa with crumpled, yellowing sheets stained sporadically with liquid iodine stood against a wall plastered with maps. An outdated plywood chiffonier with missing doors, a black velvet armchair, two white stools, a lacquered writing desk; on the windowsill: papers, piles of documents, offset printouts, bulging cardboard folders with white strings, and brown notebooks that looked like pieces of burnt pie. A shelf with tchotchkes—cartridge cases, stones, shells, a chipped glass with a church candle inside.

Briefcases were tossed all around the room—broken, busted, some missing handles, others intact. Tymofiy counted seven of them. On the floor right by the door, like a devoted fighting dog, lay the black ceremonial coat of the Obersturmbannführer. It was torn and the leather cracked in places, but it had stood the test of time; it was reliable.

Felix walked in behind him, closed the door, made himself comfortable in the armchair, and pointed at a stool for Tymofiy.

"She has me on a hook, Cornet. She turned me in to the cops," Felix said, turning his head toward the door.

"What d'you mean, she turned you in?"

"I got drunk . . . You know how it goes. Yelled a bit."

"A bit?"

"A bit!" Felix was offended. So, Chimera, Felix's daughter, had called the cops on him. "They found two bullets, dumdums. Fuck. Got two years."

"A year for each," summed up Tymofiy. "When's your sentence start?"

"Oh, I got a conditional one." Felix dismissed Tymofiy with his hand. "They wanted to give me five years. They can stick it up their ass, big time! Then the order came from upstairs to promote me to colonel. I don't give a shit!" he yelled. "Whatever," he waved his hand again.

"You're like a child," Tymofiy said unexpectedly to himself, making a note of the fact that Felix, though not drunk, clearly wasn't sober either; he was balancing between two worlds, in a kind of purgatory.

Felix glanced at Tymofiy, looking lost, perhaps remembering the history of their relationship—those times when Tymofiy was a child. Talkative, nervous, sometimes cruel. And now, look at him: a rather tall young man with an adult voice. Dressed like a clown, of course, but who the hell knows how they dress in the capital. That place seems to be populated exclusively by clowns. Felix sat in the armchair, his back to the door; his face was black, his hair gray. Fresh scratches on his forehead and emaciated, saggy cheeks, traces of scraped skin on his nose (from the asphalt, perhaps), pink sleepless eyes. He resembled an exotic fruit, rotten and manhandled. He kept looking at Tymofiy with his sotted gaze, clearly wanting to say something in particular but instead saying something else.

"What's new with the Iron Lady?" he asked.

"She's working. We're fighting constantly. She doesn't seem to get me. But honestly, she's the only one who comes close. I'm not home a lot, and . . ."

"I'll have a glass," Felix interrupted Tymofiy. "I need a drink."

"Go ahead, Ignatiev."

Felix got up and moved the chiffonier, procuring an unopened bottle of vodka.

"Gonna drink," he repeated. "I see your grandma sometimes, but I'm no longer in her good graces." He grabbed a cup with tea-brewing leftovers on the bottom, tossed the dried leaves out on the floor, swept them under the bed, and poured the alcohol.

"Are you gonna join me?"

Tymofiy nodded.

Felix passed the teacup to Tymofiy; he himself was swigging from the bottle.

"You know, I just remembered you promised to give me your manuscript to read," Tymofiy said, scrunching up his face.

"Take a bite!" Felix leaned over toward his ceremonial coat and fished a handful of raisins densely covered with tobacco from the pocket. He threw a few of them into his mouth and poured the rest into Tymofiy's palm. "If I promised, you'll get it."

They had another round. Felix got tipsy fast, and he looked relaxed. His eyes were tearing up. He put the bottle on the floor. He sat on his black armchair and gazed at the bare window caked with dust. Tymofiy recalled Felix's mood swings—once again, he would find himself by the large, pointed stone. Felix would watch the bloody mishmash of green military uniforms, crying and remembering the landscape—yellow sand, yellow stone, yellow sky. Tymofiy wished he could just leave. Now, without delay. Just take off and forget the whole thing. Right this moment. He just needed to make sure Felix gave him his manuscript first.

"I'm gonna go," Tymofiy said. "The book . . . can I have it?"

"Sit down!" Felix yelled. "Let's drink to those poor souls," he said, nodding roughly in the direction of the ceiling.

"Okay." Tymofiy sighed and looked up, as if expecting to see those souls to which they were toasting. He did not dare to take a seat, still hoping to depart.

They drank.

"I'm not giving you shit, you rookie," Felix barked, out of the blue. "Who the hell are you?"

"I'm leaving," Tymofiy said calmly.

"Who the fuck are you?" Felix's eyes widened, as if he was trying to get a better look at the person standing in front of him.

"I am leaving," Tymofiy repeated. "I don't need anything. I'm just leaving."

"I told you to *sit down*! Chin up, chest *out*!"

Felix was staring at Tymofiy heavily, with the kind of oppressive and menacing glare one would give to a captive general in a cellar, or a furious *bache* who just jumped you in a *qishlaq*.[75] The child is naked, swollen with tears, Kalashnikov hanging from his frail, tanned neck.

"I'm not giving you shit, goddamnit! *Get-yerasss-outtaheer!!*

Tymofiy made for the door.

"Sit down!" Felix started growling. "I used to kill people with one blow!"

Tymofiy stood still, glancing hesitantly at the door, as if it was an emergency airlock that opened up to freedom, life, and—above all else—sanity.

"You little bitch," Felix said with despair and started crying.

He gripped his face with his rough palm, as if trying to remove a mask, and wiped his tears. He kept staring at the dark window, as if something were taking place out there, nebulous, black and indestructible, something one couldn't look away from. He mumbled and sobbed. His hands—grayish yellow, mangled, dried out like the talons of a gutted chicken—dug into the polished armrests. Everything as it had always been. Everything as it used to be. He sat there and wept, growing numb and falling into oblivion, into worlds from which one could not emerge without sobering up. And even if he did, he would still know that these dimensions existed, always, just behind his back. Vast, yellow dimensions. Tymofiy noted that Felix had managed to get drunk on just three sips. The man had grown weak, lost his touch, his liver was no longer strong. He was sitting with his back to the door, so it was hard to squeeze past him. Tymofiy had to get out. Felix had never hit him when he was small, but now he might.

The whole thing felt like some absurd game. Or an awful, never-ending dream. Tymofiy tried to squeeze by Felix to the door, but Felix would not let him come close. Like a dog protecting his food, Felix bared his teeth and growled, ready to leap at any moment. Ready to hit. To kill with a single blow. Tymofiy saw different sides of Felix—the man *could* kill with one blow, for sure. Later on, he would curse himself bitterly, throw up his hands in grief, desperate for atonement. But that would be after, once he came to his senses, and it would be too late.

Suddenly, the door opened, and a gray, tired face peeked inside. Gypsy gold and leather, Tymofiy remembered. Only now, she'd wrapped herself into a baggy tracksuit that matched the color of her hair. Did she have anyone? A husband? A boyfriend? She must be working someplace, hanging out with friends; there must be soap operas and Russian talk shows that she likes. Or maybe not. Maybe she just stayed put, enduring Felix. She looked tired, unhappy . . .

Felix opened his eyes abruptly, leapt forward, and whirled around, ready to fight.

"Sit down, honestly!" the daughter ordered languidly. "Who are you?" she asked Tymofiy.

"Who the fuck are you?" Felix yelled, spitting, and collapsed back into the armchair.

"I'm leaving," Tymofiy said.

After drinking, his feet didn't feel like his own. Carefully, so as to not touch the armchair, he skidded to the exit. He hit his shoulder on the jamb, apologized, ran to the entrance door, and got stuck trying to open it.

"Hey, you!" the daughter yelled to Tymofiy. "So *you're* the one who brought him vodka!" she hissed. "Who are you?"

"Who the fuck am I?" Tymofiy answered, finally kicking the door open. He jumped out into the darkness of the stairwell.

◊   ◊   ◊

Two years later, taking a stroll through his native city, Tymofiy ran into Felix by the intersection near the market. Felix stood there, swaying; he wore a military field jacket, a black cap, and pathetically worn-out sneakers with no laces. Tymofiy ran up to him and called out, "Petrovych!" Felix looked at him indifferently, shaking Tymofiy's hand in silence.

Felix had grown old. He looked completely spent. Colorless eyes with discharge at the corners, yellowish skin, chronic scars on his chin, dirty cotton in his ears.

"How's it going?" Tymofiy asked.

"I'm on duty," Felix replied, turned his back, and headed toward the market.

December 2018 – October 2019 – July 2020
Mryn, Kyiv

Notes

1 Dushmans: What the Soviet troops called the Mujahideen in Afghanistan.
2 Serhiy Chervonopyskyi (b. 1957) was the head of the Veterans' Union for veterans of the Afghan war. While serving in Afghanistan in 1981, he was heavily wounded and lost his legs.
3 German: "For God's sake!"
4 Leonid Andreyev (1871–1919) is known as the father of Russian expressionism. With its candid treatment of sex, his first collection made him a literary star.
5 Referring to playwright and short story writer Anton Chekhov (1860–1904).
6 Maximilian Voloshin (1877–1932) was a Symbolist poet.
7 Lenin
8 "Two Colors" was sung by Dmytro Hnatiuk (1925–2016), who popularized Ukrainian songs throughout the world. The song was written in 1964 by composer Oleksandr Bilash and set to the words of poet Dmytro Pavlychko. It represents the life of each Ukrainian: red stands for happiness and love, black stands for tragedy and grief.
9 Mikuláš Dzurinda is a Slovak politician who was the prime minister of Slovakia from October 30, 1998, to July 4, 2006
10 "A hundred years in solitary. A hundred years in solitary, Oleksiy."
   "Fuck off."
11 From Slobidska Ukraine, a region in northeastern Ukraine that corresponds to the area of Cossack regiments.
12 There is an Ukrainian superstition that, sometimes, forty days after death someone among the family or friends of the deceased might also perish as a result of a curse.
13 The goal of the game is to knock all the opponent's pieces off the board. Named after Russian civil war hero Vasily Chapayev.
14 The Kholodny Yar Republic (1919–1922) was a self-proclaimed state formation and partisan movement. It was the last territory in which Ukrainians continued to fight for an independent Ukrainian state before the incorporation of Ukraine into the Soviet Union.
15 Used by noble families in medieval Poland.
16 The White movement was a loose confederation of anti-communist forces that fought the Bolsheviks. The movement's military arm was the White Army, also known as the White Guard.

17 Józef Klemens Piłsudski was a Polish statesman who served as the Chief of State (1918–1922) and First Marshal of Poland.

18 Film about the relationships between paratroopers.

19 Buyers were officers from different military units who came to the training centers to select soldiers for their units.

20 Gustáv Husák was the First Secretary of the Communist Party. In Ukraine, he was disparagingly given the nickname Huska.

21 Michał Ogiński (1765–1833) was a Polish diplomat and politician. Ogiński was well-known as a composer, primarily for his polonaise "Farewell to My Motherland"— a melancholic piece he wrote on the occasion of his emigration after the failure of Kościuszko Uprising in 1794.

22 Ukrainian political party and first opposition party in Soviet Ukraine.

23 Symbol of the Komsomol, The All-Union Leninist Young Communist League

24 Three-colored military uniform that was used throughout the USSR beginning in 1984. It was used in Ukraine until 2013.

25 A song from the 1975 Soviet film Afonya to which the protagonist of the film dances energetically.

26 Record player.

27 Polish: "Dammit!"

28 The Second Division of the GRU was responsible for special operations in the North and South America

29 Pikul's (1928–1990) novels often focused on Russian nationalistic themes.

30 Viktor Suvorov (b. 1945) was a former GRU officer who is an author of nonfiction books.

31 Yury Antonov (b. 1945) is a singer of the Soviet-era pop music. In his music video for the song "Moon Road," he dons his signature aviator glasses.

32 Nikolai Garin-Mikhailovskii (1852–1906): a Russian writer known for his novel Tyoma's Childhood, which focuses on the psychology of a young boy.

33 A district in Cherkasy located near the port.

34 Polish: "That's great!"

35 Polish: "Damn it!"

36 A district in Kyiv located on the left bank of the Dnipro.

37 A state-owned farm in the Soviet Union paying wages to workers.

38 Konstantin Balmont (1867–1942) was a Russian Symbolist poet.

39 Ivasyk-Telesyk: the name of a Ukrainian fairy-tale character.

40 Evokes Nestor the Chronicler, the twelfth-century author of the earliest East Slavic Chronicle.

41 UNR: Ukrainian National Republic, the Ukrainian state that existed in the territory of central and Western Ukraine in 1919–1920.

42 Vasily Shulzhenko (b. 1949) is a Russian artist working in the style of grotesque realism. His artwork often depicts the gruesome reality of life in remote areas of Russia.

43 A type of grape-based moonshine popular among the Soviet troops in Afghanistan.

44 Dmitry Ustinov (1908–1984) was a Soviet politician and Minister of Defense during the Cold War.

45 Andrei Gromyko (1909–1989) was the Foreign Minister of the USSR during the Cold War. He was known as conservative politician who distrusted the West.

46 Marko Vovchok (1834–1907; real name Maria Vilins'ka) was a Ukrainian writer of Russian origin, well-known for her collection Folk Stories, which described the lives of peasants under serfdom. Vovchok's style can be described as ethnographic romanticism.

47 Nestor Makhno (1889–1934) was an anarchist leader, commander of the Revolutionary Insurgent Army of Ukraine during the Ukrainian Civil War.

48 An archipelago near Lake Ladoga, in the Russian Federation. It is best known as a site of the fourteenth-century Valaam monastery.

49 An-12, or Antonov-12: a transport aircraft designed in the Soviet Union.
50 In military jargon, 200 refers to the soldiers killed in action.
51 From Pashto, meaning child.
52 A colloquial term for a member of GRU (Chief Intelligence Office), a foreign military intelligence agency that existed in the Soviet Union until 1991.
53 Diminutive form of PAZ, a small bus that was used in the Soviet Union in the 1980s, and in Ukraine in the 1990s.
54 Victory Day: a Soviet holiday that commemorates victory over Nazi Germany in 1945.
55 A mansion in the center of Cherkasy built in 1892 by the local engineer Andrian Shcherbyna.
56 An album by the British band The Prodigy released in 1997.
57 A village of about 5,000 in the Cherkasy region of Ukraine.
58 Yava Ren and Pavlusha Zavhorodniy: the main characters of Toreadors from Vasyukivka Village, one of the most well-known Ukrainian children's books by Vsevolod Nestaiko, first published in 1970.
59 A reference to Boyan, a legendary figure of an epic poet-storyteller from the time of Kyivan Rus'.
60 Cherkasy was founded around the year 1284; its 700th Jubilee was celebrated in 1984. Typically, such anniversaries were celebrated with pompous major renovations, and then forgotten for decades.
61 Names of industrial plants in Cherkasy.
62 Western Thunder Records was a pirate record label that operated in Ukraine in the 1990s.
63 Nickname of a Ukrainian star soccer player, Andriy Shevchenko.
64 A small store or a restaurant in the Caucasus or Crimea.
65 An acronym of Ukraine's Security Service.
66 Alexander Herzen (1812–1870) was a Russian political thinker and activist, the supporter of a uniquely Russian kind of peasant populism.
67 Vira Kryzhanivska (Russian: Vera Kryzhanovskaya) (1857–1924) was a Russian novelist of Polish origin. She was actively involved with spiritism and occultism. Kryzhanovskaya left Russia for Estonia in 1920.
68 A subculture of young men from working-class backgrounds, poorly educated, and criminally inclined. Gopniks were very active in the poorer suburbs of the big cities of Ukraine, as well as other Soviet republics and later on, independent states, in the 1980s to the early 2000s. Gopniks had their own dress code and jargon.
69 In Ukraine, Christmas is traditionally celebrated according to the Eastern Orthodox calendar on January 7th, although in 2017, December 25th was announced a public holiday as well.
70 A town in the Cherkasy region of Ukraine, best known as the burial place of Taras Shevchenko.
71 Densely populated, more affordable neighborhood in Kyiv.
72 Rita Rait-Kovaleva (1898–1989) was a Soviet literary translator and writer, particularly known for her translations of J. D. Salinger and Kurt Vonnegut into Russian.
73 Polish: "What happened?"
74 A reference to the main character of the novel Misto (The City, 1928) by Valerian Pidmohylny (1901–1937). A young man from a provincial town, Stepan is trying to make it big in the capital.
75 Rural settlement of semi-nomadic peoples of Central Asia and Afghanistan.